WHAT OTHERS ARE SAYING

Andrea Boeshaar never fails to deliver a story rich with spiritual truths and filled with God's healing for broken relationships. In *Threads of Hope*, she truly gets to the heart of God's healing grace in a way readers can carry into their own lives.

—LOUISE M. GOUGE
AWARD-WINNING AUTHOR OF *THE GENTLEMAN TAKES A BRIDE*

Andrea Boeshaar plucks the home strings with her newest historical romance. Not only does she tell a ripping good tale about émigrés from Norway in early settlement times, she also draws from her own family history. As a Wisconsin historian, I am well pleased with her efforts to make life at the dawn of our state authentic. A worthy addition to Ms. Boeshaar's delightful body of work.

—LISA LICKEL
AWARD-WINNING AUTHOR OF *A SUMMER IN OAKVILLE*

Andrea Boeshaar's story pulled me back into the middle 1800s. Her knowledge of the history of the times and her strong, three-dimensional characters kept me in the story. The feuding reminded me of Romeo and Juliet, but with an ending I liked much better. Human frailties were dealt with head-on with wisdom winning in the end. An excellent read that I didn't want to put down until the last page.

—LENA NELSON DOOLEY
AUTHOR OF *MAGGIE'S JOURNEY*, BOOK ONE OF THE MCKENNA'S
DAUGHTERS SERIES, AND THE WILL ROGERS MEDALLION AWARD–
WINNING *LOVE FINDS YOU IN GOLDEN, NEW MEXICO*

Threads of Hope is a beautifully tender story of the way God works in the lives of His own to teach lessons of forgiveness and love. Andrea's talent at weaving genuine characters, vivid descriptions, and a compelling story line together drew me into the story from the first page, and I felt Kristin's and Sam's heartaches and joy. It touched my heart, and I highly recommend this book.

—SALLY LAITY
AUTHOR OF *REMNANT OF FORGIVENESS* AND COAUTHOR OF
ROSE'S PLEDGE

Author Andrea Boeshaar weaves timeless themes of honor, equality, and mercy in this tender love story. Heroine Kristin Eikaas is sweet yet resourceful as she faces difficult situations in a new land. *Threads of Hope* is a wonderful addition to historical inspirational fiction bookshelves.

—KACY BARNETT-GRAMCKOW
AUTHOR OF *THE GENESIS TRILOGY*

Andrea Boeshaar has long been one of my favorite writers. Her blend of heartwarming romance is compelling and not to be missed!

—COLLEEN COBLE
AUTHOR OF THE HOPE BEACH SERIES

If you enjoyed the first book in Andrea Boeshaar's Fabric of Time series, you'll love the second, *Threads of Faith*! As always, Andrea offers her readers a cast of believable characters, a rich and inspiring story that overflows with faith and hope, and a conclusion that will leave them breathless . . . and looking forward to the next book in the series. Dust off your "keepers shelf," folks, because this is a novel you'll want to hold on to!

—LOREE LOUGH
BEST-SELLING AUTHOR OF NEARLY NINETY AWARD–WINNING
NOVELS, INCLUDING *FOR LOVE OF ELI*, PART OF ABINGDON'S
QUILTS OF LOVE SERIES

Threads of Faith by Andrea Boeshaar is another fabulous, page-turning winner with its spunky heroine, hunky hero, and sweet romance. A real keeper.

—DEBRA ULRICK
AUTHOR OF *NEW YORK TIMES* AND CBA BEST SELLER *A LOG CABIN CHRISTMAS*

Sweet, heart-tugging, page-turner; these are words that Andrea Boeshaar's books always bring to mind. *Threads of Faith* is no exception. Boeshaar has given us a beautiful and complex heroine, a compelling plot, and a heartfelt reminder that family ties are strengthened through forgiveness and grace.

—SANDRA D. BRICKER
AWARD–WINNING AUTHOR OF LAUGH-OUT-LOUD FICTION FOR
THE CHRISTIAN MARKET, INCLUDING THE ANOTHER EMMA RAE
CREATION SERIES THAT BEGAN WITH
ALWAYS THE BAKER NEVER THE BRIDE

Ambition, family, and honor are at the heart of *Threads of Faith*—the story of a man who has prospered at the cost of his family and faith and comes to realize what matters most in life. Heartwarming and touching, this is a book to "cozy down" with and enjoy.

—KATHRYN ALBRIGHT
AUTHOR OF *THE ANGEL AND THE OUTLAW* AND
THE REBEL AND THE LADY

Rich detail, lively dialogue, and downright smart storytelling make this second book in the Fabric of Time series a marvelous read. Andrea Boeshaar delivers another masterpiece!

—SHARLENE MACLAREN
AUTHOR OF FAITH-BASED CHRISTIAN FICTION
LITTLE HICKMAN CREEK, DAUGHTERS OF JACOB KANE, AND
RIVER OF HOPE

THREADS of LOVE

BOOK THREE

FABRIC of TIME

SERIES

ANDREA BOESHAAR

REALMS

Most Charisma House Book Group products are available at special quantity discounts for bulk purchase for sales promotions, premiums, fund-raising, and educational needs. For details, write Charisma House Book Group, 600 Rinehart Road, Lake Mary, Florida 32746, or telephone (407) 333-0600.

Threads of Love by Andrea Kuhn Boeshaar
Published by Realms
Charisma Media/Charisma House Book Group
600 Rinehart Road
Lake Mary, Florida 32746
www.charismahouse.com

All Scripture quotations are from the King James Version of the Bible.

Cover design by Bill Johnson

Visit the author's website at www.andreaboeshaar.com.

Library of Congress Cataloging-in-Publication Data:
An application to register this book for cataloging has been submitted to the Library of Congress.
International Standard Book Number: 978-1-62136-239-5
E-book ISBN: 978-1-62136-240-1

The characters in this book are fictitious unless they are historical figures explicitly named. Otherwise, any resemblance to actual people, whether living or dead, is coincidental.

First edition

13 14 15 16 17 — 9 8 7 6 5 4 3 2 1

Printed in the United States of America

For my beloved readers.
May the Lord bless you and keep you,
make His face shine upon you, be gracious to you,
and grant you peace.

A very special thank-you to editor Lori Vanden Bosch for praying for me, helping me with this story, and believing in me during a time when I didn't believe in myself.

And to Annie…thank you. You were a friend when I needed one. I will always have a special place for you in my heart.

CHAPTER 1

May 1902
Manitowoc, Wisconsin

*A*N EXPLOSION OF shattering glass sounded from directly behind Emily Sundberg, and a thunderous weight crashed into her. The world spun, and then she fell hard and facedown on the dirty Franklin Street plank walk.

Breathe! Breathe! She struggled to inhale.

"Are you all right, ma'am?" A male voice spoke close to her ear. "I'm terribly sorry about knocking you over."

He helped her sit, and a moment later a rush of sweet, springtime air filled Emily's lungs. She let out a breath of relief.

"Are you hurt?"

"I...I don't know." Emily spit dirt from her mouth. Her left cheek began to throb. Her vision swam.

He steadied her, his arm around her shoulders. "Easy there."

She took several deep breaths.

"Allow me to help you up and over to the bench. Like I said, I'm sorry 'bout knocking you over the way I did."

Emily wiggled her toes inside her ivory-colored boots. Nothing broken. She moved her jaw. Despite the pain around her cheekbone, she seemed all right. Her hand moved to the back of her head. Her fat braid had come out of its pinning and her hat—*her hat!*

She pointed to the paved street seconds before a set of buggy wheels rolled over it, grinding the lovely creation into the paved road. Not once. But twice!

Emily moaned.

"Careful, now." The man helped her to stand. "There're shards of glass everywhere."

Emily thanked God she hadn't slammed her head into the nearby hitching post.

"Hooligans!" A woman's voice rang out amidst the strangely silent street. It sounded like Mrs. Hopper's. "Hooligans, ever' one of 'em!"

Definitely Mrs. Hopper's.

The man held Emily securely by her upper arms, and Emily's gaze fell on his walnut-colored waistcoat. "You sure you're not hurt?"

"I–I don't think so."

"Well, I hope you can forgive me, ma'am."

Emily's gaze finally reached the man's tanned and golden-whiskered face. Shaggy blond hair framed his face and blood stained the corner of his mouth. In his canvas duster and matching trousers, the stranger looked out of place for Manitowoc, Wisconsin. But odd costumes weren't totally uncommon, given the city's lively port.

And yet, he seemed a bit familiar too…

"Unhand that girl, you hooligan!" Mrs. Hopper rushed forward and whacked the man on the shoulder with her cane.

He winced and released Emily. "I meant her no harm." As Emily staggered backward slightly, the man caught her elbow. His velvety-brown gaze bore into hers as if to ask yet again if she'd been injured.

Funny how she guessed at his thoughts.

"I'm just shaken." Emily glimpsed the remorse in his eyes before he bent and picked up the dark blue capelet that her grandmother, *Bestamor*, had knit for her. He gave it a shake before handing it over.

"And what about my hat?" Sadly she pointed again to the street.

The man collected its colorful but irreparably flattened remains.

"A travesty!" Mrs. Hopper's age-lined face contorted in rage. "A travesty, I say!"

Travesty indeed! It had taken months for Emily to save for that fine bit of millinery with its silk ribbons, Chantilly lace, and pink roses on a velvet bandeau. Now Andy Anderson would never see it. She took the mangled remnants from the stranger's hand. "I certainly hope you plan to reimburse me for this. I paid one dollar and fifty cents for it."

"A dollar and a half? For a hat? I could buy a shoulder holster, cartridge belt, and ammunition for that sum."

Unimpressed, Emily extended one hand of her torn netted glove. Another casualty.

Resignation softened his gaze before the man reached into his inside pocket and then placed two dollar bills into Emily's outstretched palm. "This should more than cover it. Again, I apologize."

"Thank you." Emily smiled. "Apology accepted." She folded the money and put it in her reticule, still attached to her wrist.

Mrs. Sylvia Hopper sniffed indignantly, but Emily caught the approving light in the older woman's eyes. She'd known the elderly woman for a long while, as she had been *Bestamor*'s best friend back in Norway. She'd come to America just before Poppa was born, and now her granddaughter, Iris, was Emily's best friend.

A small crowd pressed in on the boardwalk to gawk. Emily's gaze moved to the man who lay sprawled out and unmoving several feet away.

She quickly turned away. "Is he dead?"

"Probably not." The stranger bent and grabbed his hat that lay nearby and gave it a whack against his thigh. "My compliments. You took that tumble a far sight better than he did."

"Who is he?"

"Name's Wilcox. He's wanted in five counties."

Emily glanced at the motionless figure again. He didn't look familiar.

"It's actually amazing that you're not out cold yourself. For a moment I feared I'd killed you."

"And you could have killed her, you low-life hooligan!"

"Please, Mrs. Hopper…" She glanced around, hating to be the subject of such a scene. "I'm fine. No need to worry."

Muttering, the elderly woman walked to where several women stood a ways down on the boardwalk, holding parasols and whispering behind gloved fingers.

Emily felt suddenly unnerved. "I guess I'm sturdy for a woman. Even so, I haven't taken a hit like that since my brothers jumped me and I fell off my horse. Those rascals pretended they were US marshals and I was one of the James Gang." Emily moistened her lips, her gaze fixed on the handsome stranger. "They flung themselves at me from a tree limb. It's a miracle we didn't all break our necks. "

A moment passed, and Emily wondered why this moment seemed sealed in time.

The man narrowed his gaze.

"Forgive my prattling." She hadn't meant to go on like that. "The fall must have shaken my tongue loose."

Despite the injury to his mouth he grinned, and Emily could swear she'd seen that smile before.

"Both you fellas are paying for this damage to my front window!" Mr. Fransmuller stomped out of his restaurant and saloon. Emily knew him and his family, as young Hans had been in her class just the year before. "Look at what your brawl has done!"

Emily took note of the gaping hole where the two men had crashed through the window.

Mrs. Hopper limped over to the tavern owner. "There ought to be a law against such barbaric behavior in our town. Someone's going to get killed. Why, Mr. Fransmuller, you should be ashamed, serving strong drink on a Thursday afternoon. Women aren't safe to do their shopping in broad daylight anymore!"

"Just for the record, I wasn't drinking," said the familiar stranger. "Just playing cards is all."

"And gambling, most likely." Mrs. Hopper hurled another angry glare at him. "Gambling is a dirty sin."

Fransmuller frowned and wiped his beefy hands on the black apron tied around his rounded belly. "Now, Mrs. Hopper, don't start in on one of your holier-than-thou rants."

"I beg your pardon?" Mrs. Hopper brought herself up to her full height of four feet nine inches. "How dare you speak to me in such a way, Mr. Fransmuller!"

"I've got a business to run, and I pay my taxes." He threw a thumb over his shoulder. "But just look at my front window!" He gave a wag of his nearly bald head. "And you should see the saloon! One big mess!" Mr. Fransmuller marched up and stood toe to toe with the man beside Emily. "Who are you? I want your name. You're paying for half the damages to my business!"

"Yes, sir."

Emily watched as the stranger moved his duster to one side. She glimpsed the gun, discreetly haltered across his chest, before he produced his billfold and a silver badge. "Deputy Marshal John Alexander Kirk Edgerton at your service." After a courteous dip forward, he counted out several large-sum bills. "Will this cover my portion of the damages?"

Emily gasped. *Jake? Could it be?*

Mr. Fransmuller stared at the money. "Yes. This will do." He gave a nod of appeasement before walking away.

Mrs. Hopper moved down the boardwalk and continued her conversation with the other ladies.

"Jake?" Emily eked out his nickname, scarcely believing it was him. He was several inches taller, filled out some, and had grown whiskers since she last saw him ten years ago. "Jake Edgerton?"

His gaze slid to her and he smiled. "Well, well…Emily Sundberg." He didn't look surprised. Obviously he'd recognized her before she'd figured out his identity. "Look at you, all grown up—you even turned out pretty."

"*Hmph!* Well, I see you haven't changed!"

"It was a compliment."

She bristled. It didn't *sound* like a compliment. What's more, she suddenly recalled that Jake was part of that US marshal stunt her brothers pulled.

Jake Edgerton was trouble. Trouble from the time they were thirteen and fifteen.

"So what are you doing in Manitowoc?"

"Attending my granddad's funeral."

Emily felt a sting of rebuke. "Oh, I–I'm sorry. I didn't know he'd passed. I mean, I knew Mr. Ollie had been ill for a long while, but…"

"Happened just last night." Jake eyed her speculatively.

"I'm so sorry."

"Me too." He glanced away for a moment. "So what about you?" His gaze returned. "Married? Working at your family's shipping business?"

"Neither. I'm a schoolteacher here in town. I only get home on Sundays."

"A schoolteacher, eh?"

She nodded as the realization of Mr. Ollie's death sunk in. A sweeping sadness prevailed. "Again, I'm sorry for your loss. Your grandfather was a good neighbor to our family." She eyed the rugged man standing before her. Mr. Ollie spoke of him often, and Jake had been especially close to the old man. Oliver Stout, fondly called Mr. Ollie by Emily and her brothers, had been a respected attorney, one who'd boasted many times over the years that his only grandson would one day take over his law practice.

But it didn't look that way. Not if Jake was a deputy marshal.

"I appreciate the condolences, Em."

Such familiarity galled her. "So you're a gambler as well as a lawman?" Emily could only imagine Mr. Ollie, weeping in heaven.

"I partake in a game of cards on occasion."

"Family funerals being one of them?" She couldn't squelch the quip.

Jake inhaled, but then seemed to think better of a reply. Instead, he guided her the rest of the way to the bench.

Emily tugged her capelet around her shoulders and sat. She eyed the crowd, praying no one would recognize her as Maple Street School's third grade teacher or Agnes Sundberg's niece or Jacob Dunbar's cousin...or Captain Daniel Sundberg's daughter. With so much family surrounding her in this town, Emily knew the odds were against her anonymity.

"Once again, I am terribly sorry you got in the middle of this whole mess."

He couldn't be sorrier than she!

Mr. Fransmuller began sweeping up glass and shooing people away from the scene when shrieks from across the street pierced the air.

Iris. She turned in time to see her best friend making an unladylike sprint from the department store.

"Emily! Emily Sundberg!"

Standing, she cringed. So much for hiding her identity.

Emily lifted a hand in a tiny wave. Iris spotted her and crossed the street. She held her hat in place on her head with one of her slender hands. In the other she clutched her wrapped purchases.

"What's happened? Oh, my stars!" A pale blue dress hugged Iris's wispy frame as she hurried toward Emily, while her wire-rim glasses slipped down her long nose. "I heard there was some barroom fight and you got trampled half to death. What would I do if I'd lost my very best frie—"

Iris's gaze lit on Jake, and she slowed her steps. Giving him a timid smile, she let go of her hat and pushed up her glasses.

He touched the brim of his hat. "Ma'am."

Iris leaned toward Emily. "Is he the one who ran you over?"

"That about sums it up. But I'm fine, so let's finish our shopping, shall we?"

Iris didn't budge. "Aren't you going to introduce us?" She nudged Emily, who felt a new soreness in her rib cage.

Jake spoke up before she could. "US Deputy Marshal Jake Edgerton, ma'am."

"Deputy marshal? How impressive." Iris's smile grew. "I'm *Miss* Iris Hopper and Emily's best friend, going on eight years now. Right, Em?"

"Right."

"My parents were killed in a horrible mud slide in South America where we were missionaries. I've lived with my grandmother ever since." She pointed to where Mrs. Hopper still stood, recounting the event to an accumulating cluster of women.

"Sorry to hear of your loss." Jake's gaze, the color of the brandy he denied drinking, shifted to Emily. "As for Em and me, we go way back too." A slow grin spread across his mouth. "Ain't that right? And I must admit it's been a pleasure, um, running into you today."

Shut up, Jake. She looked down the block, wondering if he had any idea how much heartache he'd caused her over the years. Because of him and his big mouth, she'd spent half her life repairing her blemished reputation in this town. Worse, Jake never wrote back to her when she'd attempted to apologize for her part in the wrongdoing.

"How're your brothers?" He gave a nostalgic wag of his head. "That summer I visited Granddad and met all of you Sundbergs was the best in all my life."

"Eden and Zeb are fine. Just fine." She couldn't get herself to say any more. "We're all fine."

"Glad to hear it."

"Emily's never mentioned you." Iris's pointed features soured with her deep frown. She leaned closer to Emily. "I thought we told each other everything."

"No? You never mentioned me, Em?" Jake's dark eyes glinted with mischief.

Tried half my life to forget you! She clenched her jaw to keep back the retort and realized that it hurt too.

His expression changed. "Maybe you ought to see a doctor, Emily."

She wished he hadn't picked up on her wince. "No, I'm fine."

"She always says that," Iris tattled. "She's always 'fine.'"

"How far's the doctor's office from here?"

"I don't need a doctor, Jake. But thanks, anyway."

"Well, goodness, Em, you certainly did take the worst of it." Iris brushed off the back of Emily's capelet. "And, oh, my stars! Just look at your hat. It's ruined."

"Yes, I know. But Jake reimbursed me."

"How thoughtful." After a smile his way, Iris examined Emily's face like she was one of her fourth graders. "I'm not mistaken a bruise is already forming on your left cheek." Iris clucked her tongue. "You'll be a sight at the Memorial Day Dance tomorrow night. But if you need to stay home now, I will too."

"No. We're still going." Emily knew her friend looked forward to this community event that honored war veterans as much as she did. In addition, Andy Anderson would be there. Maybe if he saw her in the new dress Momma and *Bestamor* had sewn especially for the occasion, he'd finally notice her, and not just as Eden's sister either.

"Andy won't give you the time of day if you're all banged up. You might as well stay home."

Iris had spoken her thoughts. Sadness descended like a fog rolling in from off Lake Michigan. Emily fingered her sore cheek. She'd decided months ago that Andy would make a perfectly suitable husband. Would this ruin her chances of finally catching his eye?

"Might help if you go home and put a cold compress on it," Jake suggested. "I'll bet no one will be the wiser by tomorrow night."

"Sure, that's right," Iris's gaze softened. "Perhaps Andy won't see any bruising. And we can cake on some of Granny's concealing cream wherever necessary."

Glimpsing Jake's amused grin, Emily blushed. How could Iris speak about such personal things in front of him?

"Excuse me, but are you speaking of Andy Anderson by any chance?" Jake hiked his hat farther back on his head.

"Yes." Again, Iris seemed happy to provide all the information.

However, the last thing Emily wanted was Jake Edgerton to get involved in her life. "We should be on our way, Iris. Let's catch up with your granny."

"Well, I'll be…" Jake leaned against a hitching post. "Andy Anderson…what's that rascal doing these days?"

"Andy works over at the aluminum factory." Iris pointed just beyond Jake's left shoulder and toward where the large, thriving business was located. "He's quite the lady's man, but Em hopes to change all that."

"Iris, really!" Emily gave her friend a stern look.

"Interesting." Jake gazed off into the distance, his lips pursed as he kneaded his jaw. He seemed to mull over the information before looking back at Emily. "I wondered if I'd see Andy while I was in town." His gaze focused on Iris. "Andy and I go way back too."

Every muscle in Emily's body tensed. If only Mr. Ollie could have waited just a week longer to pass from this world to the next. Her hopes ran high for the Memorial Day Dance tomorrow night, and it vexed her that Jake might have the power to destroy her well-laid plans.

"Emily is counting on Andy to ask her for a dance tomorrow night, but—"

"Iris!" Aghast, she gave her friend's arm a jerk. "I'm sure Deputy Edgerton doesn't care about such things."

"Sure I do." He straightened, still grinning. "And I'll tell you what, Em, if Andy doesn't dance with you, I'd be happy to."

"Thank you, but I can't possibly accept." She tamped down the urge to scowl.

"It's the least I can do." After another charming smirk, he arched a brow. "What time's the grand affair?"

"Aren't you in mourning?" He just *couldn't* show up.

"Of course I am." Jake rolled one of his broad shoulders. "But I know Granddad fought in the Civil War, and I think he'd want me to attend."

Iris happily divulged the details, and Emily wanted to scream.

"I'll be there," Jake said.

"How grand!" Iris adjusted her colorfully decorative hat. "Then, of course, you must save a dance for me."

"Iris!" How could her friend be so bold?

Jake didn't seem offended. "It'd be my honor, ma'am." He smiled rather sheepishly.

Enough! Emily turned on her heel and strode down the walk, passing Mrs. Hopper and the other women. Her heels clicked hard on the weathered planks. While she walked faster than a lady should, if she didn't hurry, she'd lose her composure here and now— and right in front of the man who'd nearly ruined her life!

CHAPTER 2

*J*AKE WATCHED EM hurry off. She'd turned into a lovely young woman with those arresting blue eyes of hers. And that thick auburn hair—why, it dared a man to unbraid it and run his fingers through it.

Why did Jake have the urge to be that man? Sure, every now and again he wondered about Emily Sundberg and always imagined her married with a couple of children by now. But it would seem she wasn't hitched quite yet. Amusing, though, that she had eyes for Andy Anderson. Jake had wondered about him too. A friend from his boyhood. An eternity ago.

Seeing Emily round the corner up ahead, he blinked. What was she so mad about anyway? Of course, he had flattened her like a flapjack. Could be that he'd bruised her pride as well as her cheek. He just prayed to God he hadn't bruised anything more. He felt awful about hurting her. And maybe it was worse than that. Maybe she'd only been putting up a public front.

"I think you ought to go make sure Emily's okay." He looked at Miss Iris Hopper, who unlike Emily was reed-thin and pale as a lily. Jake was glad he hadn't landed on her.

"I suppose I should. Seems Em took a nasty fall."

"That she did."

Miss Hopper surveyed the scene around her, her gaze lingering on the fugitive, still unconscious on the ground. "So he's the criminal, hmm?"

"Yes, ma'am." Jake had recognized the wanted man shortly after he'd arrived in town this afternoon to meet with the undertaker and leave a message for Granddad's friend and attorney. Spotting Wilcox, Jake had followed him into the saloon and engaged him in a poker game.

"Poor Em." Miss Hopper looked back at Jake.

He shifted his weight. "Before you go, let me ask you something, if I may."

"Of course." Miss Hopper gave him an eager smile.

"Is, um, Andy courting Emily?"

Miss Hopper shook her head, threatening the flowery hat she wore. Her flaxen curls bounced like bad buggy springs. "Emily wishes he'd court her. The problem is Andy doesn't notice her a bit. Either that, or he speaks to her like one of his pals. You see, Em used to be quite the tomboy, and she and Andy, along with her brother Eden, were childhood friends."

"Yes, I know." Jake couldn't help a chuckle as his gaze ran down the length of the boardwalk in Emily's wake. "But she's all grown up now." *And lovely.*

"True. However, she can't seem to get Andy's attention."

"What a shame." But was it?

Jake straightened, unable to figure out why he felt more challenged now than during that last poker game. It felt rather refreshing too after watching Granddad breathe his last.

Granddad. Gone.

Sorrow weighed like a brick on Jake's chest. He'd miss the old man. Should've made an effort to spend more time with him. Jake, of all people, knew how fleeting and precious life was.

"I best hurry along and see after Emily."

Miss Hopper's voice reeled him into the present again. Jake forced himself to pay attention. She batted her eyelashes at him through thick lenses that seemed to magnify them. "But I'll be sure to save a dance for you tomorrow night."

"You do that." He politely touched the brim of his hat and glimpsed the sheriff striding toward him. The man's badge glimmered against the sunlight, and somehow Jake sensed the lanky fellow would be reasonable enough. The sheriff paused to bend over Wilcox, who seemed to be coming around. Jake looked back at Miss Hopper. "Until tomorrow night then."

"Oh, *Tante* Agnes…" Emily held the cool, damp cloth against her bruised cheek. "Poppa's going to insist I come home for the summer when he hears what happened just now."

"Your mother will want you out of town, that's for sure!" Her aunt stood with her hands perched on her ample hips. She tipped her head. "You know you can always stay here, sweetness. With four children and a husband to feed plus a shop to run, I can always use some help."

"I know…" Emily figured it would, at least, be an option.

Her gaze skipped to the wide doorway and the entrance to the shop. *Tante* Agnes had continued the boutique business that *Bestamor* began decades ago, before Poppa curbed his seafaring ways, as Momma liked to put it. *Bestamor* had grown too old and tired to run it, although she and Momma knitted and crocheted all kinds of lovely things from capelets and caps, to shawls, hats, and gloves, either finely laced or thick and warm. Both Momma and *Besta* said it was good for a woman to have a little of her own money. Poppa said he couldn't fight the both of them.

Tante Agnes moved the curtain to peer outside and check on the girls, playing in the backyard. The boys were helping their father today at the Manitowoc Shipbuilding Company, where he was the foreman. Uncle Christopher liked to brag, in a fun-loving way, of course, on Manitowoc's nickname, "Clipper City," because of all the ships it produced and repaired. Today Emily's cousins, Kjæl and David, were probably sawing wood for another ship's construction. Too bad she couldn't be a shipbuilder. Then she'd have an excuse to stay in town and near Andy.

With her free hand Emily brushed some leftover dirt off her fawn-colored skirt.

"You could visit your grandfather in New York City." *Tante* Agnes turned from the window.

Emily shook her head. Ever since her Gramma Ramsey died, she didn't care to visit there anymore. Grandpa Ramsey, as generous as he was, didn't appreciate feminine sensibilities, and Emily wasn't a tomboy any longer. Besides, Grandpa had his hands full with Eden living out there while attending college. Her twin brother, Eden, would eventually step into an executive position at R S & D Shipping and Freight Company, her family's business.

"Go stay with Aunt Mary and her family in Green Bay." After a soft laugh *Tante* Agnes wagged her head. Errant strands of her coiled, wheat-colored hair caught in the sunlight. "It's still hard to believe she married that widower with seven children." *Tante* Agnes gave a short laugh. "A new mother at forty-six. I was convinced she'd be a spinster till the day she died."

Emily mulled over the suggestion. But no. As much as she loved her great-aunt Mary, she had no intentions of spending her summer in Green Bay. She simply had to stay here in Manitowoc! It was the only way she could see to it that her paths crossed with Andy Anderson's. He was the only man she knew who didn't seem intimidated by Poppa. However, Andy just didn't seem to intercept the signals she sent to let him know of her romantic interest. But perhaps that would all change tomorrow night at the Memorial Day Dance.

That is, if her cheek wasn't horribly bruised.

Emily removed the damp cloth. "Is it better?"

Tante Agnes's blue eyes became narrow slats. "Too soon to tell, Em. We'll just have to wait and see what it looks like tomorrow morning."

She just couldn't miss that dance!

Her two cousins burst in from playing outside. At thirteen years old Kate reminded Emily of herself as a girl. Tall, long-legged, and capable of outrunning any boy in the neighborhood. Hildi, on the other hand, was all girl, with her quiet, demure disposition. She enjoyed stitching, reading, and tending to her momma's herb garden. Emily knew her traits well, having just passed her earlier this week from third grade to fourth.

"Momma, Kate pulled my hair." Hildi walked over and wrapped her skinny arms around *Tante* Agnes's thick waist.

"You're such a baby." Kate stuffed her hands into the pockets of her dark brown pinafore.

"Now, Kate, you're not to hurt your sister." *Tante* Agnes shook her head. "Hildi is only eight. You should look out for her."

Kate huffed and her lips fell into a frown. But seconds later her gaze lit up when she spotted Emily seated quietly at the kitchen table. She sprinted across the room, but then stopped short. "Snakes alive! Where'd you get that shiner?"

Emily gasped and fingered her cheek. She glanced at her aunt, feeling somewhat betrayed.

"Now, Em. Let's see how it looks tomorrow…"

She didn't wait to hear the rest of the sentence and hurried toward the shop where a large, oak-framed mirror hung on the wall. Her reflection revealed a completely disheveled young woman, from her unpinned hair to her dirty skirt. And that ghastly shadow on her cheek seemed to be spreading by the second!

"Who socked you, Em?" Kate suddenly stood at her side. "One of those dumb boys at school?"

"Nobody socked me." She turned from the mirror to regard her young cousin. "I got knocked down in front of Fransmuller's Tavern by two brawling men." Jake Edgerton came to mind, and she rued the day her path ever crossed with his.

"Did it hurt?"

"A little…" Truth be known, Emily's muscles already felt stiff and sore. "I won't likely be moving very fast later tonight and tomorrow." The Memorial Day Dance came to mind, and she hoped she'd feel agile enough to take a spin around the floor with Andy.

If only he'd ask.

Emily imagined herself in his arms as they stepped in time to the music. Andy loved that ragtime sound. But maybe the band would play some traditional waltzes.

"Why are you smiling so funny?" Kate nudged her.

"Oh, nothing." Emily turned back to the hanging mirror and pretended to examine her bruise.

"You're thinking about a beau, aren't you?" Kate puckered her lips and closed her eyes as though she were kissing her beloved.

"Shame on you, Kate. Such a thing to do! Besides, you're just a child. What could you possibly know about love?"

Kate's blue eyes sparked with mischief. "I see my poppa kissing Momma plenty of times."

"Well, that's private business which you should not discuss with me or anyone else."

Tante Agnes called to Kate. "Time to finish your chores before supper."

Not a moment too soon. Emily wagged her head as her impudent little cousin spun on her heel and headed off to do her chores.

Moving toward the front of the shop, Emily passed the workroom in which alterations were made. Occasionally customers came to Sundbergs' Creations to have their dresses hemmed or seams let out or taken in when the ladies at Grauman's Dressmaker's Shop found themselves overwhelmed with orders. *Tante* Agnes and her older sister *Tante* Adeline also spun wool into various yarns and fibers in this room. Then Momma and *Bestamor* did the needlework at home on the small farm located about a mile outside of town. With Poppa being in the shipping business and her aunts running the boutique, the Sundberg name was well known in Manitowoc. And with all the wagging tongues in town, everyone would soon know how US Deputy Marshal Jake Edgerton had bowled her over during a brawl.

Poppa would have a conniption!

The tiny bell fastened above the door jangled, signaling customers. Emily glanced up and watched as Iris and Mrs. Hopper entered the shop.

"I knew I'd find you here." Iris trotted over to her. "Deputy Edgerton is quite concerned about you."

"Well, he shouldn't be." Emily lifted her chin. "He should just mind his own business and watch where he's going."

"I'm sure that's difficult to do in a fistfight, Em."

Mrs. Hopper sniffed.

"Deputy Edgerton?" *Tante* Agnes walked farther into the shop. "Who's he?" Her gaze shifted to Iris's aging grandmother. "And hello, Mrs. Hopper. Won't you please have a seat? You look as though you could use a glass of cool tea."

"Indeed I could, thank you."

Iris pushed her spectacles higher onto the bridge of her nose. "Deputy Edgerton is in town for his grandfather's funeral."

"Oh?"

Emily regarded her aunt. "I just learned Mr. Ollie passed last night."

"How sad." *Tante* Agnes's features fell. "He'll be missed. He was a good man."

"The deputy is the one who crashed through Mr. Fransmuller's big plate window," Iris said, "while apprehending a notorious criminal."

Emily rolled her eyes at the exaggeration.

"As I walked from the scene, I overheard Deputy Edgerton tell the sheriff the whole story. Apparently Mr. Wilcox is wanted for postal theft, which, you know, is a federal offense. But he's also done other terrible crimes."

Everyone in the room drew in awed gasps.

Everyone except Emily. She almost smiled. Almost. How just like Jake Edgerton to turn the situation around and make himself look like the town hero!

CHAPTER 3

I APPRECIATE YOUR VISIT, Jake."

"No trouble, sir, since I was in town anyway." From his chair in Emily's father's prestigious office, Jake watched as the man strode to the edge of the imported carpet and stared out the tall windows banked at one end of the room. Captain Daniel Sundberg had always been a commanding figure, and now, as he straightened his shoulders and clasped his hands behind his back, he appeared even more so. Jake felt a remnant of that boyhood intimidation, like when he and Eden Sundberg were about to get a stern talking-to. The only evidence that ten years had come and gone were the silvery strands streaking the captain's auburn hair and thick beard. "I felt I should let you know about what happened earlier."

"But you say Emily wasn't injured?"

Jake had explained the whole story. "She was breathing, talking, and walking last I saw her, sir." He worked his palm along the rim of his Stetson. "Still, I'm a little worried about her. She took a hard hit for a woman." He grunted out an amazed laugh. "For a man too."

"Hmm...I find myself caught in quite the dilemma."

Jake frowned. "How so?"

Captain Sundberg expelled a weary-sounding sigh and turned from the view of the expansive lake. "Well, you see, my paternal instincts tell me to rush out of here and find my daughter." Again a heavy exhale. "But I can't. Emily fancies herself an independent young woman and has made it clear to her mother and me that she doesn't appreciate our interference."

Jake rubbed his thumb over his mouth to keep from grinning.

"The only consolation is that my youngest sister, Agnes, lives nearby with her family. My brother-in-law's brother owns the hotel almost directly across the street from them, and Mrs. Hopper's boardinghouse, in which Emily resides with her friend Iris Hopper, is only two blocks west of there."

"Sounds like Emily's got places to go if she needs help."

"My point exactly."

And the captain's got his spies. Jake made a mental note.

Captain Sundberg crossed the room and claimed an adjacent armchair. He gave Jake a speculative glance while stretching out his long legs. "As I recall from years ago, you and Emily have something of a regrettable history."

"Regrettable?" That's not the way Jake remembered it.

"Yes. I recall posting letters for Emily addressed to you in Montana."

Guilt nipped at Jake. "Her letters arrived." He remembered now. "And I always meant to reply." Poor Emily had poured out her heart in each one, apologizing and asking Jake to forgive her. Nothing to forgive as far as he was concerned. Her conscience was a bit overactive, if you asked him. But her concern for his person did speak well of her character.

"You might have penned a short note in return."

Jake heard the tightness in the captain's voice.

"You tarnished my daughter's reputation, after all. She bore the whispers, taunts, and teasing as well as a load of guilt for years."

"Captain Sundberg, I had no idea." Remorse set in, and Jake glanced down at his dusty boots. "And I'm sorry for my part in it. I never meant to hurt Emily. I was a kid—we both were."

The captain said nothing, did nothing.

Jake decided to explain himself fully. "I'm sure you already know this, but shortly after I returned to Montana, my father was gunned down in cold blood. I watched from the barn. I heard my mother and sister screaming, and I never felt so helpless in all my life." Jake could talk about it now. He'd had to recount the events for the sheriff and marshal, then a federal judge. "My senses returned, and I ran to Pa while the two men ransacked our home. They scared Ma and Deidre and roughed me up a little. Then they stole anything they could pack and carry before they took off. After Pa was laid to rest, I became the man of the family. I had to provide for and protect my mother and older sister." Jake met the captain's gaze. "Guess you might say life got a bit overwhelming. Kissing your daughter was a minor incident comparatively."

"I suppose in that light it was." The captain's features softened. "And I'm sure that was a very difficult time for you."

"Yes, sir, it was. But it made me the man I am today."

"And what sort of man is that?"

Jake heard the ring of a challenge and glimpsed the captain's grin beneath his beard. Jake didn't mind giving the man an honest reply. "I'm not bragging, but I'm a man with deep Christian convictions and one who believes in justice, not revenge. I'm dedicated to upholding the integrity of our laws as well as our courtrooms."

"Noble…"

"I try. I'm hardly perfect, Captain. I know it. But I figure if I aim to shoot straight, the bullet's bound to go in the right direction."

"I like that analogy." The captain stroked his beard, his assessing gaze moving up and down Jake's face.

Well, let him do his appraising. It wasn't the first time Jake had been scrutinized and it wouldn't be the last. Not in his line of work.

"Captain, I'm sorry my boyhood foolishness hurt Emily." As Jake recollected, she'd been adventurous and willing. Still, it hadn't been right. Then she'd grown into a young lady, writing letters to him, hoping to set things straight. Jake saw the matter clearly…now. "I'll make my apologies to Emily whenever I get a chance."

"And I trust that you'll never take advantage of her or disrespect her in the future."

"No, sir." He'd always held Emily in high regard. Always would.

"Good. Because the man who kisses my daughter marries her."

"I'll consider myself fairly warned." Last thing Jake had on his mind was marriage.

"You do that." The captain sat back in his chair, and the tension in the room abated.

Jake eased back too.

"I'm a man who believes in second chances. Lord knows I got mine." The captain's expression softened. "And, yes, Ollie told me about your father's death. I know about your mother too."

Sorrow wafted over Jake like a hot, sticky summer breeze. "It happened a little over a year after Pa's death." *Suicide.* Still so hard to fathom Ma doing such a thing. "It's coming up on nine years now."

"And no one knows what really happened."

"Most of us reckon she couldn't cope without Pa. Unfortunately we, being her family and friends, never sensed her pain and suffering. We never saw it coming."

"Devastating to be sure." The captain shook his head, a sad glimmer in his eyes.

Jake nodded. "I'm told there's a purpose for everything." Although he had yet to figure out the purpose behind Ma taking her own life.

"At one point I'd heard your mother planned to move back here to Manitowoc."

Jake thought hard. He hadn't been aware of those plans. And to this day he wondered if he could have somehow prevented his mother's death. She must have been so unhappy...but she never said so. She didn't act like it. She hid it well, smiling often and assuring Jake and his sister that God would provide for their every need. But inside she must have felt dismal, desolate, or she never would have gone to Suicide Bluff that awful day. If only she would have communicated how sad she really felt, then maybe Jake could have called a doctor—or contacted Granddad.

And he certainly wouldn't have argued with her that fateful morning over a grocery list. He said words to Ma he regretted. Words he couldn't take back now.

"Ollie took the news very hard. Your mother was very special to him, since your aunt ran off with that penniless vulture so many years ago. They nearly bankrupted Ollie, what with all their requests for handouts." The captain cleared his throat. "Please forgive me if I spoke out of turn."

"You spoke the truth." His aunt and uncle were the reasons why he'd packed his bags and moved out of Granddad's house. He'd stay at the hotel now that Granddad had passed on. He couldn't bear their constant chatter about what they'd do now that they'd inherited Granddad's money and possessions.

"In any case, I sympathized with Ollie because I'd be devastated if something dreadful happened to Emily, the way it happened to your mother."

"I understand."

Jake's gaze wandered to the painting above the mantel, a likeness of Mrs. Sundberg wearing a fancy, ruffled gown. But then, looking back at the captain, Jake decided Emily definitely favored her father—without the beard, of course. Same wavy auburn hair and sky-blue eyes, except where the captain was stern and commanding, Emily was soft looking and…lovely.

"Let's change the subject, shall we? How is your sister?"

"Deidre?" Jake smiled. "She's just fine. She and her husband live on the ranch that Pa built. No young'uns yet, but they're very happy."

"What about you? Are you happy?"

The question threw him, but only momentarily. "I'd say so. I own a small parcel of the ranch's land and live in a two-room cabin behind the main house. I'm not there much. Work calls me away a lot."

"I assume your father's death prompted you to choose your profession."

"Yes—and I feel it's the Lord's calling on my life—to protect the innocent and see that justice is served to the guilty."

The captain grinned. "Your grandfather bragged on you frequently. He was extremely proud that you chose a career in law."

"Well, I'm not an important attorney like Granddad was. Just a deputy, assisting the US marshal."

"I heard you're thinking about becoming a judge someday."

Jake chuckled at the notion. "I don't know about that. Might have been Granddad's dream more than mine."

"Even so, Ollie was very proud of you."

"I appreciate your saying so." Those words were like a salve on his beaten heart. "And I always knew it."

"My family and I will miss your grandfather, as I know you will also. If there's anything my wife and I can do for you during this sorrowful time, please let us know."

Jake merely inclined his head again. Sorrowful didn't even come close to describing his feelings. Granddad's passing busted a dam of regret. Should'ves. Would'ves. Could'ves. Those words swirled around and around in Jake's head. Just like with Ma, Jake wondered if he *should've* done more. But just like her, Granddad kept silent about his failing health. If he only *would've* said something, then maybe Jake *could've* arrived ahead of Aunt Bettina and Uncle Dwight and spared Granddad some aggravation.

"When did you get into town?"

Jake snapped from his musing. "I arrived yesterday evening, just hours before Granddad passed."

"At least you got to say good-bye."

"Yes…" It was hard to ignore the captain's look of sincerity. "Thank you, Captain."

"I imagine your uncle is the executive of your grandfather's estate." He held up one hand. "I take that back. It's none of my business, really. My only concern is our shared property line. My father acquired the land on which my home and your grandfather's sit from an Indian chief." The captain wagged his head. "Unfortunately my mother was forced to sell it after my father had a stroke. I managed to purchase back some of it, along with my original boyhood home, although we've built on additions to accommodate our family's needs."

Jake chuckled. "I believe Eden and I did some painting on one of those additions. It was punishment for one of the many stunts we pulled, but we ended up right proud of our accomplishment."

"Ah, yes..." Captain Sundberg's smile grew with obvious fondness.

"But back to your initial question..." Jake had no qualms about answering it, and more. He knew of the captain's trustworthiness. "Granddad's funeral will be held on Tuesday, so the undertaker can do his business. My aunt and uncle want Mr. Schulz, Granddad's attorney, to read the will tomorrow. They want to claim their inheritance... *now*. They cared nothing for Granddad. Only coveted his wealth."

"Unfortunate, isn't it."

Jake pulled in a long breath. "But I'm afraid Aunt Bettina and Uncle Dwight are in for something of a shock."

"Oh?" The captain regarded him askance.

"Yes, sir." Jake sensed he'd soon have a fight on his hands too. "Granddad left his entire estate to me."

"Emily, we're best friends. We're supposed to tell each other *everything*."

"Iris, I knew Jake Edgerton back when I was thirteen years old." And she wished she'd never met him!

A swell of regret plumed inside of her. Jake was the first boy—and the only one—to kiss her. It wouldn't have been so bad if she hadn't enjoyed it so much. She'd allowed Jake to kiss her on numerous occasions that summer. She'd even initiated them a few times. It was a shameful thing, feeling all those emotions when his lips met hers, awkwardly at first. However, it had been amazing how expert at kissing they'd become by summer's end.

Oh, God, I'm so sorry…

She'd whispered that prayer countless times over the years.

And then his betrayal. Jake must have bragged to all the boys after church one day. He wouldn't have lied, she had faith in that much, but the truth became embellished and vicious rumors spread around town like the Peshtigo Fire. Emily was so ashamed. She hoped and prayed that Jake would return and set the matter straight. But he never did. She wrote, asking for his forgiveness for her less-than-appropriate behavior, and prayed he'd reply that it was nothing. Kisses by curious kids, that's all. He never wrote back, never relinquished her from all her guilt and shame. Mr. Ollie kept her abreast of the events in Jake's life. She knew his father had been murdered and his mother fell off a bluff in some freak accident. She supposed he had an excuse for not corresponding. But just when she'd finally thought she'd put the matter behind her, Jake returns— bursting into her life, no less! A little too late.

"Well, I guess I can forgive you, Em." A mischievous spark brightened Iris's gaze.

"Don't you always?" Emily smiled then realized it hurt. "Is the bruise on my cheek any worse?" With every muscle protesting, she lifted the tortoise-shell-framed mirror from off the top of her lace-covered bureau. The mirror had been a gift from Poppa, and now, as she stared at her reflection, Emily realized the bruise was the least of her worries. As stiff and sore as she felt, she'd be fortunate to walk tomorrow, let alone dance tomorrow night. "I rue the day I met Jake Edgerton!"

"Oh, now, Em. Live and let live. Besides, he's awfully handsome, in a rugged sort of way." Iris blushed. "I'm sure Granny would come to at least like him a little bit, don't you think?"

"I think your grandmother should stop pressuring you to marry."

"That'll never happen."

Emily sent her friend an empathetic glance. But Iris didn't see it. Sitting in the wingback armchair in the far corner of the spacious room they rented, Iris lifted her feet onto the matching ottoman. Even though Iris was Mrs. Hopper's granddaughter, she was expected to pay rent like all the other unattached ladies who boarded at the rooming house. Mrs. Hopper frequently said she didn't want to show favoritism, now that Iris had reached the spinsterly age of twenty-four.

"What's more, I always dreamed of marrying someone like him and living out West."

Emily noted the faraway glimmer in Iris's eyes. "Rein in that imagination, cowgirl. Jake Edgerton is too much man for you."

"Why do you say that?" Iris pouted. "Am I really as bony as fine china, like Granny keeps saying?"

"No, no…" Emily didn't mean it that way. It was just that Jake's kind of woman would be one who…who…could get barreled into the street during a barroom brawl and live to tell about it?

Perish the thought! True, she'd fancied herself in love with him once when she was tomboy, a mere child really. But nothing had endeared him to her since. Besides, much of her memories of him were tainted by what happened after he left.

"I really can't help it, Em. I wish I had curves like you do."

"Now, Iris, you know as well as I do that ladies are created in all different shapes and sizes. I take after my father's side of the family, and the Sundberg women tend to fill out their bodices and have an easy time of childbirth." Emily felt a blush coming on. "At least that's what *Besta* told me." Emily had no firsthand experience there, of course. "Likewise, there's no point in me trying to fashion my body after yours. You're a good two inches taller, and you're slender, like a graceful willow."

"A graceful willow." A pleased expression drifted over Iris's face.. "Yes, that's me."

Emily smiled, glad to have appeased her dear friend. A moment later she stifled a moan as she forced her hurting body to crawl beneath the bedcovers. Next she reached for the book on the night-stand. "Sometimes I envy you too, Iris, especially when we go dress shopping. You have a much easier time of it."

"I suppose that's true." Iris smoothed her white nightgown over her knees.

"Back to Jake..." Emily wanted to squelch her friend's interest in him. Iris would only get her heart shattered like Mr. Fransmuller's plate window. "He's one step up from an outlaw."

"He's a deputy marshal and that's the opposite of an outlaw."

"It takes one to catch one." Emily opened her book. "Just remember that!"

CHAPTER 4

*E*MILY WILLED HER hand to bring the porcelain cup to her lips despite the pain the simple action incurred. Every muscle and sinew felt the effects of the hit she took yesterday. Both knees were black and blue, her elbows scraped, and the bruise on her face had spread from her cheekbone to her jaw and resembled a permanent dirt mark. *Thanks a lot, Jake!*

Carol Schmidt sent her a curious glance and reached for a second helping of fried potatoes. "Are you feeling all right today, Emily?"

"Feeling fine."

Carol's brown eyes narrowed suspiciously. "How did you get that bruise on your face?" She smoothed the napkin across her ample lap.

"Oh…a nasty spill." Emily sent a glance in Iris's direction.

"That's right. Granny and I were there when it happened."

"Hmm…" Carol chewed, her pudgy cheeks bulging, then swallowed. The woman enjoyed a good piece of gossip as much as her second, sometimes third helpings at mealtime.

But Emily refused to say more to her and the other four women seated around the table. Iris had been sworn to secrecy. However, as they read from the Friday morning edition of the newspaper, they, along with everyone in Manitowoc, were sure to find out the most embarrassing details.

Martha Martin began reading the society column aloud. It

detailed tonight's Memorial Day Dance. Emily shifted in her chair, and her stiff muscles protested the movement.

"Let's all go together." Sarah Jenkins sat up a bit straighter and smiled at her idea.

"Fine by me." Iris gave a careless shrug. "Although I'm meeting someone special there. He asked me to save him a dance."

"Who?" The ladies spoke in unison and all leaned forward over their plates.

"He's just visiting our fair town because his grandfather died. I thought his coming to the dance tonight might cheer him up."

"Who? Who?"

Emily thought the women sounded like overeager hoot owls, for heaven's sake!

"His name is Jake Edgerton. He's a deputy US marshal from Montana."

"Goodness! I just read about him here in the newspaper!" Martha flipped back a page.

Emily's hand began to tremble, but she managed to set down her teacup before it spilled. *In the newspaper!* That means Poppa would learn about the incident before she could tell him.

"I read the article earlier," Martha said. "Seems the good deputy apprehended a fugitive wanted in four counties."

"That's right." A look of pride enhanced Iris's pointed features.

Emily couldn't believe her friend had succumbed so quickly. Jake obviously had a certain effect on females.

Martha began reading the article, and Emily stared at the linen napkin in her lap. Her stomach cramped with each word. "'Deputy Edgerton recognized the fugitive and followed him into Mr. Helmut Fransmuller's restaurant and saloon. He engaged the wanted man in a game of poker and caught him cheating. A fight ensued, during which Mr. Fransmuller's front window was broken, but the deputy got his man. Sheriff Smith handcuffed the fugitive and escorted him to jail.'" Martha looked up at Iris. "And you say this same deputy asked you to save him a dance?"

"Yes." Iris blushed. "We met yesterday, shortly after that incident you just read about occurred. I'd just come out of—"

"Excuse me, Iris." Emily's gaze slid to Martha. "Is that all the newspaper had to say?"

"Yes, would you care to read it for yourself?"

"No, thank you. I just wondered." Relief poured over Emily. Her name hadn't been mentioned. Andy would never know. Poppa wouldn't find out!

"Anyway," Iris continued, "I was properly introduced to Deputy Edgerton, and we had a conversation." Her eyelashes fluttered, magnified by her thick lenses. "When I mentioned the Memorial Day Dance, he said I must save a dance for him."

Awed sighs were followed by soft giggles.

Emily stared at Iris, and when she caught her friend's eye, she gave a subtle shake of her head. Iris ignored the implied warning. Apparently she'd taken nothing Emily said last night to heart.

Emily excused herself from the table and stood, determining not to moan when her body only grudgingly cooperated. "I need to go to school today and finish cleaning out my classroom for the summer." But first she'd indulge in a hot bath and soak her sore muscles. With a parting smile at the ladies, she added, "Have yourselves a good day."

They didn't seem to hear but began peppering Iris with questions about *her deputy.*

Turning toward the stairwell, Emily silently wished the best for her dear friend—but an odd little niggle inside seemed to warn that the worst was yet to come.

Clanging church bells signaled the noon hour as Jake walked out of the hotel. He pushed his hat onto his head, squinted into the sunshine—and then proceeded to crash into a pedestrian. A female. He grabbed her arm so she wouldn't lose her balance.

"'Scuse me, Miss." All at once recognition set in. He smiled. "Why, Miss Sundberg." He politely dipped the rim of his hat. "We meet again."

She pushed his arm away and glanced around quickly as if making sure no one had seen their collision. A quick assessment of his own told Jake no one took a particular notice of it.

"Will you please stop running in to me?" She adjusted the fashionable hat that cantilevered over her face.

"It was an accident, Em. I didn't set out to run you over or embarrass you."

"Then what are you doing, lurking around the hotel?"

"Not lurking. I checked in yesterday afternoon." Jake saw the questions in her eyes. "It's a long story."

"Then I have no time to listen. Sorry." She jerked her chin and tugged on the hem of her blouse, straightening it. Jake noticed how nicely it complemented her shapely figure. She caught his appreciative stare and glowered at him.

Jake cleared his throat. "Where you off to on this beautiful day?"

"I have some work to do at school. Now if you'll excuse me."

"Mind if I walk along?"

"Yes!"

"Good thing it's a free country." He grinned. She obviously didn't want his company; however, Jake had something to say to her. "Please, Em? I need to talk with you."

She sighed. "Oh, I suppose."

He gave a grateful dip of his head.

They walked a few paces during which Jake heard the distant

but incessant hammering from the shipyards. Wagons and buggies rumbled by on the paved street. Didn't have any of those in Fallon, Montana. Only dirt roads and cow trails there. He had to admit it was nice not to eat plumes of dust as you made your way down the walk. Then two men rode by on bicycles. Now there was a sight!

They reached the corner. Emily's aunt's shop was across the street. Jake watched several ladies point and gaze into the large front window.

"Your aunt does a good business, eh?"

Emily glanced at the shop and then at him. "Yes, *Tante* Agnes does quite well. *Bestamor* owned Sundbergs' Creations up until about five years ago."

"Oh, and speaking of…I saw your grandma last night. Still quite spry for a woman her age."

Emily stopped, her foot poised over the edge of the walk. "You saw *Bestamor*?"

"That's right. I stopped in to tell your father about what happened yesterday. He insisted that I come to dinner, which worked out for me. I wanted to pick up a few more things at Granddad's place."

"Wait. What did you just say?" Emily gave him such a fierce look that Jake considered taking a step backward. "You told Poppa?"

Jake fought off a grin. He'd known hardened criminals who couldn't make him pause like Emily Sundberg did just now.

"How could you?"

"Calm down, Em. I merely wanted him to hear it from me." He suddenly glimpsed the bruise on her cheek and cringed. "I hope I didn't hurt you too bad. I'm truly sorry."

She tipped her head, curiosity replacing anger. "What was Poppa's reaction?"

Jake felt somewhat insulted that his apology went ignored. "He was concerned, of course, but he and your mother have agreed to respect your independence."

"Really?" Emily's features softened, and her eyes turned as blue as his view of Lake Michigan over her right shoulder. "Poppa said that?"

"Well, not in so many words, but that's what I got out of it."

"My goodness!" A smile slowly worked its way up her pretty pink lips. "My parents finally respect me as a grown woman."

Jake noted that she sure was a lot prettier now, wearing that friendly smile, than moments before. Over the years he'd made countless foes, but for some odd reason he didn't want Emily Sundberg to be one of them.

He offered his arm as they crossed the thoroughfare, and Emily surprised him by threading her hand around his elbow.

"What a relief...and I suppose I should thank you for breaking the news to Poppa so I didn't have to tell him about it—or worse, have him hear it from a stranger."

"My thoughts exactly—and you're welcome."

She sent a glance skyward. "For your information, I had planned to go over to the shipping office this afternoon and tell Poppa. He's usually in town on Fridays."

As they strolled down the next block, Jake politely nodded to a cluster of men talking outside a store. He overheard one fellow grumble something about the price of hog feed.

"I was equally as relieved to see that my name wasn't mentioned in the newspaper."

Jake smiled at Em's sweet babbling.

"But you're certainly a hero."

"Hardly. Just doing my job."

Emily didn't reply, and they walked along in silence for half a block. He wondered what went on inside her pretty head—and that surprised him. Normally he didn't care what a woman thought unless she happened to be his older sister or the female had something to do with a man he was tracking. But Emily was different, and he realized right then that she'd always occupied a special place in his heart.

She stopped short, and Jake did also. After giving her a curious look, he followed her gaze across the next thoroughfare to a group of four men, sitting on a weathered bench in a corner park. Behind them children played ball and chased each other while women sat idly by, talking or knitting.

One man in particular caught his attention. "Well, what do you know? There's Andy Anderson. I'd recognize him anywhere!"

Jake slowly brought his gaze to Emily and realized this was no coincidence. He chuckled. "You come here often?"

"Almost every day."

The fact she admitted it surprised Jake. "So how far out of the way do you come?"

"A few blocks while school was in session. I'd take a walk instead of eating lunch. Today I went out of my way because…"

"Because of the dance tonight." Jake released a long, slow whistle. Sounded like Emily had serious feelings for Andy. He recalled what Iris Hopper told him—about how Andy didn't pay Emily any special attention. *Unbelievable.* Jake removed his hat and combed his fingers through his hair. A man should feel lucky to win Emily Sundberg's affection.

Repositioning his Stetson, Jake watched her, waiting for Emily to make the next move. But she stood stock-still.

"The sky ain't gonna get much bluer today, Em."

She sent him an annoyed glance.

He grinned. "And I don't expect Andy gets all afternoon to eat lunch."

She said nothing—*did* nothing.

"Em?"

"The men with whom Andy's sitting today…well, I don't appreciate their vulgarity."

"Ah…"

"Andy typically spends his lunch break with David Hansen, and then I don't mind approaching him to say hello."

"I see." Jake's heart bent for her. "How 'bout we approach those fellas together? That way I'll get to say hello to Andy too. I told you yesterday that I hoped to see him again. My experience tells me those men will mind their manners if I accompany you."

"You think so?" Emily gazed up at him, her eyes round and hopeful.

"Positive." Jake clenched his fist, thinking he'd knock someone's front teeth out if he treated her with anything less than respect.

They waited until two wagons noisily rattled past before stepping off the walk. Together they strode across the street, and Jake sized up the men and the situation. He doubted Emily was in any danger, not with additional women and children nearby. He did, however, catch the way they leered at Emily, elbowing each other, snickering. But when they caught sight of Jake and figured out he wasn't merely passing by, they put on their best faces.

"Andy Anderson?"

He sat in the middle of his comrades. "That's me." Slowly he got to his feet and raised his chin. "Who are you?"

Jake held out his right hand. "Jake Edgerton."

Andy's thick brows dipped in a frown as he repeated the name. Seconds later his expression brightened. "Well, I'll be! Jake!" Andy laughed and pumped his hand. "Good to see you again." He turned to his friends. "Hey, boys, this here's a friend of mine, Jake Edgerton."

They muttered greetings, and Jake gave each one a polite nod, keenly aware that Andy hadn't even glanced in Em's direction yet.

"So how've you been, Jake? What are you doing in town? How long are you staying?"

"I've been getting along all right." He glanced at his boots, feeling rueful. "I'm in Manitowoc for my granddad's funeral."

"I'm sorry to hear it. You've got my sympathies."

"Appreciate 'em. I'll head back home to Montana on the eight-fifteen train Wednesday morning." He slid his gaze to Emily, wondering why he disliked the idea of leaving her. His feelings made

37

no logical sense. He barely knew Em, and she obviously cared for someone else. What's more, the jury was out on whether she even *liked* him.

Still…

"So you'll be around for tonight's Memorial Day Dance, eh?"

"Yeah, I'll probably show up for a while since Granddad was a military veteran."

"Great. Maybe we'll find some time to catch up."

"Maybe." Jake nodded toward Emily. "Say, um, Andy, aren't you going to say hello to Emily Sundberg?" He leaned forward. "She looks mighty fetching today, wouldn't you say?"

Emily coyly lowered her head. A pretty pink blush stained her cheeks.

"Oh, right. Hi-ya, Em."

"Hi, Andy." She took two steps forward. "I wondered if—"

"Listen, Jake…" Andy turned his shoulder away from Emily in obvious disinterest. "Me and the other fellas got some girls coming tonight from Two Rivers. Real girls, if you know what I mean."

Jake understood.

"I can arrange to get one for you too."

"No, thanks." Jake watched Emily walk away with a defeated sag to her shoulders.

"You're sure?"

"Positive. I can get my own girl." Jake started off after Emily.

"All right. See you tonight," Andy called. "The first round of beer is on me."

His friends cheered in the background.

Same old Andy. Always the big spender.

Jake easily caught up to Emily, slowed his stride, and fell into step beside her. "Are you all right?"

"Of course. Why wouldn't I be?" She clipped each word.

Jake decided to let her be until they neared a two-story,

cream-colored brick structure. The name, embossed in concrete above the main entrance, read *Maple Street School.*

"What do you see in him anyway, Em?"

She didn't reply until she reached the steps, leading up to the front doors. "For your information Andy Anderson is a good man, a hard worker. He rarely misses church service on Sunday mornings, and everyone likes him. Andy makes people laugh with his antics and impresses them with his daring. Once he climbed to the top of a partially constructed building downtown and took a photograph because Ira Lemke at the *Chronicle* was too afraid of heights, and yet he wanted the picture for his newspaper story." A soft giggle bubbled out of her mouth. "I could go on and on all afternoon about Andy."

"No need." Jake held up a hand. "I didn't ask for a list of the man's attributes, Em. I'm asking what you see in him—as a possible suitor or husband."

"Well…" She had to think about it and that told Jake plenty. "Andy's very kind—"

"To whom?" Jake removed his hat. "Begging your pardon, Em, but I'd say Andy was extremely rude to you just now."

"He didn't mean it."

"You sure? Maybe he's trying to tell you that he doesn't share your particular fondness."

"He doesn't know I'm interested."

"Andy would have to be deaf, dumb, and completely blind not to see it."

"Is that so?" She tipped her head in just a way as to reveal the unsightly bruise on her cheek. It pained Jake something awful to see it. "And what makes you such an expert?"

"I'm no expert, Em. I'll admit it."

"Hmm…I rather thought so." She began climbing the stairs, and Jake wondered if he imagined her sassy swagger.

Regardless, he wouldn't be deterred. "All I can say is that when

Web was interested in my sister, she didn't have to go out of her way to make him notice her."

Emily paused at the top of the steps long enough to send him a scathing glance.

Jake shrugged. "Just trying to help."

"I think you've done just about enough, *Deputy Edgerton.* Thank you so very much."

"Is that sarcasm?" Jake did his best not to grin.

In reply Emily swung open one of the two tall doors and disappeared inside the school.

CHAPTER 5

*O*HHH, THAT JAKE *Edgerton makes me so mad!*

Even three hours later, after cleaning her classroom, Emily still couldn't shake off her irritation. The lengthy walk from school to the riverfront didn't help it abate either.

Reaching Ramsey, Sundberg & Dunbar Shipping and Freight Company, Emily walked into its tidy greeting area and found her younger brother Zeb at the front desk.

"May I help you, miss?" He feigned importance and his blue eyes danced with mischief.

"Where's Poppa?" Emily wasn't in the mood for games.

"In his office." Zeb's brows narrowed. "Something wrong?"

"Never mind." Emily strode toward the office.

"Nice hat."

Emily heard her brother's teasing tone. "Oh, quiet." She adjusted it slightly.

"Say, Em, do you remember Jake Edgerton? He's in town and ate supper with us last night."

"Yes, I remember him."

Zeb chuckled. "I was just a kid about nine years old the summer he stayed with Mr. Ollie. All I recollect is following him and you and Eden everywhere—"

"Like a puppy," Emily put in.

"Amazing to think that Jake's a US marshal now."

"*Deputy* marshal."

"And he apprehended a fugitive. It's in today's paper."

"I know, Zeb. I know!" Emily knocked on her father's office door a bit harder than intended.

Moments later the knob turned and the door swung open. Poppa glanced at Emily, then Zeb. "What's going on out here?"

"Oh, Zeb just teased me, and I reacted poorly." She pushed out a smile for his benefit and stared into his bearded face. "I stopped in to say hello."

He smiled. "I'm glad you did. Come in, darling." He glanced at Zeb. "Mind the store and get those invoices logged."

"Aye-aye, Captain."

Immaculately dressed in cocoa-brown trousers and vest and a crisp, white dress shirt, Poppa arched a brow. The hue of his blue eyes turned to bluish ice. "Watch yourself, lad."

"Yes, sir."

Poppa turned to Emily. His smile returned, and he closed the door. "You look lovely." Stepping forward, he bent to kiss her cheek, then paused to examined her hat. "Why must you ladies wear such contraptions with all the frill and fuss?"

He looked so annoyed that Emily giggled. "Oh, Poppa…" She removed the hat pin that she'd woven through the tightly wound chignon at the back of her head. "It's fashionable."

"Of course it is." He snorted and placed a kiss on Emily's cheek. "I'm glad you stopped for a quick visit. I hoped you would." His gaze narrowed when he glimpsed the bruise on her face.

"Jake said he talked to you yesterday."

"He did. I know the whole story." Poppa gently cupped her face in his palm and tipped her head to one side. "Does it hurt?"

"Not as much as the rest of me does." Emily wrapped her fingers around his wrist and Poppa took her hand. "My muscles are stiff and sore."

"I'll bet." Poppa led her to the burgundy velvet-covered armchairs in the corner of his office. She sat down in one and he in the other. "You know, your mother is going to insist that you move home for the summer when she learns you were even mildly injured in yesterday's incident."

"Yes." Emily knew all too well how much Momma disliked all the comings and goings in town. She felt safer in the countryside where neighbors lived acres away and yet close enough if you needed them—or wanted to arrange clandestine meetings by the stream where kisses could be shared beneath the oak tree.

The memory haunted Emily. Dropping her gaze, she willed it away and forced herself to concentrate on this present conversation. "I'm certain that I'll find summer work."

"Hmm…"

When Poppa offered no further comment, Emily looked over at him.

"Something's troubling you. I can tell. You can't fool your poppa." He gave her a gentle smile. "Does it have to do with Jake Edgerton?"

She couldn't lie and replied with the tiniest of nods.

"I thought so." Poppa eased back in his chair. "But don't hold a grudge because he didn't answer your missives, darling. He admitted he received them, but his father was killed. Murdered. Then his mother killed herself."

"No! No, she didn't!" The words were out before Emily could stop them.

"Excuse me?"

"Mr. Ollie said it was an accident."

"Ollie wasn't there, my dear." Poppa stroked his thick reddish-brown beard. "Regardless, I say all this only to ask you to forgive Jake for not returning your letters. He's had a very difficult life."

"I don't think Jake wants my pity. Moreover, shouldn't he be the one asking for my forgiveness?"

"Give him a chance, Emily."

Poppa's blue eyes beseeched her in a way that made Emily's stubbornness dissolve.

"Oh, all right. For you."

"Good. I'm glad that's settled." Poppa clapped his palms together. "And now Zeb and I should head for home. Your mother and *Besta* won't be pleased if we're late for supper."

Standing, Emily tamped down a moan over her stiff muscles. She smoothed the folds of her dark blue skirt. "And I must return to the boardinghouse and get ready for the dance tonight."

"Ah, yes, the Memorial Day Dance." Poppa's grin showed through his beard. Clasping her elbow, he walked her to the office door. "I imagine all the boys at Maple Street Elementary School will stand in line for a dance with the pretty third grade teacher."

"Oh, Poppa, no one under nineteen is allowed in." Emily paused to don her hat and pin it in place. Next she helped her father into his well-tailored, brown suit jacket. "And I hope you'll keep Zeb at home."

"He's nineteen now."

She stifled a groan. Another family member with whom to contend.

"Well, lucky for you, Zeb has hired on as one of my crew. We set sail at dawn's first light."

"Where are you going and how long will you be gone?" Emily almost envied her brother.

"We're sailing to Milwaukee. It'll be a short journey." He adjusted the cuffs of his shirt. "I'm anxious to get out on the water again. It's been a long winter."

"I've heard Momma say the same thing."

"Oh?" Poppa arched a brow.

Emily giggled at his reaction, and his features relaxed.

"You and your teasing…"

Raising herself up on tiptoe, she kissed his cheek. "Bye, Poppa. I will pray for good weather for your trip."

His features relaxed. "Thank you, my darling. Have fun tonight."

"I will." Thoughts of dancing with Andy Anderson sparked a renewed hope inside of her. "Give *Besta* and Momma my love."

"Will do."

"See ya, Em," Zeb said.

Smiling, Emily waved good-bye to her brother and left the shipping and freight company.

"I expect your aunt and uncle to contest the will."

"I figured as much." Jake eased back in one of the two black leather chairs and watched G. M. Schulz pace the richly paneled office, lined with thick law volumes.

"Well, let them bring the matter to the court of law." The aging attorney rubbed his palms together. "I enjoy a lively, courtroom debate, should it come to that. However, I suspect the case will be thrown out."

"Normally, I'd agree to a settlement, but Aunt Bettina and Uncle Dwight are behaving like a pair of vultures." Jake's biceps and shoulders tensed just thinking about them. "They circled Granddad's deathbed, hoping he'd tell them where he'd hidden his treasures."

"Despicable couple." Mr. Schulz wagged his head. "No, no... then we won't settle. Ollie was of sound mind when he wrote his will. Influential people will testify to that fact." The attorney paused and peered at Jake from above his round spectacles. "Your grandfather would be sick to learn that you're staying at the Dunbars' Inn while Bettina and that conniving husband of hers live the high life in the home he loved."

Jake agreed. "But once Granddad passed, I couldn't abide staying under the same roof with them. All they discussed was Granddad's money, his possessions, his home, but never Granddad himself.

They pushed off the funeral arrangements onto me, although it's just as well."

"Probably so." The older man with a shock of white hair and bony features ceased his pacing. "Ollie always felt like he'd somehow failed Bettina."

"I think she failed him when she ran off with that devil, Dwight Cleaver."

"Good point." Mr. Schulz regarded him with a keen gaze. "How did they find out Ollie was dying?"

"Aunt Bettina still has contacts in Manitowoc."

"Of course." The older man resumed his pacing. "You're a sharp man, Jake. I'd be glad to help you find employment, either here in this office or elsewhere."

"I've got a job, thanks."

"You wish to remain a deputy marshal forever?"

"Not...*forever.*"

Mr. Schulz stopped short. "You're young enough to make a new start, Jake. Why not grab this chance to learn a new profession? Ollie's money will sustain you through any additional or required education until you find your desired occupation. I'll help you any way I can. Sometimes it's not entirely what you know but *who* you know." His crooked grin gleamed with harmless conspiracy.

Jake was flattered and mulled it over, but not for long. "Look, Mr. Schulz, I sure appreciate the offer, but I—"

"Ollie said you're a praying man."

"I suppose I am."

"Then please pray about the matter."

Oh, fine! "If you insist." But he knew the answer already. *No!*

"Now, then, about Ollie's home..."

"Just to be clear, I've got a home too. In Fallon, Montana."

Mr. Schulz snorted a laugh. "Consider your options, son. Wisconsin needs federal marshals and deputies too. Your grandfather and I have plenty of contacts. Why not get married and settle here in Manitowoc?"

"Married?" Jake laughed. "Don't tell me Granddad left me a woman in his will too."

"Of course not." Mr. Schulz's laughing eyes said he found the jest amusing as he pulled out his desk chair and sat down.

"Any idea what you'll do with your inheritance—if you don't take me up on my offer?"

Jake released a long, slow breath. "Reckon I'll sell the house. I'll give some money to Deidre and Web. The ranch could use some fixin' up." Jake couldn't help a grin as he imagined his sister's happy expression when she glimpsed the new stove he'd purchased for her. All set to ship on Wednesday. He sent Web a telegram, telling him to bring the wagon and another set of hands when he met Jake at Fallon's platform next week. Here's hoping Web could figure out how to get the new stove into the wagon, up to the ranch, and into Deidre's kitchen.

"You're a generous man, Jake."

He replied with a little shrug. Deidre and Web were always there for him. With Granddad now gone, they were the only ones on earth who cared if he lived or died.

"I'm concerned about your aunt and uncle's presence." Mr. Schulz sat back and steepled his fingers. "Perhaps we should ask the sheriff to remove them this very evening."

Jake waved a hand. "No, no, but I appreciate your offer. I don't want any confrontations until after Granddad's funeral."

"You're a better man that I." Mr. Schulz stood and resumed his pacing, his hands behind his back. For a moment he paused and pulled out his watch, glimpsed the time, and snapped the cover closed before returning the timepiece to his vest pocket. "You know, Ollie told me time and time again how impressed he was with you. He respected your desire to see justice served."

Jake gave a single nod. Granddad had said as much during each of his semi-annual trips he'd made to Fallon. Always bumped up Jake's confidence a few notches and kept him going when lawlessness seemed to go unchecked.

A smile flashed on Mr. Schulz's narrow face. "And recently you protected the citizens of Manitowoc."

"Just a fluke."

"Or divine intervention."

"I'd agree with that." Jake grinned. He always felt the Lord was on his side.

"I should also mention that the year Ollie returned to Manitowoc after your mother died, he took a sabbatical from practicing law. He wanted time to think—to mourn."

Jake shifted, disliking the topic.

"Ollie sent telegrams to Bettina, begging her to visit him. It seemed important for him to reconcile with the only daughter he had left. He even traveled to Chicago to visit her, but that husband of hers ended up swindling Ollie out of thousands."

"So she already got her inheritance."

"A good way to view it. Nevertheless, Ollie always held out hope for his younger daughter, but he knew better than to trust her and Dwight. That's why he left nothing to them. In fact, after he became so ill that he couldn't get out of bed, Ollie asked me to remove all his cufflinks, watches, and your grandmother's fine jewelry." Mr. Schulz leaned to his right and pulled open a desk drawer. He lifted out a brass lockbox and held it out to Jake. "Here, son, this is yours. You'll also find the deed to the house, bank statements, and other important documents in there."

Jake grunted out a laugh. "Aunt Bettina and Uncle Dwight have been taking Granddad's house apart looking for this lockbox. Bettina asked me about it, but I'd never seen it before."

"Ollie gave a box just like this to each of his daughters for their safe-keepings." Mr. Schulz slid the key to the lockbox across the desk.

"I don't recall Ma having a box like this."

"She did—at least at one time. Ollie purchased them in India. Beautiful solid brass."

"Hmm...that explains why it's so heavy."

Jake sized it up, taking a moment to appreciate the ornate cover, and guessed it measured a foot long, half of that wide, and the same six inches high. Carefully he opened the lid and gently rummaged through the box's depth. Precious stones sparkled. Gold glittered. Later he'd take his time with each item. "Can I keep this locked up here?"

"Certainly."

Jake found one of Granddad's pocket watches and his throat tightened. Tears stung. Swallowing down the sudden onset of grief, Jake put the watch into his vest's front pocket and fastened the gold chain.

"Ollie would be proud to know you want to wear that, son."

"Something of Granddad can be with me wherever I go."

Mr. Schulz's expression said he too was pleased by Jake's decision. "Ollie fell into a kind of slump after your mother died, so Captain Sundberg began sending his children over to keep Ollie company." He snorted a laugh. "That Emily used to bend his ear by asking all sorts of questions to which Ollie had to find the answers somewhere in his library of books. She played the piano and sang for him, and Eden and Zeb kept Ollie on his toes with their mischief and interest in his weapons collection. But Ollie enjoyed it. In the evenings Mrs. Sundberg often brought him meals, and I believe the older Mrs. Sundberg, Kristin, accompanied Ollie to several business dinners and community events."

That was news to Jake. "Were they...in love?"

"I don't believe so." Mr. Schulz shook his head. "Good friends."

Jake still found it amusing. Emily's grandmother and his grandfather, something of a couple.

But why should that tickle him in any peculiar way?

"The Sundbergs were good neighbors to Ollie and vice versa once he recovered from your mother's death. I think it'd be fine if you chose a small token to give them in remembrance of Ollie." Mr. Schulz sat back and lifted his hands as if surrendering. "But you're not obligated. Just a suggestion."

"I'll make sure they each get something special."

"I believe that would please Ollie. In the meantime if your aunt and uncle remove anything from Ollie's home without your consent, you're free to contact the sheriff." A crooked grin dented one side of the elderly attorney's face. "You've met him already."

"Sure have." Yesterday's incident came to mind, the one in which Emily got hurt.

Spying a black velvet-covered box, Jake removed it from the brass casket and opened it. A tiny silver cross hung from a sterling chain.

"That belonged to your grandmother."

"It's pretty." Jake wondered if maybe Emily would like it. Might even serve as something of a peace offering.

The treasure fit into his palm and he pocketed it. Then he closed the lockbox.

"Mr. Schulz, do you think it would be terribly disrespectful of me to show up at that Memorial Day Dance tonight, seeing as Granddad hasn't even been laid to rest yet?"

Mr. Schulz lifted his narrow shoulders and pursed his lips. "Depends how you behave at the dance, I suppose. But simply attending and—" He narrowed his gaze. "Meeting someone special there, are you?"

"I heard Emily Sundberg talking about it, and I promised her a dance."

"Ah…" Mr. Schulz put the weighty brass box back into the drawer, locked it, and tucked away the key. "Then I will say what I think Ollie would say, go and have a good time."

"I thought so too." Jake stood. "Thank you for your time, Mr. Schulz, and I'll be in touch."

CHAPTER 6

*T*HE DRESS FIT perfectly!

Up in her room at the boardinghouse Emily stared at her reflection, pleased by what she saw. Momma and *Besta* had outdone themselves on this dress. A pale green, it had a loose-fitting bodice, V-neck with horizontal ribbing, and a white lace modesty inset. The trumpet-shaped skirt flowed nicely over her hips, its hem brushing the tops of her shoes.

"Em, you look stunning. Wait until Andy Anderson gets a glimpse of you."

"You think so? Truly?" She willed her sore muscles to make the turn away from the walnut-framed mirror. She'd discovered that if she kept moving, her body didn't hurt as badly. Once she stopped, it was hard to get going again, and sitting still while Iris had styled her hair had been difficult. "What about my cheek?"

"The bruise hardly shows. The way we've piled your hair and curled the tendrils against your face...why, you look like one of Mr. Charles Gibson's girls." Iris retouched the locks at Emily's temples.

"Really? You think so?"

"I wouldn't fib about something like that." Iris pushed up her glasses. "We're best friends, aren't we?"

Emily managed a nod while taking in Iris's ensemble. She looked attractive in the bargains she'd discovered while shopping at Schuette Brothers Department Store. The feminine off-white shirtwaist was a dignified mate for the fashionable nine-gored skirt. Around her tiny waist Iris wore a silk sash of robin's egg blue.

She swung her slender hips. "Do you think the good deputy will want more than a dance from me? Like a kiss, perhaps?"

Emily drew in a breath, shocked. "Why, Iris Hopper! The things you say sometimes! We're respectable schoolteachers."

"School ended last week." A gleam entered Iris's pale blue eyes before she took Emily's place in front of the full-length mirror. "This summer I'm going to find a husband. I'm determined." Scrutinizing her reflection, Iris carefully removed her glasses.

Goodness, she was serious! Iris never took off her spectacles unless she meant business. "Iris, about Jake Edgerton..."

"What about him?" Iris pirouetted and came to stand in front of Emily.

"Jake's not husband material, not in the way you're thinking." She and Iris frequently shared their dreams for the future. Iris wanted a husband who worked all day and came home in time to wash up, eat, and attend parent-teacher conferences. She wanted a man who'd involve himself with their children's lives and their community. "Jake's work makes him an unpredictable man. I mean, think of it, Iris. Deputy marshals escort dangerous criminals to federal prisons. They lead posses, carry guns, and frequently kill other men." Emily folded her arms. "Do you really think that sort of husband will be home in time for supper every night?"

"Well, I..." A shadow of doubt crept over Iris's narrow features. "I hadn't considered his occupation just yet, other than to find it quite fascinating."

"Then perhaps you could write a piece on Jake and submit it to the *Chronicle*." Emily winked. "A great excuse to converse with him alone, and the editor at the newspaper said he'd especially consider articles from the community's teachers anytime."

"Hmm...what a clever idea." Iris set her forefinger on her lips, thinking.

"After the interview, you may discover for yourself that Jake's not husband material."

"I'll have a clue then, won't I?"

"More than a clue, I'd say."

Iris's broad smile revealed two crooked eyeteeth, and Emily found her expression endearing. It seemed to confirm Iris's unconventional nature. Who else would have accepted a rejected, former tomboy as a best friend when they were fifteen years old? No one else but the sometimes prudish, sometimes pert and zany Miss Iris Mae Hopper.

"You're brilliant, Em. I adore the idea of interviewing Deputy Edgerton."

"Yes, I know how brilliant I am." With a laugh Emily glanced back into the mirror. If only Andy Anderson would be so impressed with her.

After another final inspection of their attires Emily and Iris collected their hats, shawls, gloves, and reticules and left for Manitowoc's community building. They passed a saloon. Its doublewide front doors stood open to let in the mild evening air, but already raucous singing accompanied by a slightly out-of-tune piano emanated from the establishment. It wasn't even dark outside yet.

Emily decided they'd walk home another way and perhaps make the trek with their boardinghouse mates.

At last they reached the community building. Inside, Emily heard the musical ensemble playing a lively tune. She and Iris followed the melody to a large recreational room, used for multiple purposes. Tonight it had been decorated with brightly colored paper flowers and streamers for this month's big event. The Memorial Day Dance.

Emily scanned the room for Andy, and her gaze lit on him almost immediately. He stood in the far corner of the hall in his dark brown suit. His loud chortles reached her ears and made her smile. Andy had a way of making everyone smile.

"Andy looks awfully handsome, doesn't he, Em? But, alas, it appears he's been imbibing." Iris clucked her tongue.

"You are sounding and more and more like your grandmother every day." Emily squared her shoulders. "Everyone knows Andy is the jovial sort—without help from beer, wine, or what have you."

Iris stepped closer to her. "I saw one of his friends pocket a flask."

"Then that man should be removed from the hall."

"It was a woman, Em. The blonde over there, wearing the black and white dress. However, I dare say her hair is likely bleached. No real hair is *that* color. And that dress...so immodest!" Iris took a step back. "And I do *not* sound like Granny!"

Emily said nothing but watched as Andy pulled the buxom blonde onto the dance floor. The muscles in her chest constricted painfully. But then Andy began a jig when he should have been waltzing, and Emily laughed at his antics.

"Oh, he's just putting on." Relief poured over her.

"Hmm..." Iris didn't sound convinced.

Another man cut in, and Andy sauntered over to the linen-covered food and beverage table.

"Now's your chance, Em. Go say hello to him."

"Should I?"

"Yes, go."

Nervous flutters filled her insides as Emily walked toward him. Besides being a childhood friend to both her and Eden, Andy had served aboard several of Poppa's clippers and steamships, impressing her father with his ambition and ability to work hard. If Poppa said Andy Anderson had potential, then it was true.

"Hello, Andy." Emily held her breath.

"Oh, hi." He ladled berry punch into a glass cup and barely gave her a glance.

"I'd been hoping that maybe...well, that you'd ask—"

"My friends are waiting. Got to go."

Andy wheeled away from the table. His rejection stung. Did Andy find her repulsive? Had she grown three heads? Were they horned?

The band began playing another tune, and more couples filed onto the dance floor of the rapidly filling hall. Emily fought back tears as she saw Andy pull a well-endowed brunette into his arms. As they waltzed nearer, Emily felt her chin begin to quiver. Blinking, she turned away and started toward where she'd left Iris.

"May I have this dance, Miss Sundberg?"

Emily halted, looked up, and, to her horror, realized she'd all but walked into Jake Edgerton's outstretched arms. She instantly sensed he'd witnessed Andy's dismissal—again.

Dodging his gaze, she tried to speak, but her throat clogged with unshed emotion.

"I'll take that as a yes." Jake's right arm encircled her waist, his left hand held her right, and, as they stepped to the music, Emily caught the most pleasant scent, something akin to citrus and cedar wood, most likely a tonic his barber used. She'd noticed immediately that his sandy-blond hair had been trimmed and slicked back in a stylish manner.

"You look beautiful tonight, Em."

She barely heard the compliment but tried to glimpse Andy over Jake's shoulder. Each time she caught sight of him, Jake would take a turn. Finally Emily realized he did it on purpose.

And she had behaved extremely rudely!

At long last her gaze traveled up Jake's raven necktie and clean-shaven jaw to meet his gaze. She mustered an apologetic smile.

"Well, that's more like it."

His dark eyes reminded Emily of Momma's velvety chocolate pudding, and she found it impossible to look away.

"I'd venture to say you're the most beautiful young lady here tonight."

"Thank you, but you don't have to try to make me feel better, Jake."

"I wouldn't dare." His eyes turned to polished ebony.

Something sparked inside of Emily as Jake drew her closer, holding her a breath away from impropriety. Emily's hand seemed to have a will of its own as it inched up his arm and came to rest on the shoulder of his black wool jacket.

He began to hum to the music. His easy pitch caused Emily to relax.

"Casey would dance with the strawberry blonde"—he sang so closely to her ear that it tickled—"and the band played on."

A little laugh erupted.

"I know this song by heart."

"Oh?" Smiling, she pulled back slightly to view his expression.

"Mm-hm." He dipped his head. "It's the only modern tune the boys back home learned how to play. You see, there's a group of fellas that play for the Fourth of July picnic and such, but they're not able to get together and practice very often on account they all live in different parts of the county."

"A pity."

"I'll say! Particularly when we're forced to hear the same three numbers for the entire afternoon."

Another laugh bubbled up inside of Emily. She glimpsed Jake's smile before he brought her close to him again. The tempo slowed and a buttery warmth spread throughout her being.

"He married the girl with the strawberry curl," he sang, "and the band played on."

The world seemed to slow. They stopped dancing. Emily watched Jake's dark eyes fixed on the tendrils surrounding her face. They were lighter than her natural auburn. Perhaps in this dimness they might look strawberry blonde…

Her breath caught when his gaze found hers once more. A light of intensity, perhaps even certainty, lurked in the depths of his eyes.

Then he chuckled lightly.

Emily realized the band had stopped playing. People began mingling noisily around them. She gave Jake a smile, unsure what he found funny. Maybe something concerning the story he'd just shared. Perhaps he simply enjoyed dancing with her just now. She enjoyed dancing with him very much.

Taking a step backward, Jack gave her a short bow before placing a kiss on her fingers. That same spark ignited deep inside of her.

"Thank you for the dance, Miss Sundberg."

"My pleasure, Deputy Edgerton."

All at once a throng of people came between them, some heading for the food and beverages. A growing sense of awareness engulfed Emily. Funny, but while dancing with Jake, she hadn't given Andy Anderson another thought!

As the evening wore on, Emily danced with everyone, it seemed, except Andy. She'd waltzed with Mr. Saunders, an accountant. When the band played some ragtime, she'd done a fairly good two-step with John Bjornson, who worked at the hardware store, and two-stepped again with Matt Smith, the son of a minister at one of the Protestant churches nearby. But now she needed to catch her breath.

Unlike Iris who hadn't stopped all night.

Emily shook her head at her best friend. Iris gave her a wave before spinning in her partner's arms. Then Emily searched the hall. No sign of Andy. She strolled outside where people had gathered in small groups to catch their breath, cool down, or enjoy a cigarette. Several couples stood arm in arm, their heads inclined as they whispered to one another. Oh, how Emily wished she and Andy could share romance beneath the moonlight in just that way. If Andy would kiss her, perhaps she'd forget all about Jake Edgerton.

She wandered to the wood plank fence, dividing the community's property from a resident's. Leaning on a thick round post, she heard Andy's fun-loving laugh and directed her gaze toward the sound of it. She smiled, staring across the way. He stood with the same two women he'd danced with earlier, only now three more had been added to the mix. A couple of Andy's buddies stood with him...and Jake too.

Emily straightened, feeling a tad betrayed somehow. But what did she care if Jake conversed with Andy, his vulgar friends, and those...hussies.

Turning her back on them, she stared into darkened yard next door. *Lord Jesus, why does Andy find those women he's entertaining more appealing than me? Aren't I just as pretty? I certainly dress and behave more respectably. I've worked so hard to be respectable.*

She detected a presence beside her and turned to see that Jake had crossed the way. Like most men at this late hour, he'd removed his suit jacket.

"Emily Sundberg, standing in the moonlight..." He leaned on the fence. "You're a fetching sight to behold."

"Apparently not fetching enough." Folding her arms, Emily flicked a glance to where Andy stood, waving his arms in animated gestures as he, perhaps, told one of his amusing jokes.

Jake leaned his back up against the fence post and said nothing for several long moments. "Your father said Eden's away at school in New York."

"That's right." She noticed he'd changed the subject. "Eden is oh-so sophisticated now that he attends Columbia University." Emily couldn't stave off a grin. As much as she teased her twin, she felt proud of him. "He'll graduate next year, as he took off time to work onboard a ship, gaining experience about the shipping industry in general. Just like my poppa did."

"I'm impressed. I reckon he'll be a part of your family's shipping business then too."

"That's the plan." Emily's gaze snuck away to watch Andy.

"And you're a schoolteacher..."

Her gaze bounced back to Jake. "Yes." But he knew that already.

"I'm impressed with your achievements as well, Em."

"That's nice of you to say." Emily resumed watching Andy and wondering over his behavior yet once more.

"I'm not just saying it to be nice. I mean it."

"Thank you." Unfortunately the complimentary words didn't carry the momentum needed to reach her wounded heart.

"Say, look, I have something for you."

"For me?" Curious now Emily gave Jake her full attention.

He reached into his vest pocket and retrieved a small black box.

"What is it?"

"Open it."

Bemused, Emily worked the tiny clasp that secured the box's lid. When she opened it and saw the silver necklace, a sort of dread fell over her. Why was Jake Edgerton giving her a gift of jewelry?

"It's lovely." She ran her finger over the delicate cross. "But I can't accept it."

"I insist. That necklace once belonged to my grandmother."

"I don't know what to say…" Emily looked up at Jake, wondering. "Why are you giving me such a keepsake?"

"I thought you should have something of Granddad's since I heard how you and your family befriended him over the years. I plan to give trinkets to your mother and grandmother and firearms from Granddad's collection to your dad and brothers. As kids we dreamed of shooting those weapons." He grinned. "I thought you'd appreciate jewelry more than a pistol. Was I mistaken?"

"No." She smiled and relaxed. "How very thoughtful of you, Jake. But it's not necessary. Mr. Ollie was our neighbor."

"I know, but when I saw this, I thought of you at once." He removed the necklace from its boxed cradle, and then stepped forward and set the silver chain around her neck. He bent so close to clasp the chain that his jaw brushed against Emily's cheek. Accident—or on purpose?

"Hold still."

At his whispered command a delicious batter of warmth poured over her being for a second time that evening. Emily couldn't understand her response to his nearness, and she actually enjoyed the fact that he seemed to take his time securing the clasp.

"There."

Another whisper and her knees weakened. He stepped back, and she felt almost disappointed.

"It looks lovely on you, Em."

"Does it?" She felt flustered.

Then all at once, she recalled another time in her life when she enjoyed being close to Jake...

Sinful! Emily put a name to her response to him as she touched the necklace. "But perhaps I'm not worthy to wear such a treasure."

"What are you talking about? Of course you're worthy." He grunted out a laugh that held a note of disbelief. But it soon faded into the night air, already filled with chortles, music, and singing, both human and spring peepers alike.

"Emily, I got your letters, and I swear I meant to reply."

She felt cemented in place. The warmth she felt before turned to stone.

"Life handed me a lot of... *distractions*, and I never seemed to get the chance to sit down long enough to write back."

"I understand." Emily knew what it felt like to be overwhelmed with obligations. "Still, it wouldn't have taken but a few moments, Jake." She kept her voice soft and low. "You could have written a few simple words in reply to let me know you didn't think badly of me."

"I never thought badly of you, Em. Never did and never will." He gently gripped her upper arms. "We were young..."

"But I knew that what we were doing was wrong. I just couldn't seem to say no to you." She almost choked on her confession, feeling mortified that she'd actually put a voice to the words that had haunted her for ten long years.

"I'm flattered, but please don't blame yourself. I shouldn't have taken advantage of you like I did."

Emily pulled away.

"The whole thing was both my idea and my fault. I was older." Jake's tone grew gently husky with obvious sincerity. "I'm sorry, Em."

She accepted his apology with a succession of quick nods, but stared off in the distance at nothing in particular. Tears blurred her vision.

"I hope you'll forgive me—and yourself too." Jake reached across the space between them and briefly touched the silver cross which now rested at Emily's neckline. "Maybe this necklace can remind you that if the Savior of the world can forgive us, we can forgive ourselves…and others." He turned and leaned his forearms on the fence. "Did you ask Him to forgive you?"

"Of course I did." *What a question!*

He faced her again. "Then trust that the work is done, Em. All you have to do is believe. Right?"

Emily blinked. How could it be that simple?

"How does that verse go? 'If we confess our sins, he is faithful and just to forgive us our sins, and to cleanse us from all unrighteousness.' Isn't that it?"

"I believe it is." Emily read the Scriptures on a frequent basis.

And obviously so did Jake.

Beneath the moon's glow she regarded the good deputy in a brand-new light. And then she allowed the truth of what he'd just said to crack the ten-year-long stronghold.

Several minutes ticked by and Jake turned, leaning his back against the fence again. He glanced her way, and Emily found the confidence to meet his gaze. She smiled. Amazement replaced her guilt and shame. When Jake spoke God's Word to her, it was as if the barred door of her soul became unlocked. All she had to do was walk out of her inner prison cell.

"Thank you, Jake. I needed that reminder, and...I needed it from you."

"Glad I could help. Sorry it took so long."

Emily rolled a shoulder. "I only wish you hadn't told all the other boys in your Sunday school class about it. The truth became vicious lies and suddenly I was no better than Mary Magdalene before she met Jesus."

Jake replied with a throaty groan.

"The other girls weren't allowed to play with me. Thank goodness Iris came along, or I might still be without a friend."

"Emily—"

"And I think every boy in my class teased and taunted me for a year after you left."

"I didn't tell another single soul about kissing you."

Emily felt like socking him. "Don't you dare lie to me now, Jake Edgerton."

"I swear, Em. I never breathed a word."

She felt stunned. If it wasn't Jake... "Who else would know such a thing? We were alone."

"I thought so too." He paused, seeming to think it over. "Well, it's over now, right? No sense dredging it all up again just to find out who might have spied on two unsuspecting kids."

"Good point." Still it troubled her that an unknown third party had glimpsed their intimate scene, one that belonged to courting or betrothed couples, not children.

She brought her hand up to the silver cross necklace. "Anyway, all is forgiven."

"I'm glad, Em. Right now I could use some friends."

"In that case, Jake—" Emily decided he'd suffered too, losing his parents the way he had and now his grandfather too. "—consider me your friend."

He stuck out his right hand. "Friends it is."

Emily slipped her palm into his. "Friends."

CHAPTER 7

*T*HE NEXT MORNING Jake awoke, stretched, and grinned as recollections of the night before flashed through his mind. Glory, but those two young ladies amused him! He'd walked Emily and her friend Miss Hopper home from the dance last night, and they sang most of the way to the boardinghouse.

> After the ball is o-ver,
> After the break of morn.
> After the dancers leaving;
> After the stars are gone.
> Many a heart is aching,
> If you could read them all;
> Many the hopes that have vanished,
> After the ball.

Jake's smile faded when he remembered Emily's admission that the song caused her to feel glum. Miss Hopper had quickly changed the subject, and she and Em chattered the rest of the way home.

Jake rested his hands behind his head and stared at the ceiling. Andy Anderson never did ask Em to dance. His loss.

Inhaling deeply, Jake let the breath out slowly. He felt a powerful attraction to Miss Emily Sundberg, and if he wasn't mistaken, Emily had sensed something special between them too. What a relief to know she didn't hate him or hold the past against him any longer.

But Emily had her heart set on Andy, and she wasn't likely to admit feeling anything for Jake anytime soon.

And what would happen if she did acknowledge there was still something between them after all these long years? Nothing could come of it. His life, after all, was in Montana. Not Manitowoc.

Jake flung off the bedcovers, washed, and dressed. Glancing at Granddad's pocket watch, he realized he was getting a later-than-usual start. But that was all right. He didn't have chores to do, and the marshal or some county sheriff didn't require his assistance. Jake felt more relaxed than he'd been in a long, long while.

Jake read through a couple of pages of his Bible, cogitating a while afterward. He said his prayers, always putting on that armor of God, which Jake trusted to protect him.

Finally he set out to find some breakfast. He'd seen a diner down the street and headed in that direction. Soon the inviting smells wafting from that small, corner establishment beckoned him inside.

Jake entered and scrutinized the patrons, mostly sailing men. A couple of them might be trouble, but they didn't seem looking for any at the moment. He let down his guard half a notch and seated himself at a corner table with his back to the wall and ordered coffee. Just as the waitress set the steaming cup in front of him, Jake spied Emily and Miss Hopper crossing the street. They wore expressions of determination, and he wondered what they were up to. Jake couldn't resist saying hello.

The legs on his chair scraped the scarred wooden floor as Jake moved to stand. He asked the waitress to save his table then walked outside and met the pair on the boardwalk.

"Oh, Deputy..." A blush crept up Miss Hopper's neck and spread into her face. "What a nice surprise."

He politely inclined his head. "Miss Hopper." He looked at Em. "Good morning, Miss Sundberg." He could tell by her smile that his feigned formality amused her.

"G'morning, Jake. We were making our way to the hotel. You're just the person we hoped to find." She elbowed her friend. "Isn't that right, Iris?"

Miss Hopper nodded with such vigor that the curls around her face bobbed and swayed.

"Hmm…" Jake immediately grew suspicious. "And what, may I ask, do I owe this unexpected but most pleasant call—that is, if you would have found me at the hotel?"

Emily shot a glance skyward at his teasing, and Jake chuckled at the response.

"I would like to interview you for the *Chronicle*." Miss Hopper fluttered her lashes. Jake had learned the gesture wasn't necessarily flirtatious. The young woman seemed to have rapid eye movement whenever she felt flustered, embarrassed, or the least bit excited.

His gaze moved to Emily. Sunlight danced off the golden strands of hair framing her face. A fitted cap complete with ribbons and feathers covered the rest of her head.

"Do you have some time, Jake?"

"For you? Of course…for both of you." He rubbed his scratchy jaw. "I'm just not sure about the interview."

"It's mostly a tribute to your grandfather." Miss Hopper wore some concoction over her platinum ringlets. Jake found the thing most distracting. "But I thought I'd add that his grandson, you, is carrying on Mr. Oliver Stout's passion for upholding United States law."

"Well…"

"Please, Jake?"

The way Em's blue eyes pleaded with him melted his resolve. "All right. But I was about to eat breakfast. Will you ladies join me?"

"What a kind offer," Miss Hopper said. "We accept."

"Yes, thank you for the invitation."

Jake opened one of the diner's two tall doors, and the ladies filed in. He showed them to his table, and they all sat down.

"This is a decent place, isn't it?" Jake noticed Emily glancing around at the other patrons.

"It's fine." Miss Hopper had claimed the chair beside him. "Especially this time of day."

Jake's gaze returned to Em, who sat across from him. "You lookin' for someone, Miss Sundberg?" He could only guess. "Andy Anderson, perhaps?"

Emily sent him a withering stare. Next she lifted the printed menu off the table.

"I don't see him, but if he walks in I'll let you know," Jake promised.

"Oh, who cares about him?"

Did she mean it? Jake glimpsed the shadow on the left side of her face, a bruise, and he cringed. He'd hurt her the other day. How could he have forgotten, although she'd been hiding it awfully well.

"I'll quit teasing you, Emily. I'm sorry."

She momentarily weighed his apology. "I accept…and thank you."

"Poor Em gets teased enough by her brothers." Iris shot her a sympathizing glance.

"And father too."

Despite her facetious tone, Jake knew that Emily adored her father—almost as much as the captain adored her, no doubt.

The waitress came and took their orders. Jake was pleased the ladies decided on more than a nibble.

As if divining his thoughts, Emily said, "Mrs. Hopper, our lovely landlady and Iris's grandmother, doesn't serve breakfast at the boardinghouse on the weekends. So it's nice that we can share breakfast with you this morning, Jake."

"Likewise." He didn't think he'd mind glancing across the break-fast table and seeing Em's sweet face every day. His gaze slowly fell to her strawberry-ripe lips, a juicy-looking neck, and—

Best stop right there.

He took another swallow of coffee and gazed around the busy

diner. Mismatched wooden tables sported neat, checkered cloths, and various styles of chairs, much like the establishment's patrons themselves, circumferenced them. Plates clapped together from somewhere behind the counter, and the sound intermingled with the chinking of eating utensils.

Jake's thoughts stayed on Emily. A lofty dream, pursuing her. Could be why Andy didn't pay her any mind. A man would have to impress the captain. Daunting, but Jake felt up to the challenge.

Pity, though, that he couldn't court her. He had a hunch that Captain and Mrs. Sundberg and Em's brothers would approve. They already considered him a friend of their family because of Granddad, and Jake sensed he'd won their trust the other night when he'd dined in their home.

"Deputy, did you hear my question?"

Jake glanced at Miss Hopper. "My apologies. What did you say?"

"I asked if I could begin my interview before our breakfast arrives."

"Go right ahead."

A fluttering of lashes behind thick lenses. "First off, when did you decide to be a United States deputy marshal?"

"It was right after my father was gunned down in cold blood."

Miss Hopper paled slightly, but made a note on the bound booklet in front of her.

He glanced across the table to gauge Emily's reaction and saw neither shock nor pity in her expression. Only a glint of sorrow in her eyes before she sipped from the cup of tea that evidently arrived while his mind had drifted.

Smoky smells of frying ham reached his nostrils, and his stomach gnawed at him. With the primping he'd done yesterday afternoon and evening in anticipation for the dance, he hadn't eaten much, but he was ready to chow down now.

"How old were you, Deputy, when your father died?" Miss Hopper asked, her voice low and sympathetic. "And may I just add that I can relate to your loss. As I mentioned yesterday, my parents were missionaries and tragically killed in South America."

"You have my sympathies." Jake lifted his coffee cup. "I was fifteen. A month away from sixteen." He finished his coffee and waved the waitress over for a refill. "I managed to finish school while I tried my best to fill Pa's shoes on the ranch. My sister and mother did everything they could too. But then Ma—"

Jake still couldn't bring himself to actually speak the words *killed herself*. He paused to allow the waitress to fill his coffee cup. "Ma died in a freakish way that I don't care to discuss. But after she passed, I wasn't interested in the ranch anymore. A fellow named Boyd Webster offered to buy it and ended up falling in love and marrying my sister in the process." At that, Jake grinned. "Things worked out well for Deidre, which made me happy. So with the ranch now in the capable hands of my brother-in-law, I decided to doggedly pursue the men who'd killed Pa." He leaned closer to Miss Hopper. "You see, I'd been keeping track of those two as best I could through newspaper articles and hearsay. I told the sheriff what I knew, and since these men also had a history of federal offenses, the sheriff handed the matter off to United States Marshal William McDermott. I proved myself a good shot with a good head on my shoulders, and not long after we met, Marshal McDermott swore me in as a deputy. Later I rode with the posse that found those men, and we brought them to justice."

"Did you kill them, Jake?"

He looked at Em, noticing the ferocity in her gaze. "No, I didn't kill them. The trio was tried in court for their crimes and sentenced to hang."

"If someone killed my father, I'd want revenge."

"No, you wouldn't, Em. You've got a conscience. That's obvious. Therefore, you'd want justice."

She appeared skeptical.

"You see, I believe that at every turn in life, a man—or woman, in your case, ladies—either follows the Lord or follows his heart, which we know is deceitful and desperately wicked, according to the Scriptures."

Emily's features softened, and her gaze sank into her teacup. "I suppose you're right, Jake."

He grinned. "I know I'm right."

She flicked him an annoyed little glance for his confidence, no doubt, and he chuckled inwardly. Beside him, Miss Hopper busily scratched everything he said onto paper.

"And what, exactly, does a deputy marshal do?" Miss Hopper's light gaze flickered on him again.

"The usual, I guess, like catching horse thieves, escorting patients to the insane asylum, per judge's orders, apprehending men who sell whiskey to the Indians, guarding railroad tracks if there's trouble, either with workers or Indians, and—"

"Playing poker and finding card cheats?"

Jake's gaze honed in on Em. She sipped her tea demurely, but he noticed the sassy gleam in her eyes.

"I recognized Thaddeus Wilcox from his wanted posters. He's robbed both banks and trains and looted ranches while folks were away at church. In spite of all those terrible crimes, being a federal deputy marshal, I couldn't get involved until I learned he'd stolen mail off one of the trains he robbed. Postal theft is a federal crime, and that's my jurisdiction. When I recognized the wanted man, I couldn't believe it was him, here in Manitowoc. Last we knew he was somewhere in Minnesota." Jake rubbed his thumb along the smooth dark brown porcelain handle of his coffee cup. "Even so, I needed to make sure the individual was the scum I thought. I followed him into the saloon, engaged him in a game of poker, and you know the rest." Jake's gaze fell onto her cheek again, and for the umpteenth time, he felt terrible about hurting her. "But all's forgiven, right?"

Emily's gaze melded into his as her fingers touched the little silver cross she wore around her neck. *She's wearing Gramma's necklace again today...*

"All's forgiven." She gave him one of her sweet grins, and Jake felt the bond between Emily and him get just one cord stronger.

"So tell me, Deputy..."

Jake tore his attention from Emily to focus on Miss Hopper's next question.

"Is there a special young lady in your life?"

"Iris!" A chiding note from Em, who leaned toward her friend.

"I'm just asking. Oh, not for my newspaper article." Miss Hopper's features pinched with her suddenly prim expression. "For the sake of breakfast conversation."

Jake couldn't hold a chuckle back. "Well, for the sake of breakfast conversation, no. There's no special young lady in my life." Regret poured through him like the coffee he drank. He couldn't fall in love with Em. Not in this stage of his life. And he couldn't let Miss Hopper get her hopes up about him either. "And there will be no special lady. You see, my job is what's called a widow-maker. Deputies run the risk of getting killed with each assignment they accept. I could never do that to a woman—make her a widow on account of my job, that is." He thought of his mother, so sweet and lovely. She'd hid her despondency over Pa's death so incredibly well...

He shook off those haunting and painful thoughts as their meals arrived. Jake determined to enjoy his present company.

Looking at Emily Sundberg, Jake wondered what was *not* to enjoy. While he didn't recollect a whole lot about that summer he'd stayed with Granddad, he did remember kissing Em and liking her real well as a friend too. She'd been able to keep up with Eden and him, which, Jake recalled, angered Eden.

And now here she sat, sharing a late breakfast with him—and at a time he needed a friend too. But could he fence in his feelings for

Em and be satisfied with her friendship? He'd have to, at least until he returned to Montana in a few days.

She gave him a curious glance, and Jake realized how hard he'd been staring.

"Will you say grace for us, Jake?"

"I'd be happy to." He bowed his head and spoke a few words of thanks for this day, this meal, and this most pleasant company.

"Oh, that was so very nice, Deputy. Wasn't that a nice prayer, Em?"

"Very nice. Thanks, Jake."

"You're most welcome." It tickled him to watch Miss Hopper's curls bob and sway. Glory, but they looked like they weighed more than she did! "So what do you ladies do when you're not teaching school or attending dances?" He forked a bite of fried eggs into his mouth. They'd been cooked in butter and tasted salty, rich, and good on an empty stomach.

"We usually find summer work," Miss Hopper replied, "which we are actively seeking now."

"I see." Jake bit into his thickly sliced bread. Mmm...so fresh it almost melted in his mouth.

"Yes, otherwise I'm going to have to move back home," Emily said, "or work at Sundbergs' Creations and help my aunt."

Jake didn't understand her dilemma. "What's wrong with either of those options?"

Emily sighed. "My family."

"Your family?" Jake set down his fork and touched his napkin to the corners of his mouth. "They're good people."

"Oh, of course they are, and I love them dearly. Please don't misunderstand. But I'm not a child any longer and shouldn't rely on their assistance."

"I'm fortunate that way," Miss Hopper put in. "Granny expects me to be independent...at least until I find a husband."

Jake had slipped in another bite so he couldn't reply. But he'd picked up on Miss Hopper's not-so-subtle hint. He didn't dare even smirk. His older sister had ground into his head how important marriage was to every young woman. Girls dreamed of that day, even lived for it. Deidre had anyway. And Emily obviously wanted to lasso Andy Anderson into saying *I do*.

A surge of jealously ran through Jake, the likes of such he'd never felt before. But he couldn't court Em—or any woman. Not unless he got an appointment from the president. As a marshal he'd have more administrative duties, meetings, dinners with state representatives, and less dangerous assignments. Although risks existed in every occupation, including ranching. Regardless, being appointed to a United States marshal by President Roosevelt didn't look like it was in Jake's immediate future.

Jake swallowed. "I'm sure the right man will come along soon, Miss Hopper."

"Oh, please, call me Iris. After all, we're friends." She glanced at Em. "Right?"

"Right." Emily smiled and her gaze met Jake's.

"Right." He smiled back. "Friends." He hoped he could get that concept through his thick skull because everything inside of him wanted to be more than just Emily Sundberg's *friend*.

CHAPTER 8

S MALL TALK ENSUED as they ate their meals. From what Emily gathered, Jake had several matters pressing in on him.

"My next order of business is taking care of all the particulars for Granddad's funeral."

Emily set aside her fork. "What kind of particulars? Maybe Iris and I can help."

"Well, now, maybe you can."

Jake settled back in his chair, hooking one arm around its square and slatted back. Emily decided he looked very much like a lawman today in the black vest he wore over a striped shirt. And handsome—Jake certainly was that! Emily caught herself time and again admiring his physical attributes, from his neatly combed sandy-blond hair and his molasses-colored eyes to the tiny cleft in his stubbly chin and his strong-looking shoulders, which could very well be broader than even Poppa's.

"I wonder if I should have some sort of luncheon after the service."

"That's customary," Iris said, "although the church basement is far too small for a reception."

Emily agreed. "What about Mr. Ollie's house?"

"Um…" He looked off in the distance, his gaze tapered.

Concerned mixed with curiosity filled her. "Is there a problem?"

"A couple that I can think of offhand. Don't misunderstand; I don't mind hosting. But, you see, Granddad was an elderly fellow, sick for a number of weeks. The house hasn't had a good cleaning in I don't know how long, and my aunt and uncle are there."

"They are?" Emily wished her tone hadn't sounded so incredulous.

Jake nodded and took a swallow of coffee. "Those two greedy souls are the reasons I moved into the hotel."

"I wondered why you weren't staying at Mr. Ollie's house."

"Now you know." His gaze captured hers for the seemingly hundredth time this morning, and once again Emily didn't possess the will to look away.

"Guess I'll find a way to work around them."

"We'll clean the house for you, won't we, Em?"

"Of course. Otherwise, if you prefer, Momma and Poppa will open their home for a luncheon. I'm sure of it."

"Kind offer. I'll keep it in mind just in case."

"Our ladies' auxiliary will make the meals." Iris turned to Emily. "We'll see most of them at choir practice tonight, and we can ask each lady to bring a dish or plate of something to share. The choir is supposed to sing at Mr. Stout's memorial service on Tuesday anyway." She smiled. "I should think the various foods will make for a grand buffet."

"Marvelous idea." Emily cast a glance at Jake, careful to keep her eyes fixed on his collar so she wouldn't get stuck in those molasses-colored eyes again.

"I agree. A perfect solution." Iris adjusted her eyeglasses.

"What do you think, Jake?" Emily smiled. "Problems solved."

His lips moved as if he wanted to decline their offers, but then he smiled. "I'm touched, ladies. Deeply touched." After sending Emily a meaningful stare, Jake turned to Iris and gave her a grin.

A blush spread across her pale cheeks.

The woman who'd waited on them came and collected their dirty dishes. After she left, Emily remembered her promise to *Tante* Agnes that she and Iris would mind the shop for a couple of hours this afternoon so she could get several errands done.

"Iris, we should go. *Tante* Agnes is probably wondering where we are."

"Oh, yes, of course..."

Jake stood, and then held the chairs for Emily and Iris. "Well, this has been a most enjoyable meal."

"Thank you for breakfast, Deputy...I mean, Jake."

"Yes, thanks, Jake."

"You're both welcome."

They strolled to the counter where Jake paid the bill. Emily and Iris waited outside as he finished his transaction. Glancing at the overcast sky, Emily thought of Poppa and said another prayer that his trip to Milwaukee would be an uneventful one.

Iris slid her hand around Emily's elbow. "The deputy is quite handsome, isn't he?"

"I suppose." Guilt pressed down on Emily. She felt like a traitor, attracted to the man who'd captured her best friend's interest.

Unable to meet Iris's gaze, she stared into the street, filled with wagons and buggies. Children ran down the walk, shouting and laughing. Oh, but how could she have betrayed Iris in this way? It's just that Jake had some strange effect on her—always did. However, she wasn't foolish enough to believe anything would come of it. Didn't he say his job was a widow-maker? He wasn't a marrying man, which Emily had already sensed. But, like many men, he was an accomplished flirt—which probably came in handy when he interrogated females. Of course they'd cave in to his inquiry, what with that charm and his good looks.

So how did she make Iris understand that?

The object of her thoughts exited the diner and donned his wide-brimmed hat. Not exactly a fashionable derby, but it complemented Jake's rugged appearance.

"What are you ladies doing with the rest of your day?"

"Oh, well, let's see...after helping Emily's aunt, we're going to cut flowers in Granny's garden and take them over to church for altar decorations. Then it's choir practice until six o'clock. After that we'll eat a light supper, followed by a bath—"

Emily jerked Iris's arm. "He asked over our day, not evening."

Iris swallowed a giggle. "Pardon me. I didn't mean to imply that Em and I bathe together."

"Iris!" She glanced at Jake. To her relief, he appeared thoroughly amused.

"I thought nothing of it, Miss Hopper."

"Iris."

Jake hesitated for a fraction of a second before inclining his head slightly. "Iris."

A man called out his name. "Jake! Jake Edgerton!"

Emily looked toward the street and saw Mr. Schulz in his sleek black surrey, motioning for Jake. She knew the prominent attorney through her parents. He frequently attended fund-raisers and dinner parties at their home.

"It's urgent, Jake. I've been looking all over town for you." He spotted Emily and sent her a quick but friendly wave.

She lifted her hand, returning the gesture.

"Ladies, please excuse me."

"Of course..." Iris stepped toward him, a bold move for a lady. "But you'll be in attendance tomorrow, won't you, Jake?"

He paused. "Attendance?" His brows came together and a curious light entered his gaze.

"At church." Iris shifted into demure. "Just a few blocks west of here. The church with the loudest bell in town."

Jake grinned as he moved toward the street. "All right. I'll be there." His gaze snagged Emily's. "See you tomorrow."

"I apologize for interrupting your day, son, but it's that confounded aunt and uncle of yours."

"Now what?" Jake hated to hear.

"I just received a bill for the purchase of a new conveyance and a team of horses! What's more, I discovered that yesterday Dwight requested a copy of the title to Ollie's house—make that your house. You're going to have to tell them, Jake. You're the executor of your grandfather's estate. He left them nothing."

"You're right. The time has come." He eyed Mr. Schulz. "Do you have all the legal documents?"

"Got them right here." Mr. Schulz patted his jacket pocket.

"Good."

As they left the city behind, neither continued the conversation, the only sounds now coming from horse hooves pounding the dirt road and twittering birds in the leafy treetops. Jake took this time to ruminate over his various options. Aunt Bettina and Uncle Dwight wouldn't cooperate if he strong-armed them.

They passed the Sundbergs' home. Jake saw none of the family members outdoors, but a spotted dog ran from the barn and onto the grass to bark at them.

"Easy, boy." Jake grinned as the dog sat and watched them ride by.

When they reached Granddad's place, Mr. Schulz pulled into the brick drive. Jake glanced up at the spacious home, constructed in a cream-color brick. Painted green trim framed each of the windows, and the four in the front had been opened to let in the springtime air.

"Be firm, Jake."

"I will. But we'll go in easy. Agreed?"

"As you wish." Mr. Schulz tugged on the reins and halted the buggy.

Jumping out, Jake eyed an impressive wagonette with four leather seats and detachable black fringy roof parked near the doorway. He guessed that his aunt and uncle's intent was to load up as many of Granddad's belongings as the brand-new conveyance would hold.

"They will have to return this vehicle at once!" Mr. Schulz eyed it with an indignant air. "Of all the nerve."

"If it gets Aunt Bettina and Uncle Dwight back to Chicago and out of our way, it might be worth letting them have it." Jake walked to the wide front door and made use of the heavy brass knocker.

"This is your house, Jake. You should walk right in."

"We're going in easy. Remember?"

Mr. Schulz gave a nod and squared his shoulders as Jake rapped on the door a second time.

A minute passed. Then another. Jake knocked again.

Aunt Bettina finally came to the door. "Well, what a surprise." Her amber eyes bounced between Mr. Schulz and him. She folded her arms, looking suspicious. "What do you want? If it's about the bill Dwight and I submitted to your office, Mr. Schulz—"

"It most certainly is."

"Aunt Bettina, we need to talk to you and Uncle Dwight."

"I told you to handle the funeral arrangements, Jake. And you, Mr. Schulz…I expect you to pay the bills. It's very simple."

"Not *that* simple." Jake pushed open the door and stepped around his aunt's slender frame.

Mr. Schulz followed.

Aunt Bettina's skirts swished as she pivoted. "This is an outrage!" She called for Uncle Dwight, who ambled into the foyer in one of Granddad's silk smoking jackets.

Jake's neck muscles tensed.

"Problems with funeral plans, Johnny?" Dwight fingered his long mustache.

Jake didn't flinch at the nickname, although no one called him Johnny except Dwight—and it wasn't an endearment.

"The funeral arrangements are made. But I thought Mr. Schulz and I should deliver your copy of Granddad's will in person." Jake strode to the parlor and halted at the sight. How did two people make such a mess? Books and papers were strewn about, cluttering tabletops. A lamp had been overturned and never righted. The printed blue settee looked wrinkled and mussed.

"Well, hand over the document and be on your way."

Hearing his uncle's impatience, Jake turned to face the man. Might as well get to the point. "Granddad left his estate to me."

"What?" Aunt Bettina made a march toward him. "But I'm his daughter."

"Biologically." Mr. Schulz gave an indignant snort.

"How dare you, you miserable attorney! Are you implying that my father disowned me?"

"Legally he did. But he never ceased praying for your soul." Mr. Schulz had already pulled the will from his jacket's inside pocket.

After snatching it, Uncle Dwight read the document. Jake watched his aunt, gauging her reaction. She stared at her husband with a grim set to her mouth. A handsomely attractive woman, Aunt Bettina's looks had most likely spared her and Dwight from numerous consequences, jail being one of them. Granddad made mention of the fact once. As for appearances, Jake remembered his mother being pretty too, but in a different way. Ma had been a hard-working woman with a soft heart. Bettina, on the other hand, looked soft on the outside, but possessed a heart of cold, hard steel.

"We will contest this piece of rubbish." Uncle Dwight folded the parchment and slapped it against his palm. "It's been altered, and you, Johnny, no doubt swindled the old man on his death bed."

Jake's right fist balled. "I did no such thing." One more insult, and he'd throw Dwight out the door on his backside. And then he'd return the conveyance, and these two could walk home for all he cared. "I suggest that if you want to *ride* home to Chicago in that fancy new buggy of yours, you'd best watch your manners."

"You have no say as to whether we leave or don't leave," his aunt said. "And I've earned this house and everything in it."

"Earned?" Jake cocked his head. "How's that? You never worked a day in your life."

She raised a hand and Jake snatched her wrist before she could slap him. *Whew-whee!* For a woman of no means she certainly put on airs. "I wouldn't do that if I was you, auntie dear."

She pulled her hand free.

"As for rights, Jake has every right." Mr. Schulz stepped up with his pointy chin lifted in confidence. "This house belongs to him." He went on to list the number of judges, attorneys, and other community members who would attest to the fact that Granddad left his estate to his only grandson. "So contest it if you must. However, you should know that it will be quite expensive."

"Plenty of attorneys will work on commission." Dwight's chin rose equally as high.

"Not when they find out it's a losing case. You have no grounds. This will was prepared long ago, not on Ollie's death bed as you've so ignorantly stated."

Uncle Dwight's face reddened.

"However, I have a proposition for you." Jake regarded his aunt. "How 'bout you take the new carriage and the team? In addition, I'll give you ten minutes to pack your belongings and grab whatever you wish from the house."

"Jake, no!" A look of outrage furrowed Mr. Schulz's brow.

He lifted a hand to forestall further argument. "But you've got ten minutes, understand? After that, I will physically usher you out the door. Then once you leave, I never want to see you or hear from you again. Am I clear?"

Aunt Bettina weighed her options for a moment then ran for the curved stairway.

Uncle Dwight's thin lips moved as if he wanted to debate the matter further.

"Time's a-wasting." Jake glanced at the grandfather clock in the front hallway. Oh, how this man tested his last nerve! And apparently he sensed it too, because Dwight whirled around and followed Bettina up to the second floor.

Placing a foot on the lower step, Jake listened to the bickering that broke out between the couple. With a measure of sadness he noticed that neither asked to stay for Granddad's funeral on Tuesday. He would have granted the request and put them up in a hotel somewhere—but not the Dunbars'. He wouldn't wish his aunt and uncle on anyone he knew. However, the fact the pair didn't ask to stay only proved again that they didn't care about Granddad and that all they'd come to Manitowoc for was financial gain and not to say their last farewells.

"Jake, giving them the buggy, horses, and *anything* they want from the house? They deserve none of it!"

"True." Jake paused in thought. "But God gave me His grace when I didn't deserve it. He's merciful, kind, patient, and generous." Jake met the elderly man's gaze. "I think Granddad would have wanted me to show my aunt and uncle the same as God showed me."

"You're right." Mr. Schulz seemed properly chagrined. "Your actions are exemplary considering what you could have done—and legally, I might add. Ollie would be proud." Some of his agitation returned. "Still…anything in the house?"

"I already have the lockbox with the most valuable items, the ones Granddad cherished."

"What of the oil paintings?"

"To unscrew the frame from the plastered walls of even one of the more valuable works of art will take time. Dwight's not that patient, and they've only got ten minutes."

"Nine, according to my watch."

Smiling at the quip, Jake kneaded his jaw. "Think you can write something up, stating my aunt and uncle agreed to my terms and have them sign it before they load anything into the buggy? Just for the record?"

"Of course, I can…and will." Mr. Schulz made purposeful strides toward Granddad's office.

Jake stood by the front entrance, waiting and wondering how

he'd get this house cleaned up before the luncheon on Tuesday—even with Emily and Iris's help. He spied an empty bottle of whiskey under a parlor chair. He didn't want the ladies to see garbage like that. No telling what else they'd find. He'd have to do a preliminary sweep of house. *Lord, the task seems daunting.*

As Emily went about her business that afternoon, she fended off thoughts and images of Jake. His affable smile, enchanting gaze, the way he held her while they'd waltzed last night, and how he'd hummed in her ear. Just as easily she recalled his reciting of Scripture. He seemed like a fine man. And other than his tendency to flirt, a good and decent man.

Her best friend certainly thought so. And each time Iris gushed over Jake, Emily felt guiltier for having similar feelings for him. True, she told Iris everything, but she could never admit to this—they were both falling hopelessly for a man who had told them up front that he had no intentions of courting and marrying. What insanity!

Thankfully Jake also said he planned to leave Wednesday morning.

That night after her bath Emily donned a fresh cotton gown, brushed out her thick hair, then wound the top sections around pieces of fabric extras she'd collected and strategically cut into strips. When she reached the end, she tied it off. She repeated the steps until all the strips of material had been used. With her hair full of knots, she made her way down to the sitting room. She and her boardinghouse mates typically gathered on Saturday night to read and sew. No men were allowed into the house after eight, so there was no danger of being caught in her bedclothes with her hair in rags.

One step into the sitting room and Emily halted. There in the midst of all the shiny faces of her housemates, stood Iris, reenacting her dance last night with Jake.

"He's such a gentleman." Iris hugged herself, a dreamy look plastered across her face. "He held me at arm's length."

He'd held Emily close to his heart.

"When the music stopped, he quickly offered to get a glass of raspberry punch for me."

When the music stopped, Jake hesitated to let me go.

Every set of pink lips in the room murmured, "Ooh..."

Emily gave herself a mental smack and sank into the burgundy-colored settee. Beside it, on the end table, a crackle lamp glowed brightly despite its frosted white glass.

"And now, ladies, I will read you a story." Iris held up the book in her hand. "It's about love and daring in the Wild West."

If nothing else, Iris made an exceptional actress. Little wonder her students adored her.

"I found this novel in a chest of drawers up in Granny's attic. It's called *Glass Eye, the Great Shot of the West*. It's an old tale, but a good one about a woman who gets separated from her wagon train in the 1870s and is pursued by an Indian. But Glass Eye rescues her and they have adventures together while trying desperately to meet up with the wagons again."

"Read on, Iris!" Carol glanced up from her mending and grinned. "My mother, God rest her soul, loved those story pages."

"Yes, well..." Iris cleared her voice. "I'm not sure Granny will approve, but I'll read until we hear from her." Iris glanced quickly at the arched entryway.

The other ladies sniggered, and Emily grinned. Lifting her knitting basket, Emily extracted the sweater she knitted. She'd originally intended to give it to Andy on his birthday in November. After last night's Memorial Day Dance, however, those plans now changed. Emily clearly saw that Jake had been right about Andy's behavior—and hers. Quite unladylike to go out of her way for a man who openly displayed his disinterest, perhaps even dislike.

Except now she needed to get her mind off Jake Edgerton.

She focused on her knitting, and as Iris began reading, Emily wondered if *Tante* Agnes would sell the sweater in her shop. Emily could undo the stitches across the shoulders so it fit a woman, and a bit of adornment on the front would sufficiently feminize the garment. The lovely and practical wrapper would surely keep a lady warm when the cold winds blew off Lake Michigan.

Emily wound the yarn around her forefinger and put her knitting needles together. They made a rhythmical click with each stitch. She'd selected a soft merino wool so the sweater wouldn't be bulky. And the rich chestnut color—

Just like Jake Edgerton's eyes.

CHAPTER 9

*H*E FIGURED HE still had about four hours of daylight left. Jake heaved another load of garbage onto the burn pile. It was the Lord's day, true enough; however, Jake didn't think God would mind him working this way, since it honored the memory of one of His own. It'd be embarrassing if Emily and Iris came to clean tomorrow and found such a sty.

Yesterday, after his aunt and uncle rode off in their new carriage, Jake had walked through Granddad's house to assess any damages. With a sick heart, he saw they were numerous. Holes in the walls, as if someone searched in vain for a hidden safety deposit box; lampshades broken beyond repair. Food and booze spilled, causing the soles of Jake's boots to stick on the floor.

Approaching horses alerted him. He turned toward the sound and watched as Captain Sundberg and Zeb rode up then dismounted.

"Need some help?"

Both men eyed the burn pile.

"Emily and Iris offered to clean tomorrow, so I was just trying to give them a head start." Jake smiled and finger-combed his hair back off his perspiring forehead.

"Zeb and I spent the weekend on the lake and docked in Manitowoc this morning. We decided on an afternoon ride through the neighborhood." The captain strode toward him. "We spotted the horses and wagon and thought we'd pay a call."

"Kind of you. And I wish I could invite you in, but I'm afraid Granddad's house isn't presentable."

"How'd that happen?" Zeb glanced at Jake, his blue eyes flashing. He only vaguely resembled Emily and Eden. Having dined with the Sundbergs on Thursday night, Jake concluded Zeb inherited his mother's finer features.

"My aunt and uncle made ill-mannered company."

"Not surprising." The captain clapped a hand on his shoulder. "Are they gone now?"

"Yes, sir. They weren't interested in staying in town for Granddad's funeral—but I expected as much."

Before the captain could reply, another rider approached, and seconds later Emily appeared on horseback.

"You two are incorrigible." She hurled an irritated glance at her father and brother. But when her gaze met Jake's, her expression transformed with her sudden smile.

"Hi, Jake."

"Hello, Em."

She made a fetching sight in her riding habit on back of the bay mare with its dark-brown mane. She swung her leg over the saddle and easily jumped down. After an affectionate pat on her horse's neck, she strode forward and addressed her father and brother again.

"That wasn't nice, sending me off in another direction."

"If you can't keep up, Em..." A teasing note sailed on Zeb's tone.

"Oh, I can keep up—as long as I'm not sent on a wild goose chase!"

Lowering his head, Jake tried to hide his amusement. Em still rode with the boys. At least that much hadn't changed in ten years.

"And I haven't any idea where Iris is. It'll probably take me all evening to find her."

Zeb snorted a laugh.

The captain wore a crooked grin. "Don't worry about Iris. She'll turn up. She always does."

Emily's gaze returned to Jake, this time her features drawn in confusion. "What are you doing here? I thought you were spending the afternoon with the Schulzes."

"I was—did." Jake thought Em's eyes rivaled a clear Montana sky. "I enjoyed a fine dinner, but then I kept remembering that a churchful of folks are coming to Granddad's home after his service on Tuesday."

"Don't you remember that Iris and I said we'd clean for you tomorrow?"

"I remember. I was just doing the preliminary stuff is all." Jake gave her a smile and she smiled back. *Lord, she's the prettiest young lady I know.*

The captain cleared his throat, and Jake looked his way. "You can count on us to help too. Right, Zeb?"

"Right." Earnestness shone in the younger man's gaze.

"My wife and mother will, I'm sure, be happy to assist both Emily and Iris with cleaning."

Emily nodded.

How could Jake refuse? "I accept your offers. Thank you." Tension that he didn't realize existed left his neck and shoulders.

"By the way...." The captain stroked his beard, his brows pressed in thought. "Are you still at the Dunbars' hotel?"

"Yep, and I plan to stay until I leave Wednesday morning." Why make any more mess in a house he planned to sell?

"This is all turning out quite well." The captain strode back to where Emily and Zeb stood. "You can join us for supper tonight and then drive the girls back into town, which will save me a trip. We'll begin our work first thing tomorrow."

"Sounds good to me." Jake felt like a blessed man indeed.

Cries of distress severed the peacefulness of the evening. And then Iris came into view, riding her horse, legs flailing out of the stirrups and her thin body bouncing up and down in the saddle. Emily rushed to help her while Zeb and Captain Sundberg grinned.

"Just another Sunday afternoon ride with the girls." Zeb sent Jake a sly smile.

Emily pitied Jake, having walked into a swarm of her family members. He met *Tante* Adeline and Uncle Will, who owned Dunbar Manufacturing. Uncle Will made sure that Jake heard all about his only son, Jacob, who attended college with Eden in New York City.

"We run a combined family business," Uncle Will explained. "Jacob and Eden have big plans about expanding it."

"That's right." Poppa beamed. "The boys are learning all the latest business strategies. I can't wait to hear more of their ideas."

Emily felt a sting of envy, until Iris whispered, "And they can thank a teacher for it."

"How right you are." Emily felt better. She and Iris shared a grin.

"I seem to recall meeting Jacob years ago." Jake's dark gaze slid Emily's way.

She caught its curious light. "You did. There was often some confusion the summer you visited because of the similar names, my cousin Jacob and you, Jake."

"Oh, that's right." He grinned and glanced at Poppa. "I believe Jacob helped Eden and me paint that addition."

Poppa chuckled.

Emily didn't remember any painting. She looked at Iris and shrugged.

Tante Agnes and Uncle Christopher entered the front hallway next.

"We heard there's company." *Tante* Agnes gave Jake a welcoming smile while Poppa made the next round of introductions.

"My sister Agnes and her husband Christopher Flagstedt." He moved on down the line. "And these are my nephews, Kjæl and David, and my darling nieces, Kate and Hildi."

"A pleasure to meet you all."

Emily scrutinized Jake's expression. He didn't seem intimidated in the least.

"Is he the one who ran you over the other day, Em?" Kate stared up at Jake.

Emily's cheeks warmed, although she dared not let it show. It would only encourage the outspoken thirteen-year-old. "It was an unfortunate accident."

Her cousins, Kjæl and David, could barely contain their amusement.

Emily sent them a quelling stare.

Kate pressed the matter. "That shiner of yours really stood out when you were singing in choir this morning."

Emily gulped in a rush of air and touched her cheek, realizing too late that she'd given the desired reaction.

"Kate Flagstedt, you apologize this minute!" *Tante* Agnes placed her hands on her round hips.

"Sorry." It lacked sincerity.

The boys lost what little self-control they possessed and laughed. Kate's face brightened, and she laughed too.

"What did Andy Anderson have to say about that bruise on your face?"

Emily gaped at the impudence.

"He didn't say a single thing." Iris stepped into the fray. She frequently rose to Emily's defense. "Emily ignored him all night, and he deserved it."

"Who asked you?"

"Hush now, Kate. You are behaving rudely in front of guests." *Bestamor* put her arm around the girl and led her into the kitchen. "Come and help me finish preparing our supper."

Smiling, Zeb gave the Flagstedt cousins a good-natured shove. "You two better behave or you'll be doing the dishes."

"You'd better listen too. Zeb speaks from experience." Poppa grinned.

Emily sent Jake an apologetic shrug. She'd read somewhere that one could have no dignity in the circumference of family. How true it was.

Jake leaned her way. "That little bruise didn't hardly show. I thought you looked real pretty this morning."

"Thank you." As always, his nearness affected her. The air around them seemed to grow thinner and Emily's face more flushed by the moment. If this continued, her parents would think she had the influenza and Iris would suspect her traitorous heart.

"Don't pay these scamps any mind, Deputy." Momma stepped in and showed Jake to a comfy chair in the parlor.

"Yes, and I apologize for my daughter." *Tante* Agnes sat down. Eight-year-old Hildi quietly leaned against her knees, but Emily didn't miss the shy little smile her youngest cousin sent Jake.

"No need to apologize, Mrs. Wilson." Jake added a charming grin to his reply. "The teasing didn't offend me in the least."

"Like my Emily when she was a girl," Momma said, "my niece Kate is far too influenced by the men in her life."

"Well, they're good men anyway, Mrs. Sundberg."

"Yes, I suppose they are." Momma strolled over to where Poppa stood and slipped her arm around his. The looks they exchanged warmed Emily's heart. Even after all these years of marriage, Momma still missed Poppa when he went away on business. He missed her too, and their love for each other shone in their gazes. Someday Emily hoped to be so in love.

Inexplicably her gaze moved to Jake. Like every other man here, he'd removed his dress jacket some time ago. His long-sleeved, white shirt accentuated his sun-bronzed face and hands—hands that knew all about hard work. His black vest and coal-gray striped trousers were a classic style for men about town.

Jake's eyes suddenly met hers. Emily blinked. He'd caught her staring. She quickly looked away, only to find Poppa's gaze on her. He sent her one of those affectionate winks that made her smile.

Uncle Christopher cleared his throat. He always reminded Emily of a bear, albeit a tame one. Tall, with a head of black curls, and a brawny frame, he'd made shipbuilding his passion in life. "How'd your trip go, Daniel? Smooth sailing?"

"Yes, it went well." Poppa sent a glance across the room and in Zeb's direction. "What did you think, son?"

"I don't think sailing is the job for me."

"He's just like I am, Daniel." Momma laughed and leaned her head on Poppa's shoulder. "I loathe sailing. I did it once when I came from London. Afterward I vowed to never set foot on a ship's deck again. I haven't either."

"Yes, that's true." Poppa placed a quick kiss on top of her head. "You haven't."

"The minister gave a good message on deck this morning though." Crossing his arms, Zeb leaned against the parlor door. "I'll never forget it, hearing God's Word preached while basking in the sun and feeling the wind blow and billow the sails overhead. An exhilarating experience, that's for sure."

Poppa grinned, and Emily caught the twinkle in his eyes when he looked at Momma. "I believe Zeb is more like his old man than you think, my dear."

"You'll have to work harder to change that, Julianna." *Tante* Adeline swallowed a laugh.

Tante Agnes agreed.

Poppa ignored his sisters' teasing. "Jake, have you ever sailed?"

"No, sir, can't say as I have."

"Hmm…a pity you're not staying even a day longer. I'd enjoy taking you out on the lake for a day. Zeb would join us, wouldn't you, son."

"I suppose I would." He didn't sound too enthusiastic about the prospect.

"We'd come along, wouldn't we, Em?" Iris nudged her then looked at Jake. "Emily and I love adventure."

"Of course we'll go—that is, if Poppa invites us."

"Well, I hate to disappoint," Jake said, "but I'm expected in the Dawson County Courthouse one week from tomorrow."

Emily saw genuine remorse in his dark gaze.

"That means I need to be on the eight-fifteen train Wednesday morning."

Reality took hold of Emily. Somehow, up until now, she'd been holding onto a thread of hope that Jake would stay in Manitowoc.

But he lived elsewhere, in a rugged land, inaccessible to ships like those belonging to her family's company. A land that Emily had only read about in textbooks or novels. Fallon, Montana. It sounded like another world.

And as far as she was concerned, it might as well be.

CHAPTER 10

*L*ATER JAKE DROVE Emily and Iris back into town in one of Mr. Ollie's fine carriages. Emily allowed Iris to sit in the padded leather front seat beside Jake. She talked almost all the way, sharing one amusing story after the other about her experiences teaching fourth graders. Emily had to admit that she admired Iris's theatrical abilities, which, tonight, were often rewarded with one of Jake's low, rumbling chuckles.

At last he pulled up across from the boardinghouse. Only a few riders and even fewer buggies rambled the residential street at this time of night. Lamps lit front windows, lending to the peaceful scene, although music and laughter from a not-too-distant shameful tavern carried on the cool, northeast breeze. Most establishments closed on Sunday, but with ships coming into port at all hours of the day and night, there were those who disregarded the Sabbath in order to help weary sailors spend their money.

Jake climbed out and reached for Iris. He easily swung her down from the buggy. "Thank you for making this ride most entertaining, Miss Iris."

She giggled and touched her gloved hand to her nose, turning her head slightly and playing coy. "No *Miss* in my name. I'm trying to eliminate that word, remember?"

Emily sighed. So much for subtlety.

"Ah, that's right." The look in Jake's eyes, evident beneath the glow of the tall streetlamp, told Emily she'd better speak to Iris…*again.*

He extended his hand, and Emily took it. Jake lifted her from the carriage. When her feet touched the ground, she stepped back and straightened her skirt, righting the buckle on her wide belt. She and Iris had changed after their ride this afternoon.

"I had a nice time meeting your family and getting reacquainted with some of them."

"I think you're the first man to ever say that to me."

"I hope I'm—" He swallowed the rest of his reply. "You've got a nice family, Em."

"Yes, I suppose I do, even if they're opinionated and love a good debate over politics."

Jake laughed. "That was my favorite part of the night."

A dim flash in her peripheral, and then Emily spotted Iris, waving from the porch of the boardinghouse. She'd turned on the outer front light.

"I need to go. Good night, Jake."

Emily sent him a final glance and took two steps forward. Only too late she heard the jangle of harnesses. An oncoming buggy! But no time to run! Iris screamed out her name. Emily's breath caught. She squeezed her eyes closed, every muscle taut, and prepared for impact.

Then a jerk backward, threatening her balance…

The buggy rattled past with only a warning called from the driver to watch where she was going.

Safe!

And then Emily found herself in Jake's arms. She felt the warmth within its circumference. Her body sagged in relief, her shoulder leaning against his chest. Her head fell back, and she stared up at him. The brim of his hat shadowed the both of them. "Thank you, Jake." *Breathe. Breathe.*

"You're welcome."

She felt the words close to her cheek.

Moments ticked by, and he didn't move. Emily sensed that he meant to kiss her. But not again. Not here. In front of Iris? The world?

With hands on his forearms, Emily struggled, forcing her legs to support her. "I'm grateful..."

"Well, there's no sense in you getting run over a second time this week."

She expelled an audible sigh, glad he lightened the moment. She even managed a smile.

Iris ran from the porch. "Emily, are you all right?"

"Yes, I'm fine."

Jake slowly released her.

"I need to be more careful when crossing the street." She felt foolish. "I teach my third graders to look both ways."

"Accidents happen." Jake placed his hand on the small of her back as he walked Iris and her across the road. "Good night, ladies. I'll see you bright and early in the morning."

"We'll be ready." Iris grabbed Emily's hand and fairly dragged her across the walk and up the porch steps. "Oh, Em, you scared the liver out of me! I thought you were going to be killed!"

"For a moment I thought so too."

"Thank God for Jake!"

"Yes..."

Myriads of emotions tangled inside of Emily. Was it shameful to feel disappointed that he hadn't kissed her? Disappointed, but immensely relieved that he didn't? Iris would have been shocked and heartbroken. Emily would have lost her good reputation as well as her best friend and then...she might as well have passed on to glory just now.

"But, listen, Iris..." They paused at the front door. Emily tried to carefully order her words. "I don't want your feelings to be hurt.

Jake stated plainly that his job is a widow-maker. Remember? He's not interested in marriage."

"Pshaw!"

Emily gasped. "Iris!"

"Well, honestly, Em. Most men say they're not interested in marriage, but they change their minds."

"How do you know?"

"I listen to testimonies at weddings. I overhear conversations—"

"Eavesdrop?"

"Of course not." Iris tipped her head and the pink floral creation on her hat flopped to one side. "For instance, I simply walked by the hardware store a while back and heard one man say that he never planned on marrying and having seven children, but he did. What does that tell you?"

"Oh, dear…" Emily realized Iris didn't plan on giving up on Jake so soon.

"Stop fretting."

Did she have a choice?

They entered the house, and Mrs. Hopper thumped her way up the narrow corridor with the aid of her cane. Her hair was flattened from pin curling, and her blue housecoat billowed slightly as Iris closed the inside door.

"I heard a scream!" The elderly woman reached the small foyer. "What's going on? Hooligans? I tell you this neighborhood isn't safe anymore!"

"No, Granny. Emily almost got trampled by a horse and buggy. Jake Edgerton saved her life."

"Wh–hat?"

By now their housemates were lined up along the stairway rail. Emily wished the polished floor would open so she could hide from their scrutiny.

"Isn't he a hero? He captured a wanted man right here in Manitowoc and now he saved Em's life."

The other ladies sounded impressed with their murmurs to one another.

"But I'm fine, and I apologize for the disturbance." Emily wished they'd all return to their rooms, because that's where she was headed. "Good night, Mrs. Hopper."

"Good night, my dear."

No tongue-lashing?

"G'night, Granny."

Just behind her, Emily heard Iris give her grandmother a perfunctory kiss before catching up at the stairs.

"Our Emily is still alive because of Deputy Edgerton."

"Iris, it wasn't that much of a fuss." Despite her statement, as she walked up each step, her fellow tenants touched her arm and shoulder and stated their gratefulness to Jake that she was still alive.

Finally in the sanctity of their spacious room, Emily undressed. She reflected on the pleasant day, an uplifting message at church this morning, her ride on her horse Ginger, and of course Jake's company.

"Emily?"

"Hmm?"

Iris took a deep breath. "I have been doing some soul-searching lately."

"And?" Perhaps her reason had returned.

"And I believe with all my heart that…"

"Yes?"

Iris gave a decisive nod. "I believe that Jake is my…my *destiny*."

It would have been so easy to lean forward just a bit and place a kiss on Emily's full, pink lips. So easy…but he didn't. He couldn't. Not again. Not after their heart-to-heart talk on Friday night. But one thing's for sure—Emily didn't love Andy Anderson, and it was just as well since Andy had decided to move to Idaho and try his hand at potato farming. As he'd told Jake that morning after church, Andy planned to quit his job tomorrow and leave on Wednesday morning's train with Jake.

He kicked off his boots and collapsed onto the bed in his hotel room. Andy wasn't the man for Em. He grinned. She could probably outride and outshoot the poor fellow!

No, a man didn't need a wife to compete with; he needed a woman to love and cherish. Andy was a dreamer. He needed a practical woman who could help him plant more than just potatoes.

Lying across the bed, Jake put his arms over his head and stretched. His mind wandered back to Emily, as it often did the last couple of days. He wondered why she'd ever set her cap for Andy. Maybe because he spoke fluent Norwegian and had been a good friend of Eden's? Jake guessed she probably didn't know many men. Captain Sundberg would have seen to that.

Jake smiled inwardly. He could well imagine Emily's father scaring off prospective suitors. As for Emily, he'd say she still had special feelings for him...just as he harbored a curious longing for her. Was his presumption correct?

Over the years he'd grown accustomed to figuring out people's motives and intentions. At times his life depended on making accurate assessments, and Emily was easy for him to read.

Lord, I want to act! But how could he? Courtship? Marriage? His life wasn't exactly stable. Sometimes he stayed gone for days, and he'd dodged a bullet through the head on more than one occasion. He couldn't—wouldn't—bring Emily into that kind of environment.

He thought of Ma. A man did not lose a mother that way and not wonder if he did something wrong. He knew he wasn't responsible for her actions, but they'd wounded him just the same as if he had been.

Jake's gaze wandered the rented room, the heavy wine-colored drapes and papered walls. The Dunbars ran a fine hotel, quiet, clean, with a fresh pitcher of water on the stand twice a day. He should have known they were related to the Sundbergs. He'd learned tonight that Will Dunbar's brother owned and managed this hotel and another one across town. Guess he could understand how Emily felt stifled in her quest for independence or some such nonsense.

A grin tugged at his mouth just before Jake commanded his weary body up from the bed. He crossed the room, rolling up his sleeves, then poured water into the bowl. He made good use of the soap, cleaning his hands, splashing his face. He glanced in the dark-framed mirror above the washstand and noted the worry lines etched on his forehead. Beads of water trickled down to a jaw that would need a shave tomorrow morning. Reaching for the towel, he dried off and willed his features to relax. He thought over his pleasant afternoon and evening. Emily's smile came to mind, her laughter, and the indignant sighs or tosses of her auburn head over her cousins' teasing. If ever there was a woman for him...

No! Jake tossed the towel onto the stand as reality hit hard once more. Courtship and marriage posed too many risks—

The most deadly of them being the one to his heart.

CHAPTER 11

*E*MILY PLACED HER hands on her low back and stretched. The temperature had soared today along with the humidity.

"Do you want to stop for a few minutes and rest?"

She glanced at *Bestamor* and shook her head. "I'm fine."

"She always says that." Iris turned from her perch on a stepstool, a rag in hand as she wiped out Ollie's kitchen cupboards. "Even after she nearly got run over by that buggy last night."

Emily rolled her eyes. Iris had told everyone she encountered today about the incident, and Emily had grown tired of hearing it.

Momma smiled. "My daughter has always kept her angels on their toes." She stood at the sink, graying strands of her jute-brown hair plastered to her temples. She set more dishes into the soapy liquid. "Haven't you, love?" Even though Momma had lived in America for the past twenty-five years, the British inflection in her voice was still quite evident.

"Now, then, we will not tease Emily." *Besta* put her arm around Emily's shoulders. Leave it to her grandmother to come to her defense.

"*Takk*." Emily replied the *thank you* in Norwegian.

Besta smiled, and the crinkles around her blue eyes multiplied. With her free hand she adjusted the scarf she'd placed over her snowy-white hair. "*Er du klar til å skrubbe gulvet?*"

Emily nodded. "Yes, I'm ready to scrub the dining room floor."

"Good." Momma spoke from over one slender shoulder. "The men will be wantin' to bring in the carpets soon. Your father said it looks like rain."

Besta gave a nod, and Emily picked up the pail and headed for the dining room.

Kneeling, she submerged her hand into the warm, soapy water and fished around until she found the scrub brush. As she made wide circular strokes on the hardwood floor, she thought of Jake. All day he seemed distant, avoiding her gaze—but she ought not be looking at him anyhow. It's just that his manner toward her had changed, and she wondered why.

After scrubbing a row across the room, Emily went back over it with a damp rag. She sat back. The wood gleamed. Now to finish the remaining three-quarters of the floor.

In the midst of the next row *Besta*'s call reached her ears. "Andy Anderson is here. He is tying his horse to the hitch."

Iris dashed into the dining room.

"Careful not to fall!" Emily sat back on her haunches.

She skidded to a halt and wiped her hands on the apron she wore over her brown skirt. "Did you hear? Andy just arrived." She made upward motions with her hand. "Quick. I'll help you tidy yourself up so you're presentable."

"He's not here to see me, silly." Emily pushed back the scarf on her head.

"What if he is? Maybe he found out somehow that we're here at Mr. Ollie's, helping clean and prepare for his funeral tomorrow."

"Then he'll have to leave his calling card." Emily couldn't keep the facetiousness to herself. "Folded at the top left corner, no less."

Iris snorted her both delicate and amused laugh.

Moments later Andy's voice wafted in from the foyer. Obviously *Besta* had met him at the door. Emily pressed her lips together and met Iris's wide gaze.

"Mr. Edgerton is outside somewhere," *Besta* said. "Try out back."

"Thank you, Mrs. Sundberg."

A pause.

"By the way, I quit my job at the aluminum factory today."

Iris gasped.

Emily laid her forefinger against her own lips, signaling complete silence.

"But why would you quit such a good job?"

Crawling on all fours, Emily reached the edge of the room where she could just make out Andy's stocky form.

"I've decided to be a wealthy potato farmer in Idaho." He finger combed back locks of his toasty-brown hair. "I have purchased my train ticket. I leave tomorrow afternoon."

"So soon?"

"The sooner the better. That's what I came to tell Jake. You see, I originally planned to ride the eight-fifteen on Wednesday morning with him."

"What do your parents have to say about this?"

"They're happy for me. They wish me well."

Emily startled at the news, but she wished Andy well too. No sadness or disappointment. Just a strange apathy, which proved she'd never cared for him in the first place.

Scooting back, her foot met up with an obstacle. A backward glance revealed black trousers. She instantly turned, sitting on her bottom, and stared up to find Jake. She tried not to show her grimace.

"I understand I have a visitor." He whispered, but an amused glint entered his gaze.

Emily nodded and pointed over her shoulder, toward to the foyer.

Jake hunkered down. "Sorry to have walked all over your just-washed floor." His gaze said he was sorry about something more, perhaps about not telling her that Andy decided to leave Manitowoc.

"No offense taken." She mouthed the words more than uttered

them. Her face felt on fire from the shame of having been caught eavesdropping.

Jake stood and walked out of the room. She heard him greet Andy.

Emily sprung to her feet, looked for Iris, and found her lurking near the butler's pantry, a small area adjoining the kitchen and dining room. "You might have warned me about Jake's approach."

"I didn't hear him coming, either." Iris looked as guilty as Emily felt. "I was trying to hear everything Andy said." Her expression fell. "Oh, Emily, I'm so sorry for you. Andy's leaving."

Emily wanted to say she didn't care, but then admitting so might make Iris suspicious of her true feelings. So she shrugged.

Iris pulled her into an embrace. "You poor thing. You're so distraught, you can't speak."

"Not distraught, Iris."

"Bereaved. Stricken. Heartbroken."

"No, no…" Emily pushed back. "Iris, I'm—"

"I know…you're *fine*." Her pale green eyes deepened one shade. "But inside you're really battling a torrent of tears."

Emily sent her gaze upward. "Not so much, Iris." She spotted a wispy gray web in the corner. "But how about taking care of that?"

Iris whirled around. "Oh, dear, and I just loathe spiders."

"It doesn't appear the spider has been there for quite some time."

The heavy front door closed with a *whoosh* of air and *Besta* murmured something. Jake replied, "So it would seem."

Emily felt rooted in place. Iris too froze. And then a shudder of dismay traveled down Emily's spine when she heard Jake walking back through the dining room. But he didn't stop when he reached them.

"There'll be time to say your good-byes to Andy tomorrow." He brushed past them with nary a glance. "He'll be at the funeral."

⊛⊛⊛

A steady rain began shortly after the rugs and furniture were back into place and all the buckets dumped and rags wrung out. Momma and *Besta* had been through the house and rearranged artwork on the walls to cover paintings that Jake's aunt and uncle took. Emily first assumed the valuables were the woman's inheritance and didn't think much of it, until *Besta* told her the real story, which she'd heard from Poppa, who, of course, heard it from Jake himself. Jake in all his benevolence had given his aunt and uncle whatever they wanted, but then he told them to leave. They did without argument, as they held no real sadness over Mr. Ollie's death. The whole thing didn't surprise Emily. She'd known for years that Jake's aunt hadn't cared about her father. Mr. Ollie once muttered that he'd spoiled Bettina rotten. Rotten to the core.

Emily gathered the last of the supplies and met her family and Iris on the back porch. A sick, smoky smell from this afternoon's burning lingered in the air. She spotted Jake immediately. He leaned casually against a wide, white pillar.

"I can't thank you all enough," he said. "You've done over and above."

"It's our pleasure to help." Poppa stepped forward and shook Jake's hand. "Anything else you need, let us know."

"I appreciate it." He looked out over the blooming flower garden. "Once the rain lets up I'll head back to the hotel, and if Emily and Iris want to ride along…"

"You're not going anywhere without a hot meal." Momma looked to Poppa for affirmation. "Besides, the girls want to wash up and change."

"Ah, yes, please stay to dinner, Jake. I won't hear the last of it if you don't."

"Well, then, I accept." A smile spread across his face.

He still hadn't glanced her way, and Emily couldn't figure out why. Not that she wanted any more moon eying, but she didn't like the tension between them either. It couldn't have been her eavesdropping, because he'd been acting strangely all day.

She ran a hand over her hair, thinking maybe he didn't look at her because she made a dismal sight in her oldest black skirt and one of Zeb's outgrown shirts. She realized she'd lost her black scarf.

"I forgot something." She headed for the door. "I'll be right back."

Inside, Emily ran through the house, searching, and finally found her fringed thing, lying on the rug in the upstairs hallway. She bent and grabbed it and caught her reflection in the large, ornate mirror on the wall. She didn't appear any worse for wear, although in this light the shadow on her cheek looked more pronounced. Even so, her family knew she received her share of bumps and bruises. They'd seen her "shiner," as Kate called it—and so had Jake.

Still confused over his behavior, she hurried back down and outside. She stopped short when she saw that only Jake remained on the back porch.

"Where's everyone else?"

"They made a run for the buggy. I said I'd wait for you and lock up."

"Iris didn't wait for me?" Odd that she'd miss her chance at a few seconds alone with Jake.

"Nope."

He still made no attempt to look at her as he turned the key in the back door lock. In fact, it seemed he made every attempt not to look at her.

"Jake, have I offended you somehow?"

"Nope."

His swift answer crimped her heart. "I think you owe me more of a reply than that. I thought we were friends."

He sank his dark gaze into her eyes. Finally a response! As she searched his face, trying to understand, his features softened.

"I'm sorry, Em. I've just got a lot on my mind."

"Well, that makes sense."

She moved toward the steps. A light spray from the rain moistened her face. How refreshing after the heat of the day.

And then she remembered why she and everyone else here today had worked so hard. *Mr. Ollie's funeral tomorrow.* Jake was probably overcome with sorrow as the day approached.

"Jake—" She turned easily on the wooden porch. "—I've been insensitive, thinking only of my feelings. I worried all day that I offended you, when you're obviously mourning the loss of your grandfather."

A slight nod in reply.

"I have to admit feeling misty myself, being here today. I have a lot of fond memories of Mr. Ollie." She smiled.

For a long moment, neither spoke. A rhythm of raindrops drummed on the roof, covering the porch.

"I'm sorry that I didn't tell you Andy planned to leave. I figured it wasn't my news to tell."

She'd almost forgotten about it. "Well...Andy made his decision, and far be it from me to stand in the way—like I even could. Andy doesn't speak to me, as you know."

"And about that, Em..."

She tipped her head.

"Your father and I talked today. He told me that he and Andy exchanged words some time ago regarding your, um, romantic interest in him."

"Poppa?" Emily felt herself pale. "What did he say to Andy?"

"Oh, something about Andy making sure his intentions were honorable. I wouldn't have said anything, but I know how hurt you've been by Andy's behavior. I even told your father that I felt the need to mention it to you."

Her blood rushed back with gusto. "Well, that just figures!" She gave her scarf a sound shake. "If it's up to him, I'll die an old maid!"

"Now, Em..."

"And it's not funny."

"I'm not laughing."

"I can see the smirk on your face."

"I'm sorry. The old maid remark tickled me." He gave his head a wag. "You're a beautiful young lady, Em." He stared off in the direction of the woods. "When the right man comes along, neither your father nor brothers will be able to scare him off."

His words touched her deeply, and yet she felt somewhat baffled. "So, let me get this straight. Andy approached Poppa about courting me?"

"Sounded like it never got that far." Jake paused. "And Emily..."

"Yes?"

"I too have been fairly warned."

"What?" Horror gripped her, not so much because Poppa spoke to Jake about her, but that Poppa had even noticed something undefined existed between them. "What did he say?"

Jake hesitated, and for a moment Emily wondered if he'd tell her. "Your father said that the man who kisses his daughter marries her."

Her jaw dropped. "He had no right!"

"He's your father. He had every right." Jake straightened. "And no man ought to be kissing you."

"No man ever has, except for you." She backpedaled. "But you weren't a man. We were children."

His expression lightened. "Look, Em, I'm not afraid of your father or your brothers. If I wanted to pursue you, I would. But I live in Montana and my work is—"

"I know. It's a widow-maker."

"It's best if we keep a polite distance."

"You mean we haven't been polite?" She felt mildly insulted. So they'd exchanged some token glances. A dance. A private conversation in a very public place. So what?

Nevertheless, Emily had everything to lose. If Iris found out about her attraction to Jake, she might feel double-crossed and never trust Emily again. She tossed her head. "I can be friends with you just like I'm friends with Andy."

Jake looked somewhat abashed. "Ah, yes…Andy. Your friendship has blossomed, hmm? Your side of it anyway."

Emily kept silent and held his narrowed gaze. Let him think what he would. Soon both men would be out of her life forever. What would it matter?

Without another word Jake reached for the black umbrella residing near the porch rail. Emily didn't bother waiting until he opened it. Whirling around, she ran down the porch steps and toward the buggy. Large raindrops pelted her from the gray sky, saturating her hair and baggy shirt. But Emily didn't care if she got soaked.

❦❦❦

"Do I detect something of a cold shoulder from my daughter this evening?"

"I'd say it's more frosty than cold." Jake relaxed in the black leather armchair and gazed at the sturgeon mounted over the blue-green mantel. The color suggested the depths of the Great Lake out of which the captain had fished the monster. With its long, whiskered mouth and armorlike skin it spanned at least six feet. Biggest fish he ever saw, alive or dead, next to a paddlefish.

"So I gather you told Emily about our conversation this afternoon."

Jake glanced at the captain, noticing again his fine smoking jacket. "Emily asked, just like I said she would. She thought she'd offended me. I assured her she hadn't."

"Hmm…so now she's angry with me. Well, so be it. I'm her father, after all."

"I reminded her of that fact." Jake's curiosity gnawed at him. "No offense intended, but didn't you expect this kind of reaction from Em?"

"I suppose I didn't."

Jake rolled a shoulder and wondered how he too could have been so wrong about her. "Captain, I think she still has a particular fondness for Andy Anderson."

A heavy frown settled on the captain's brow as he turned the '58 Remington in his hands, Jake's gift to him as a remembrance of Granddad. "You think so? Andy?"

"She didn't deny it this afternoon." Jake made a grave error when presuming a woman's mind. He should've known better. But he'd let his emotions overrule his common sense. "I'm thinking Em just used me..." That didn't come out quite right. He cleared his throat and started over. "She used our friendship to make Andy jealous. Obviously it didn't work."

"Emily doesn't play those sorts of games."

All women play those sorts of games. "Either way, it doesn't matter."

"I suppose you're right." The captain scrutinized the weapon in his hands. "Are you certain you want me to have this revolver? It's quite collectable."

"I'm sure, as long as you don't use it on me." Jake grinned.

The captain grunted. "No promises." His blue eyes twinkled. "Especially where my daughter is concerned."

"You don't have to worry about that, not with me."

"Hmm...well, I think you're mistaken about her feelings for Andy. He's been Eden's friend for years, and I've never detected any sort of chemistry between them."

Chemistry? Is that all? There existed some magnetic lightning between Emily and him. Jake sensed it when he'd seen her in town on Thursday, felt it again when they'd danced on Friday night. Couldn't stop thinking about it all weekend.

"Zeb is thrilled with his pistol..."

The captain's voice drew Jake back to the present.

"...and Eden will be also."

"Good. Granddad would be pleased."

The captain stroked the shiny barrel. "We always admired Ollie's collection."

Jake smiled. "He had a veritable arsenal. I'm taking plenty of weapons back with me."

A rustling of skirts, and Jake looked to see Mrs. Sundberg enter the study. He stood and politely took the tray containing two cups of rich-smelling coffee. He placed it on the rectangular table between the chairs.

"As a boy I dreamed of firing this very gun." The captain practiced his aim and pointed the unloaded weapon at the windows. "To my great disappointment I never got the chance, although I've fired myriad others, of course."

"Well, now you can shoot off that Remington to your heart's content." Jake grinned.

"But not in the house, dear." Mrs. Sundberg folded her slender arms. "That's what I always told our children."

Jake's smile widened.

The captain chuckled and gazed at his wife. "Thank you for the coffee, darling."

Mrs. Sundberg replied with a hard stare before leaving the room and closing the door more forcefully than necessary.

Jake sat. "Another cold shoulder, Captain?"

He sighed. "So it would seem." He set the Remington on the side table nearest to his chair. "Thank you for this keepsake."

"You're welcome. I wanted you all to have something of Granddad's." Jake had bestowed two sets of his grandmother's earbobs to the two Mrs. Sundbergs, the captain's wife and his mother. Each looked pleased by the gift. And, of course, Emily got that necklace. He noticed she'd even worn it today while cleaning. Maybe she never took it off. Jake rather liked that idea.

I've got to stop thinking about that woman.

"Do you mind if I bring up some business?"

Jake helped himself to coffee. "Don't mind at all. What's on your mind?"

"I'll get right to the point. I'd like to purchase your grandfather's house."

Jake had prayed along those lines. *Thank You, Lord!* "That surely will simplify things."

"I thought you might be agreeable."

"I am." If he could somehow know that his place passed back into the Sundbergs' hands, Granddad would be pleased.

"I'll even incur any shipping expenses on furniture you'd like to keep, and I'll dispose of whatever items you decide to leave behind."

"That makes things even simpler."

"Right now an acre of land in Manitowoc sells for roughly eighteen dollars and thirty-five cents."

Jake let out a long, slow whistle. "That much, huh? An acre will run you about a dollar-fifty to eight-fifty in Dawson County." He thought of his father, once a farmer here in Wisconsin. He'd married Ma and then headed for Montana. "Hence the westward homesteading."

"Exactly." The captain narrowed his gaze and pursed his lips. "Now, then, here's my offer..." He tapped the side of his chair.

Jake sipped his hot coffee. "I'm listening."

CHAPTER 12

*W*HEN THEY RETURNED to the boardinghouse Monday night, Emily collapsed into bed. If she'd thought her muscles hurt after the run-in with Jake last Thursday, they screamed at her now. She'd also caught something of a chill from the rain as the weather change brought a cold damp wind from off the lake.

The bedroom door squeaked open and Iris entered. "I finished writing my article about Jake and Mr. Ollie."

How can she still have so much energy? Emily lolled her head in Iris's direction. "That's wonderful."

"I plan to drop it off at the newspaper tomorrow." She stared at the sheet of paper in her hands. "If the editor publishes it, it'll be too late for Mr. Ollie's funeral service, of course, but it'll make a nice article anyway."

"How thoughtful of you."

Iris held the paper to chest. "Jake said he wants a copy if it's really published."

Emily forced a smile. "That's quite the compliment, isn't it?" Thanks to Poppa, she and Jake were barely speaking. *Polite distance, indeed!*

Iris crossed the room and hung up her yellow housecoat. "We'd best get some sleep. Another busy day tomorrow, with Mr. Ollie's funeral service. The church service begins at ten o'clock, followed by the entombment and then the light luncheon at Mr. Ollie's—or, rather, Jake's."

"Or rather my father's home and property, after tomorrow morning." *Besta* had told her about it.

Iris gasped and her slender hand fluttered at the throat of her gown. "No! Really?" Agape, she stared at the rose-papered wall, opposite their beds. "So that explains why your father and Jake were holed up in his study for so long after supper."

"That's why, and I can't tell you how happy my grandmother is about it. She said my grandfather, Sam Sundberg, would be thrilled if he could somehow know that the land he had once been given by Chief Oshkosh belonged to the Sundbergs once again. "

"What will your father do with that house?"

Emily pushed herself up onto her elbows, which was no simple task. "Momma said Eden has a special girl now. We'll meet her at Christmastime, and it's likely that Eden will propose at that time—just like Poppa proposed marriage to Momma one Christmas Eve long ago. Momma thinks Eden will want the house as he plans to take over much of Poppa's business."

"Eden is going to be married before you?"

Emily dropped back down onto her pillow, feeling as dismal as the weather. "Everything is so unfair, Iris. I found out that Poppa scared Andy off."

"And now he's leaving tomorrow for Idaho. Oh, you poor dear. Your heart is breaking, isn't it?"

"More than you'll ever know, Iris." Emily gazed at the familiar plaster ceiling with its spidery cracks. The image of Jake's face appeared in her mind's eye. She saw those weather-worn lines etched down from the dimples in his cheeks that made his jaw look more square and, yes, more rugged. She'd see his face forever. He was the only man she'd ever loved—and ever would. Andy had never evoked anything even remotely similar within her being. But Jake had won her heart of hearts ever since she was thirteen.

"Write him a letter, Em. You can give it to him tomorrow."

"Jake?" She peered at Iris.

"No, Andy."

Emily's face heated as though the sun beat down on it at noon-time and she'd forgotten a hat or bonnet. "I'm not up to letter writing tonight."

"Then in the morning."

"Maybe."

She brought her fingers up and touched the silver necklace. The tiny cross pendent had slid across her throat and lay near her earlobe.

Iris reached to turn down the lamp, and Emily caught her gaze before the room went dark.

"I meant to ask you where you'd gotten that pretty necklace you've been wearing the past couple of days."

A wave of guilt crashed over Emily. "This old thing?" No lie. It had been Jake's grandmother's.

"Oh, so you found it in your room at your parents' house? That makes sense. It must have been something you acquired before we knew each other."

"It was a gift."

"How special." Iris yawned. "Good night, Em."

"G'night."

"You're my very best friend, and I love you as much as I would love a sister."

"I love you too, Iris. And I'd never hurt you for the world."

"Of course you wouldn't." She yawned again. "We're sisters in Christ."

Emily smiled. The room quieted, and Emily grew drowsy, lis-tening to the rain's gentle drumming against the side of the house.

The next morning Emily indulged in a hot bath before she dressed. Moving and stretching helped the soreness she felt in her back and legs from scrubbing floors and lifting and pushing furniture, which, in hind's sight, had been far too heavy for woman's work. Delegating had never been among the list of Emily's stronger attributes. Perhaps it came from growing up on a small farm and competing with brothers, particularly her twin, Eden.

Once she'd dressed in somber attire, fashionable brown skirt and a plain ivory shirtwaist, Emily brushed out her hair. *Besta* had taught her how to tame her curls with one thick braid and then wind it into a tight coil, which was finally pinned at the nape. She smiled at her grandmother's story about a smitten Indian brave whacking off several inches of her braided blonde hair for a remembrance. *Besta* said she'd been terrified until Grandfather Sundberg stepped in to protect her.

With her hair finished, Emily glanced at the many hatboxes stacked on top of her wardrobe. Which one to wear. She nibbled her lower lip. After several moments she selected one with a wide brim and swathed in tulle, brown ribbon, and rosettes. It complemented both her hair and her outfit.

Ready at last, she left her room and took to the stairs. Iris had returned from her errands, excited about the prospect of her article being published in the *Chronicle*. It would be her first.

"Oh, Granny, won't it be grand if I can tell my students in the fall that I'm a published author?" Iris helped the elderly woman don her hat while Emily filled a basket of foodstuff that Mrs. Hopper so kindly prepared yesterday.

At last the three of them left the boardinghouse and waited out in front for Jake's arrival with the buggy. Emily was surprised when Zeb showed up.

"The pastor requested that Jake arrive ahead of time so mourners could express their condolences to him if they wished." Zeb climbed down, careful not to catch the hem of his good jacket on the side of the vehicle.

"Makes perfect sense." Iris placed her gloved hand into Zeb's palm, and he helped her into the carriage.

Next Zeb assisted Mrs. Hopper aboard and, finally, turned to Emily. Although she was older, he'd grown taller and broad-shouldered, strong like Poppa. With a grin, he took Emily's hand and placed one hand at her waist. Then he sort of tossed her into the buggy. She landed quite unceremoniously beside Iris. She heard his chuckles.

Iris clucked her tongue. "Such abuse, you poor darling."

"At least someone pities me." Emily slapped the back of Zeb's head after he positioned himself in the driver's seat, reins in hands. Again, Zeb laughed. Mrs. Hopper sent her a curious look, and from out of the corner of her eye, she caught her best friend's grin. "So you think it's amusing too?"

"No, no…but your brothers love you, Em."

"Sure we do." Zeb still wore a wide grin.

"Of course." Mrs. Hopper seemed charmed by her young, hand-some driver. "You've become a fine man, Zeb Sundberg."

"Thank you, ma'am." He gave Emily a grin.

She hurled a glance at the blue sky.

The buggy jerked as Zeb urged the team forward.

Iris leaned close to Emily. "Despite your family's love, I under-stand how you might feel…*suffocated*."

"I do, Iris." Emily thought of Poppa and how he'd humiliated her.

"You've never really been on your own, not like Eden."

Emily fought off a pout.

"I haven't either, and you know how Granny continually presses me to get married." Iris whispered the remark. "It's disheartening. She doesn't see my personal achievements."

"Well, I do. The play you wrote at Easter time was brilliant. The message of our Savior's death and resurrection came alive, and the children were so happy to have a part in the service."

"Thank you, Em."

She smiled.

"Our families don't understand that we're independent women of the twentieth century."

Emily squared her shoulders. "Yes, we are."

"So you'll enjoy the plans I've made."

"What?" Her confidence waned. "What plans?"

"I'll tell you later, after the funeral."

Anticipation and dread mingled inside of Emily. But Iris's plans weren't always harebrained. She'd been the one to suggest they both earn their teacher's certificate. They'd acquired jobs, albeit at different schools, and they each had a small savings. However, there were those plans that hadn't ended so well. Like the time they'd placed orders for two goats, intending to make goat's milk soap and other luxurious bath accessories. It had sounded so profitable, although they hadn't investigated the breeder. What had arrived from within a boxcar were ornery old things that butted anyone and anything within close proximity. Momma hated them, and the goats tormented the other livestock on the farm. Finally Poppa had to put them down. So much for their investment.

"This isn't one of your goat plans, is it?"

"Oh, no…" Iris grinned happily before gazing over the busy street. "This is a sure thing."

Emily wondered.

Jake knew it was a bad idea right from the moment he began to read Granddad's favorite Psalm. "'Yea, though I walk through the valley of the shadow of death, I will fear no evil: for thou art with me.'" His throat went dry and his voice cracked as he read the rest.

He drew in a deep breath before finishing. "'Surely goodness and mercy shall follow me all the days of my life: and I will dwell in the house of the Lord for ever.'"

The congregation said, "Amen!"

Jake closed his Bible and stepped off the platform. He headed for his place in the front pew, only to discover that Emily Sundberg had taken his place. He slowed his pace and glanced at the adjacent pew, but it was filled. The entire church was packed from wall to wall.

Emily must have realized his dilemma because she quickly scooted over, but not before Jake glimpsed the tears in her eyes, shining from beneath the rim of her hat. The sight gripped his heart. He hated the sight of a sad woman—ever since Ma…

Jake halted his thoughts and strode the rest of the way to the pew and eased himself in beside Emily. On her other side, he heard Iris sniff loudly and, next to Iris, he'd glimpsed Mr. and Mrs. Schulz. After he was situated, Emily's gloved fingers briefly touched the back of his hand. Oddly, Jake felt comforted by her simple gesture.

The rest of the service went off without a hitch, and Jake decided his grandfather had been rightly honored by the Scripture readings and short testimony from Mr. Schulz. Afterward, at the burial, Jake tossed the first handful of dirt onto Granddad's coffin. He murmured a last good-bye, remembering Granddad's intelligent and patient gaze, his words of wisdom from the Scriptures, and his sound business advice. *You love the law like I do, Jake. You're a fair man. You believe justice will be served…*

And then it was over.

CHAPTER 13

*J*AKE PRESSED HIMSELF into a space between Granddad's parlor and dining room and watched the goings-on. After relaying their condolences to him, people mingled while holding their luncheon plates in one hand and enjoying the array of food. Dishes lined the sideboard and cluttered the linen-cloth-covered table. Awestruck, grateful, and mightily overwhelmed described his feelings at the moment. Almost every female in Granddad's church brought something tasty to share. If he kept sampling, he'd bust a seam.

Emily's mother came toward him, carrying a tray of sweet baked goods. She stopped. "Help yourself, Jake."

"Oh, no, thank you, Mrs. Sundberg, I'm filled up."

She smiled and moved on.

Soft piano music wafted to his ears from Granddad's library. Curious, Jake strode in the direction of the library and recognized the melody of "Be Still, My Soul." Granddad loved that hymn.

Four dining room chairs blocked the entrance of the library, discouraging guests. Evidently one guest hadn't been deterred. Jake slipped past through the middle of the chairs and paused at the doorway. Emily sat at the piano.

"Leave to thy God to order and provi-ide." She began to sing in a smooth soprano. "In every change He faithful will remain. Be still, my soul, thy best, thy heavenly Frie-end, through thorny ways leads to a joyful end."

Jake felt sort of choked up. "You trying to make everybody cry?"

Emily glanced over her shoulder. "Hi, Jake."

"Hi, yourself." He walked forward. "You play beautifully."

"Thank you."

She began again, and Jake sidled up to the piano and leaned against its polished edge.

"Poppa thought I should play some of Mr. Ollie's favorite hymns."

"Nice idea." The melody plucked a soulful chord deep inside of him.

"Poppa likes to hear that his money has been put to good use on all my many piano lessons." Glancing up from the keys, she smiled at him, and Jake's insides warmed.

"I think your father made a sound investment."

The comment earned him another smile, and Jake wished he wasn't leaving tomorrow morning. He tried to burn this moment into his memory forever. Beautiful and talented Emily Sundberg, serenading him at the grand piano.

Her fingers rested on the keys. "Any requests, Jake?"

He thought a moment, his mind devoid of all thoughts except the ones of her and the way the sunshine danced off her reddish-brown hair, and how fetching she looked in the ivory, high-necked blouse she wore. He spotted the necklace he'd given her, its only evidence the tiny cross, resting at her throat. A feeling of pleasure spread through him. Just as he suspected; she wore it every day.

Because of him?

Maybe more because Granddad had been a grandfatherly figure in her life too.

"How about 'Nearer My God to Thee'? Mr. Ollie liked that one too."

"That will do just fine, Emily."

She arranged the sheet music in front of her and then began

to play. Jake forced himself to back away from the piano, but he couldn't make himself leave the room. Emily had some inexplicable way of drawing him in and making him stay...

But what of her feelings? Sometimes he thought he sensed they shared a powerful attraction, but other times she made it clear that he was only her friend.

Jake walked to the second set of bay windows. Sheer white draperies covered them, and he pushed them open. Outside people mingled on the back lawn, ladies in their feathery and flowery hats and somber-colored skirts and dresses, and men attired in their Sunday best on a Tuesday afternoon. He inhaled deeply as his gaze wandered farther, beyond the guests and toward the little stream that ran through the property. Back toward...

He nearly groaned. "Emily, come over here. There's something you need to see."

She stopped playing in mid-chord. Jake turned and watched her slide off the piano bench. She crossed the room, a spark of curiosity in her eyes. The thought of taking her in his arms and holding her next to his heart wouldn't seem to shake loose and abate. Especially after he'd spotted that massive oak, under which he'd first kissed her.

"What is it, Jake?"

Taking her arm, he guided Emily to the window and stood behind her. "What do you see?" A whisper of lavender tickled his nose. Mercy, but she sure smelled sweet!

"I see Mr. and Mrs. Hansen and Lois Applegate."

"Look beyond the folks, Em."

"Well...the garden needs tilling. It's probably not too late to plant."

"Past the garden."

"More lawn, wildflowers..." She gasped.

Jake grinned.

"Oh, my...the oak tree!"

"Clear view from this window, wouldn't you say?"

She whirled around and paled. Her eyes grew wider. "Oh, Jake…" Her fingers covered her lips.

"I'm wondering if Eden came over looking for me and…well, found me."

"No, it couldn't have been Eden. He knew how badly I felt and the guilt I carried for so long. He would have confessed if he'd been the tattler, at least to me if not to Poppa."

"Think so?"

She nodded. "Positive." She flicked a glance over her shoulder. "We were so stupid to think we were alone."

"I know it. God saw everything."

Emily groaned.

"I'm sorry, Em." He cupped the bruised side of her face. Her skin felt petal-soft beneath his rough hand. "Forgive me for all the hurt I caused you."

She leaned into his touch, doing something crazy to his insides. "All's forgiven. Remember?" She turned in her pretty fingers the tiny, silver cross at the base of her neck.

"I remember." He barely eked the words out, and when he dropped his hand and lifted his gaze to hers, he battled another onslaught of emotion. *Lord, how did she get under my skin?*

"Will you ever come back to Manitowoc, Jake?"

He never wanted to go. Not now. "Emily, I, um…"

"I know Poppa is purchasing Mr. Ollie's home, and I know your life is in Fallon, Montana."

Her words brought his senses back. "Right."

"But it would be nice if you'd visit sometime."

"Why?" *Give me a reason, Em.* Not that he had any business asking for one.

"Well…" She moistened her pink lips, her gaze never leaving his. "Momma said Eden met a nice young lady in New York. He might propose over Christmas. Maybe you'll be invited to the wedding."

"I doubt it. I haven't seen Eden in—"

"Ten years."

Jake gave a slight nod. *Come on, Em, you can do better than that.*

Her gaze fell to her now-folded hands. "But my family holds you in high regard."

"I hold them in high regard too."

"You do?" Her blue eyes sailed up until she met his gaze once more. "Even though Poppa said what he did to you?"

"Even though."

"Really?"

He nodded. "I wouldn't mind seeing you again, Emily."

Her smile and pretty blush made him grin. "Then I hope you'll come back."

"Do you, Em?"

She nodded then quickly took to studying her hands again.

Jake reached out and touched the tendril, curling down from her temple. Hair like silk. "Then maybe I'll have to conjure up some excuse to come back." He traced the soft curve of her jaw with his forefinger.

"Iris would like that."

"Iris?" His insides turned stone cold, and he withdrew his hand.

"I shouldn't speak for her, though."

"No, you shouldn't." Disappointment made his words come out more forceful than necessary. Jake set his hands on his hips. "I'd appreciate it if you'd speak for yourself."

"I did." Her gaze jumped to his. "It's just that...well, it's complicated."

The reply didn't help Jake one bit. She had allowed him to touch her hair and her face. That told him one thing, but out of her mouth came something else.

Emily's gaze suddenly darted toward the door. "Hello, Poppa!"

Jake stepped away and turned toward the entrance.

"Glad I found you both here." The captain entered the library with

Andy Anderson in tow. "Look who's with me. Andy. He's saying his good-byes."

Jake watched Emily's reaction. After a polite smile she glared at her father. Shifting his gaze, he saw the captain reply with an affectionate wink. Jake sniffed, scratched his jaw, and looked at the tops of his boots to keep from smiling at the exchange.

Andy approached him and extended his right hand. "Good to see you again, Jake." The man looked slicked and polished, a far sight better than Friday night. "It's because of you that I'm heading west."

"No, no..." He'd hate it if Emily ever blamed him. "You made your own decisions."

"But you told me how affordable land is out there."

"Sure, but you're your own man, Andy." Jake looked at Em, who mouthed something to her father. Was she even paying attention?

"That I am." Andy tugged on the lapels of his stone-brown jacket. "My own man and soon to be a wealthy potato farmer and land-owner. Not like some of my relatives in Norway." He moved back around. "See ya, Em."

"Bye."

Jake scrutinized her every feature. No misty eyes. No crestfallen expression. Now, see, that told him something else.

"Emily?" The captain captured his attention and halted Andy's strides. "You may never see Andy again. Isn't there something more you'd like to say to him?"

Jake sucked in a breath and held it.

"Yes, of course there is."

There is?

"Have a nice life, Andy."

Jake exhaled.

"Thanks, Em. I will." Andy smiled and shook the captain's hand before leaving the library.

Captain Sundberg strode toward Emily. Seeing his approach, she folded her arms and lifted her chin.

"Darling, don't be angry with me." He slipped one arm around her shoulders.

She shrugged it off. "Poppa, forgive me for speaking so candidly in front of Jake, but you should know—you both should—that I'm embarrassed over what transpired the other day." She sent a furtive glance Jake's way. "I'm referring to your conversation with Jake about me, Poppa."

"I know full well to what you're referring, my dear." The captain trained a hard look on Emily, although she didn't seem intimidated in the least.

"Perhaps we should have talked about it first."

"I'm your father, Emily." The captain pulled back his shoulders. "Jake understands."

"Yes, I do." He picked up the undercurrent; the warning still remained: *The man who kisses my daughter, marries her.*

"Poppa, I'm an independent woman twenty-three years old." Emily stepped closer to her father and straightened his already impossibly straight bow tie. "Need I remind you that I have a twin who is the same age?"

"You needn't." The captain tolerated her fussing.

She brushed a speck off his black jacket. "Eden is allowed far more freedoms than I have ever known." She whispered something before rising on tiptoe and placing a kiss on the captain's cheek. Facing Jake once more, she sent him a pleasant smile. "I hope you will visit again."

"We'll see."

Her smile looked perfunctory. "If you'll excuse me, I'll see if Momma needs my help."

Jake replied with a small nod, and his gaze trailed Emily out of the room. When he turned back to the captain, he caught his watchful stare.

"My daughter doesn't seem heartbroken over a certain young man's departure."

"No, she doesn't."

"I know my daughter, Jake, and I'm afraid your hypothesis is incorrect." He lowered his voice. "She harbors little to no feelings for Andy."

"I'll take your word for it." Emily was a puzzle to him.

Commotion at the doorway drew Jake's attention. Men's laughter carried into the library, and moments later Mr. Schulz appeared, accompanied by a very distinguished-looking man with a white, bushy mustache.

"There you are, Jake! And Captain Sundberg, I'm glad you're here too." Mr. Schulz rushed toward them. "I'd like you both to meet someone." He waited for the other man to catch up before continuing. "Allow me to present Mr. Joseph Quarles, Wisconsin's United States senator."

A US senator? Impressive! Jake shook the man's hand. "Pleased to meet you, sir."

"Likewise."

Mr. Schulz introduced the captain and they clasped hands.

Senator Quarles regarded Jake. "I was a very good acquaintance of your grandfather, although we typically met on opposite sides of the courtroom aisle."

"Ahh…" Another attorney. Jake might have figured. Lawyers typically went on to run for public office.

"Simon, here—" He directed a brief nod at Mr. Schulz. "—has been telling me of your exemplary persuasive skills."

Jake knew he meant his handling of Aunt Bettina. "Oh, mine aren't close to Granddad's."

"I wouldn't be too certain of that. Oliver lost his fair share of arguments."

"Thank you, sir." Jake humbly accepted the compliment.

"Good of you to drop by, Mr. Quarles." The captain clasped his hands behind his back.

"I'm back in Wisconsin on business, and when I learned the

news of Oliver's death, I knew I had to make the journey here from Madison."

"Do you need a place to stay? There's an extra room at my house."

"No, but thank you, Captain Sundberg. I have family in Kenosha with whom I'll reside." He turned back to Jake. "But I'd like to speak more with this young man. A United States deputy marshal from Montana?"

"Correct."

His mustache twitched. "Simon tells me you're a fair man in your dealings. I'd like to hear about them."

"Please get comfortable." The captain indicated to the light-blue chairs on their left. "I'll ask my wife to fix you a lunch plate."

"No need, Captain. Your wife is already seeing to the matter."

They sat down. "Now, tell me, son…" Mr. Quarles unfastened the single button on his expensive-looking black jacket before sinking into the armchair. "Tell me of the buffalo hunters, cowboys, and outlaws. Is Fallon, Montana, anything like Dodge City, Kansas?"

"No, sir." Jake had a good chuckle, thinking of the five buildings that made up Fallon's main street. "Not even close."

After Zeb drove them home later that night, Emily helped Iris carry a basketful of clothing upstairs to their room at the boardinghouse. She'd left various articles in Emily's room at the farm and only this evening packed them up and brought them home.

"What is all of this?" Emily unburdened her arms onto her bed and recognized a number of her own belongings among them. "Iris?"

"It's part of my plan."

"I think you'd better tell about this plan of yours."

Iris never looked up from folding the clothing and separating them into two piles. "A pity Jake couldn't take us home tonight."

"He's dining with Senator Quarles, the Schulzes, and my parents." Emily folded her arms and leaned against Iris's bedpost. "We could have dined with them tonight too, but you insisted on coming home early."

"It's been a long day." Iris yawned. "We've got an even busier day tomorrow."

"Looking for summer work?" *Ah, that's the secret plan!*

"No."

"Iris…" Mild irritation welled up inside of Emily. "If the plan involves me, I think you'd best divulge it now or I won't cooperate."

"You're right. Now's the time." Sitting on the side of the bed, Iris smoothed her skirt over her knees. "I told you that Jake is my destiny, and I've decided to act upon my steadfast belief."

"He doesn't want to get married."

"He'll change his mind."

"Iris, how can I get through to you?" Oh, how her friend tried Emily's patience!

Crossing the room, Iris opened the top drawer of the oak desk they shared. "This morning after I dropped off my article at the newspaper office, I went to the train station and purchased two tickets."

"What? Two tickets? To where?"

"Montana, Idaho, and Washington State." She smiled. "I want to see the Pacific Ocean."

"No!" Emily shook her head with vigor. "No, no, no!" She stared hard at her friend. "Have you lost your very mind?"

Iris's chin quivered ever so slightly. "You won't make me ride the Northwestern Pacific Railroad all by myself, will you?"

"Northwestern Pacific? That train doesn't service Manitowoc."

"No, it doesn't. You see, we board the train to Milwaukee, and then transfer there to St. Paul. We'll transfer again once we reach Minnesota, and we'll be on our way to the Pacific. The clerk at the station told me all about it and even gave me a map."

Iris may have done her homework, but the idea was still insanity. "Be reasonable, Iris. My father will not allow me to get on a train and follow Jake across the country."

"Don't look at it as following Jake. We're following our hearts. Wouldn't you like to catch up with Andy?"

"Not particularly." Emily decided she needed to tell Iris the truth, at least in part. She sat down on the edge of her bed and ran her hand over the quilt *Besta* made for her. "I don't love Andy. I never did. He was a convenient choice for a husband, or so I thought. But I feel nothing for him, Iris. Nothing." She met her friend's bright gaze. "I don't care that he left this afternoon. I wish him the best."

Iris merely shrugged. "I still want to see the rugged west and the Pacific Ocean."

"Ohh…" Emily collapsed across her bed. Iris had gone crazy. That's what happened. Crazy!

"Think of the grand stories we can tell our students in the fall. We'll have an adventure. I want to experience America. See the prairies and the mountains. Emily, you and I have attended school here and now we live and work here. The way things are going, we'll die old maids right here in Manitowoc."

Emily would concede to at least that much.

"Besides, your poppa would allow Eden to ride the train alone and, actually, he already has."

True. Eden had taken the train to and from New York City several times in the past years while Emily experienced only guarded freedoms.

"Are we really independent women of the twentieth century or not?"

Emily sat back up. "Yes, but despite my best argument, Poppa still won't let me go."

"That's why you'll write him a letter, which we will drop off in his box before boarding the train in the morning."

Emily laughed, imagining her father's outrage. "My father will hop on the next train and collect the both of us and put us over his knee."

"No, he won't, Emily. He knows you're upset with him for prematurely and needlessly, I might add, discouraging Andy from courting you."

He'd warned Jake too. But Emily wouldn't tell Iris about it. How could she without revealing her treasonous heart?

"Your poppa and my granny have no legal right to stop us, Emily."

"Yes, I know, but…"

"But you're right. They'll worry."

"Yes, they will."

"Therefore—"

Emily should have known Iris would think up something more.

"We'll leave them letters stating that we're riding the same train as Jake so they don't worry. After all, Jake won't let anything happen to us, now will he?"

"Once he learns we're following him—that *you're* following him—Jake will be furious."

"Pshaw!"

"Iris Hopper!" Emily stood and placed her hands on her hips. "Stop that talk—stop all this nonsensical talk."

"Oh, all right. I will watch my tongue, but that's all I'll promise. As for my brilliant plan, Jake will enjoy our company on the train, just as he has enjoyed this last weekend. We're friends, after all."

"Why didn't you tell me sooner and I could have talked to Poppa about it. We could have discussed this. And we could have informed your grandmother."

"Think about that Emily. For one, your father would have locked you in your bedroom on the farm *forever.* Secondly, Granny would guilt me to death about how she cannot cope if I don't take her shopping or scrub the floors or *get married soon.*" Iris's shoulders slumped. "Granny is healthy and quite capable. She has her friends and the other girls for companionship, and you and I will only be gone a short time." She paused, a determined glint in her eyes. "Your family, Em, and my granny would all have tried to stop us. That's why I kept my idea from them—from even you until now."

"I have to think about this." Emily paced the narrow aisle between their two beds. Why was this beginning to make some sense? Why did she feel a delicious spark of daring and, yes, defiance? Besides, they'd only be gone, what, a couple of weeks, wouldn't they? As for Jake, saying good-bye to him had been excruciating this evening, especially with Iris, her family, the senator, and Mr. and Mrs. Schulz clustered nearby. She'd never had a chance to say everything she'd wanted, and she'd never heard from Jake the words she longed to hear—that he'd be back someday.

However, if he waited another decade, Emily would definitely be an old maid. Although everyone thought that of Aunt Mary, and look at her now, with a husband and stepchildren, but a family all the same. And in eleven more years, perhaps Iris would no longer think that Jake was her *destiny*.

"Start packing while you think, Em. We have to check our bags tonight, and the attendant is only in the office until ten o'clock."

Emily paused in mid-stride. "Why tonight?"

Iris pushed up her spectacles. "So no one sees us carrying our valises to the train station in the morning."

CHAPTER 14

WEARING DARK HATS and shawls, Emily and Iris found a driver and buggy for hire just two blocks east. With the bearded driver's assistance, they managed to check their valises at the train depot before the office closed at ten o'clock. Thankfully the driver asked no questions and deposited them a half-block from the boardinghouse. They slipped back into their room undetected.

The next morning, however, proved another story. At the bank Mr. Zane eyed Emily suspiciously as she withdrew most of her savings. The sum equaled almost six months' pay.

"Making a large purchase, Emmy?" The banker, wearing his usual white shirt, black vest, and matching sleeve garters, worked the corners of his mustache between his thumb and forefinger. He peered at Emily over round spectacles.

"Yes, and it'll be quite the surprise for my family." Emily hoped the news didn't reach her father before she boarded the train.

At the station they climbed aboard the passenger car, praying Jake would board another. If he saw them, Emily felt certain he'd order them off, and he'd have the help of Poppa and Zeb. No, it was best he didn't see them until they transferred in Minnesota.

Emily selected a place by the window in a group of four cushioned seats that faced each other. Iris sat across from her. They placed their smaller bags, containing books to read and needlework, on the empty seats, praying the car didn't fill up.

"Isn't this grand?" Iris gazed around the car then ran her hand over the plush burgundy fabric covering the seat next to her. "Cushioned seats, mahogany trim, and electric lighting." Her face lit with happiness. "I must be sure to write this down in my journal."

"I don't think we'll be forgetting this trip soon." Glancing at her friend, Emily smiled and wondered why her father disliked the railroad, even though Grandpa Ramsey had a vested interest in it.

She wiggled into the seat's soft padding. She and Iris would be most comfortable on their journey to Milwaukee.

The conductor made his way down the narrow aisle, checking to be sure passengers had tickets and that they'd boarded the proper train. Emily didn't see any sign of Jake and relaxed.

But what if he'd decided to stay on another day? Or longer?

"There's Jake!" Iris pointed a gloved finger at the window.

Emily saw him jog toward the passenger car one up from theirs. "Good. At least we know he's on his way out west too."

"And there's your father."

Emily's gaze slid to the crowded platform where she spotted Poppa and Zeb, waving good-bye. They must have taken Jake to the station after signing papers this morning. Poppa now owned Mr. Ollie's house and the acreage surrounding it.

"How nice that your family is so fond of Jake."

"Yes, I suppose so." She didn't want to give any indication of her interest, lest Iris suspect her deep feelings for Jake.

As she watched Poppa and Zeb make their way off the platform and toward the street, she missed them already. In her letter she begged Poppa not to try and stop her somehow or send Zeb after her. She needed to make this trip alone, to prove to him and the rest of her family that she'd become an independent and respectable young woman. Momma would understand—in time. Poppa would be furious and stay furious.

"We won't be gone long." She'd spoken more to herself than to Iris.

"Back in a couple of weeks." Iris readjusted her hat. "Today's trip will take us to Milwaukee then on to St. Paul, and another two days to Fallon."

"Fallon?" Emily looked at Iris. "I thought you wanted to see the Pacific Ocean."

"Only if Jake doesn't invite us to visit his ranch."

"The ranch belongs to his sister and brother-in-law, not Jake."

"Mere technicalities, Em…Oohh!" The train lurched forward. Iris laughed. "Won't this be a thrilling adventure, one we'll tell our students this fall?" Her eyes grew round. "Why, we'll tell our own children about it someday!"

Emily grinned at her friend's enthusiasm, glad she didn't allow Iris to travel alone. What's more, this trip would prove to Poppa that she could think on her own two feet. Risking his outrage was worth it.

Jake hadn't been able to do it. He'd held the pen to the paper, but he couldn't sign it.

From his seat by the window, his back to the wall, he watched the passing scenery as the train chugged its way across the Wisconsin River. Pretty countryside. And why did Emily's face keep popping into his mind at the word *pretty*?

She'd been the reason he couldn't sell Granddad's house this morning. He kept seeing her, sitting at that shiny, black grand piano, playing so well, singing so beautifully. And that view from the library window, that giant oak tree, under which he'd first kissed Emily Sundberg.

Father God, could it possibly be Your will for Emily and me to—

"Everything all right, sir?"

Jake snapped from his silent prayer and looked up at the conductor. "Excuse me?"

"Can I be of service?"

"Ah, no, thanks." He pushed himself up higher into his seat.

"Very well. Please feel free to enjoy the dining car, club car, and observation deck at the back of the train."

"Maybe I will. Thanks."

The dark-suited man with his boxy railroad cap moved up the aisle and gave the same invitation to the folks sitting in front of Jake.

His stomach rumbled, and he pulled out Granddad's pocket watch. Almost noon. Eating a meal in the dining car sounded good. He hadn't packed a picnic basket like many folks did when they rode the train.

Jake stood and made his way through the causeway and down the aisle of the second passenger car. He briefly scanned the riders, always alert for signs of trouble. His gaze touched on two ladies, each wearing one those ostentatious hats that they were wont to wear these days, all feathers, flowers, and ribbons piled on wide brims that shadowed their faces.

But the one kind of reminded Jake of Emily somehow.

Lord, I imagine I see that girl everywhere!

Trying to shake Emily from his thoughts wasn't easy, and yet he knew he couldn't completely let his guard down. After all, a man never could tell whom he might run into on the train.

Relief washed over Emily. She adjusted her hat then peeked over the top of the seat in time to see Jake disappear into the flexible gangway, adjoining this car and the dining car. For whatever reason, she hadn't considered the fact that Jake might want to eat.

"Too close for comfort, Iris."

"We are within our rights. We can ride this train if we want to. We paid for our tickets." She removed the hat pin and next her hat.

"I don't care if Jake sees me." Her blonde curls seemed to dance with defiance.

"Then you're saying you don't want to go any farther than St. Paul?" Emily shook her head, imagining the consequences. "Jake just might throw us in jail until Poppa comes for us."

"He wouldn't dare."

"Let's not tempt him."

Iris considered her a moment before donning her hat and repinning it. "Oh, all right."

Emily dropped her gaze back into her book. About an hour later Iris tapped her ankle with the toe of her boot, signaling Jake's return. Emily held her breath and watched beneath the brim of her hat as Jake passed.

She exhaled.

"Is it safe now?" Iris's voice rose above the din of the car.

Several rows up, Jake hesitated.

Emily pushed her foot into Iris's.

Jake kept on walking.

When he'd left the car, Emily lifted her gaze. "Your *destiny* almost found us out."

Iris merely grinned. "There is a greater force that will see us all the way to Fallon, Em. God has it all planned. I just have a feeling…"

"We're headed for the Pacific Ocean, remember? Not Fallon." Although Emily couldn't say she'd mind if Jake asked them to visit a real, western ranch.

"Oh, right. Pacific Ocean."

Emily breathed a sigh then asked God once again to protect them and see them through on their journey west.

At six forty-five the train pulled into Union Station in St. Paul, Minnesota. It was ever-so-much larger than the depots in Manitowoc or even Milwaukee. Constructed in brick, the building stood several stories high, and the throng of passengers bustling through the station amazed Emily. Fortunately several attendants were most helpful. They purchased their tickets, opting for the regular passenger car rather than paying ten dollars more for a sleeper. As there were almost three hours to kill before their train left, they checked their valises, wired their families, and then found a small eating establishment nearby that served up a tasty and filling supper. Emily knew that at any given time Jake might spot them, although she didn't see him in the eatery.

As they strolled back to the station in twilight, Iris halted on the street corner. "Look at the grand clock, Em, built into the base of the train depot's steeple. I wonder who winds it each night."

Emily smiled. "It's most likely electric, wouldn't you think? And we have remarkable structures in Manitowoc too."

"Yes, but this is St. Paul. We're actually here in St. Paul!" Arms spread, she looked at the sky and twirled around in a circle.

"One of the many things I love about you is your enthusiasm, Iris." She hooked her arm around Iris's.

But as they crossed the street, Emily wondered if her father would be any less furious after receiving the telegram, stating she was safe. In the missive she'd left in his postal box, she'd promised to send messages along the way so her parents would know of their whereabouts and wouldn't worry.

Back inside the station they sat down and waited for the boarding to begin. By the accumulating crowd, Emily guessed there would scarcely be an extra seat. Men and women, and scores of children, waited for the conductor's call. Emily wondered if they were homesteaders, going west to find their fortunes, like Andy Anderson did.

Finally the boarding call came, and Emily and Iris stepped into the queue. This train was considerably shorter than the one they'd taken from Manitowoc. Several freight cars, one Pullman, a dining car, a club car, complete with a ladies' parlor, men's parlor, and the observation deck. Only ten cars in all.

Stepping onto the train, Emily scanned the car. No golden-blond head or one covered by a Stetson. She led Iris to a seat near the back so that they'd have easier access to the dining car without traipsing past rows and rows of people.

They sat down, and moments later two unkempt men sat in the seats opposite them.

"Evenin', ladies." A toothless grin. The man removed his hat, revealing stringy, rusty-colored hair. "I'm Hank Batson and this here's my brother Ulysses."

Ulysses removed his hat. Locks of dirty-brown hair fell over his high forehead. "Hello, ladies."

His murky gaze gave Emily a measure of discomfort, and she merely smiled guardedly. Even Iris didn't speak, but gave a polite nod.

"Hope you don't mind our company. Looks like the train's going to be filled up."

"This is a public car. People sit where they must." Iris quickly pulled her book from the decorative bag she'd carried onto the train. It, like Emily's tote, contained a couple of books, a knitting project, and her reticule.

And their money.

Up until now, Emily hadn't sensed any danger. But unease prickled along the back of her neck. She wished more than ever that she'd catch sight of Jake.

"I think these two are kinda uppity, Hank." The stony-eyed Batson brother appraised Emily in an unseemly manner.

Then Jake walked by without seeing them. Hope welled inside of Emily. If they needed help, Jake wouldn't be far away.

She nudged Iris, who gazed up from behind the pages of Kate Chopin's *The Awakening*.

"How's the story?" Perhaps if she changed the subject the gaping men seated across from them would grow bored and seek out the club car.

Iris slapped down the book. "This is one of the most tragic stories I've ever read. I cannot figure out what all the literary raves have been about. Florence Cooper at the library insisted that if I want to be an independent female I must read it." Iris wagged her head, sending the blonde ringlets around her face swinging. "But I can't understand why. This female character leaves her perfectly nice husband and children to go on a self-searching journey, which leads her to drown herself in the end."

"How tragic indeed."

"If only her self-exploration could have led to a relationship with Christ instead."

Emily agreed.

"One must look up to see the truth. Poor Edna Pontillier's awakening came in the form of allowing herself to be swallowed up by the ocean."

"Poppa wouldn't call drowning oneself an awakening, and he ought to know. He sailed the world."

"Precisely." Iris dropped her book back into her bag. "I'll talk to Florence about not recommending this novel to others, especially women in a fragile state of mind."

Emily thought of Jake's mother. She'd killed herself, or so they said. Mr. Ollie believed something else called her to up to the bluff, although he'd been up there himself and returned none the wiser. Could Jake's mother have been struggling with some sort of emotional illness, like the character in Iris's book? Poppa made mention once that Mrs. Margaret Edgerton hadn't been able to cope with the death of her husband.

Such sadness. Emily's heart went out to Jake. Just as swiftly guilt nipped at her as she watched Iris remove her knitting and place it in her lap. Iris believed Jake was *her* destiny, not Emily's. What would happen if she discovered Emily prayed otherwise? To find love but lose one's best, most dearest friend...talk about tragic!

Emily sent a furtive glance across the way and felt the tension in her body abate. Sweet success. Their unwanted traveling companions wouldn't bother them for a while. The two men had fallen asleep.

CHAPTER 15

*R*ESTLESSNESS CREPT OVER Jake, and for the life of him, he couldn't get comfortable. Luck hadn't been on his side tonight, that's for sure. He'd done some walking, thinking, and praying this evening, and then his dinner was late when he finally got around to eating. Altogether he'd nearly missed the train out of St. Paul. To further his disappointment, he'd tried to purchase a ticket in the sleeper car, but it was full, and he hadn't arrived early enough to claim his usual seat at one of the car's ends, so he could keep an eye on passengers. He felt like that proverbial sitting duck in this location. Well, maybe he'd walk over to the dining car and buy a cup of coffee. Didn't seem he'd get much sleep tonight anyhow.

Standing, Jake made his way down the narrow aisle toward the diner. Two men caught his eye. If they weren't trouble, he didn't know who was. He glanced across at the two sleeping ladies sitting across from them and—

Emily!

Jake stopped, staring, wondering if his mind played tricks on him. But, no, he'd recognize Em's sweet, round face and red-brown hair anywhere. She looked so peaceful as she slept, angelic even. His gaze slid to her companion. Iris. He should have known.

The scruffy men in the adjacent seats held their heads together, whispering in obvious conspiracy, and Jake glimpsed the ladies' reticules in their book bags. He moved forward and then leaned on the side of the one man's chair.

He looked up, his gray eyes wide with surprise.

"If you touch those purses or harm even a single hair on these ladies' heads, you'll deal with me. Understand?"

The guy closest to Jake gave a nod, but tiny lines around the other man's eyes went taut.

"How dare you insinuate we'd do such things, sir. We've done nothing wrong."

"Yet. You haven't done anything...yet." He shifted, appraising the two. He'd bet they only owned the clothes on their backs. He rubbed his jaw. Maybe some town sheriff purchased train tickets west just to get rid of them. Happened frequently. "I appreciate the fact you haven't acted on any temptations. How 'bout taking a walk to the club car?" He reached into his pocket and fished out two quarters. "Or get yourselves some coffee at the diner. Both cars are open all night."

The men accepted the money. Jake softened and pulled his billfold from his jacket's inner breast pocket. He gave the men each a dollar. "Have a meal or two while you're at it. Looks like it's been a while, eh?"

"Yes sir, it has at that." The men exchanged glances. "Thanks, pal."

"When you return, find yourselves different seats. I happen to know there's two up front."

Jake moved aside to let the men rise and file out of their seats. He pointed the two toward the dining and club cars. As they passed, Jake got a whiff of their unwashed bodies and grimaced. Obviously it had been a while since they'd bathed as well as eaten.

Emily coughed and her eyes fluttered open. She sucked in a startled breath until recognition set into her sleepy gaze. "Jake!" A sheepish smile played across her pink lips.

Shrugging out of his jacket, he sat down. As good as it was to see Em again, questions plagued him. "What are you doing on this train?"

"Oh…" She wiggled up to a straighter sitting position. "Iris and I…well, we decided on an adventure." Her gaze briefly touched on her friend before returning to Jake. Again her lovely smile.

"Your parents know about this?" He felt certain they didn't.

"They do now. I left them a detailed note and sent a wire from St. Paul."

Why this train? Why now? "Where you two headed?"

"The Pacific Ocean." Emily laughed softly, maybe even nervously. "Iris got this idea in her head to ride this railroad to the end of the line, see the ocean, and come back. We'll have something to tell our students in the fall, plus we'll have proved ourselves capable women in our families' eyes."

"If your father doesn't kill you first." He should have known the nutty scheme had been Iris's. He leaned forward and clasped his hands over his knees. "Emily, you don't always have to follow Iris's lead on things. Trains going west aren't always safe." He whispered so as not to disturb other sleeping passengers. "There are robberies, train accidents. In fact, just recently a bridge collapsed, killing most of the folks on board. And those men, sitting across from you…"

"What about them?" A frown creased her brow.

"I'm pretty sure they were about to steal yours and Iris's purses. I was on my way to the dining car and happened to catch those wayfarers before they snatched your money."

"We'll be more careful." She lifted her purse from out of the carryall bag and put its long strap around her neck.

"Careful? That's not good enough. Are you prepared to encounter the likes of Butch Cassidy and his gang or the wanted outlaw Kid Curry?"

Emily didn't look a bit deterred. "Mr. Ollie never had a problem."

Jake sat back. He couldn't argue. Granddad always made it safely to Fallon and back. Considering the determined tilt to her chin, he tried not to grin. One other thing was for sure, Emily Sundberg didn't scare easily.

"As for Poppa, I'm of legal age, Jake. I've proved my independence financially. He needs to respect me and stop interfering in my life at every turn."

She gave him a pointed stare, and Jake knew she referenced her father's warning the other day. So this was revenge.

He rubbed his hand along the side of his scratchy jaw and gazed at the shuttered window, closed for the night. Suddenly the image of Em eavesdropping on Andy Anderson's conversation with the elder Mrs. Sundberg flashed through his mind. Andy. On his way to Idaho. So that's what this trip was really about. *Chasing after Andy.*

Jealousy, ripe and green, pumped through his arteries and thudded against his temples. What a fool he'd been, considering life-changing options just so he could return to Manitowoc. To Emily.

Except she loved Andy. Didn't that beat all...the man had been more than rude to her. Couldn't she understand that he didn't have the slightest interest in her?

Jake couldn't sit here anymore. He couldn't stand to look at her pretty blue eyes. It hurt too much.

Without a word he stood and made his way to the diner.

What just happened?

Emily watched Jake stand and leave the passenger car. The door closed behind him, and he disappeared into the gangway. She turned back around in her seat. He seemed furious—no, something else. Something beyond description. She'd seen the emotion glint in his dark gaze but couldn't be sure what it had been. Did he think she lied? The Pacific Coast really was their point of destination, unless they garnered an invitation to Jake's ranch, which didn't look promising at the moment.

The train's rhythmical sway caused Emily's eyes to feel heavy again. Then she spied Jake's jacket on one of the seats across the way and hoped those scruffy men wouldn't return...and Jake would.

She checked on Iris, sleeping soundly. Emily grinned. Iris could sleep through cannon fire, not that either she or Emily had ever heard cannon fire. But if it exploded around them in the middle of the night, Iris would sleep through it!

Easing back, Emily closed her eyes and saw an image of Jake with that emotion in his gaze. Had she wounded him somehow? Maybe he was just irked. She'd known all along that he'd side with Poppa. But perhaps he felt responsible for Iris and her, and that didn't sit well with him. Well, he needn't worry. She mustered her resolve. They wouldn't trouble him.

Emily awoke to find Iris shaking her shoulder. She'd dozed off again. Sunlight streamed through the windows across the aisle, and for that reason, many passengers didn't open their wooden shutters.

"I'm famished. Let's go fix ourselves up in the ladies' parlor and then head for the dining car."

Emily bobbed out a reply and yawned. Her stomach gnawed at her. Breakfast sounded good. She walked down the narrow aisle, through the noisy flexible gangway, and had to actually pass through the dining car to first make use of the ladies' parlor and toilet. The men's parlor, she'd heard, was nearer to the club car.

The train jostled and swayed them as she and Iris waited their turn in the dressing room. Emily felt the rumble of the wheels on steel rails beneath her feet.

"Jake saw us last night."

Surprise rounded Iris's eyes. "When did that happen?"

"In the wee hours of this morning, while you were sleeping."

"And?"

"I don't think he was very pleased to see us."

Iris seemed to tuck the information into the folds of her mind before she shrugged. "Just like your brothers, Emily. Remember how aggravated they'd become years ago when we'd follow them around and do whatever they were doing?"

Emily remembered.

"I think Jake is behaving a bit like your brothers."

"But why would he?"

"Because we didn't ask him first." She gave a decisive nod of her head. "It's just as Granny says. Men like to feel that they're in control."

Emily wondered, although the statement certainly rang true in the Sundberg household. How Momma and *Besta* put up with it, she'd never know.

At last their turn came, and in a box-size room, she and Iris managed to straighten their many petticoats and repin their hair and hats. In the mirror on the wall, Emily glimpsed the dark circles beneath her eyes from lack of sleep. The few hours she had slept had been fitful ones. She'd been distrustful of the men seated across from them and then Jake had awakened her. The way he stalked off had been disconcerting, and Emily kept dreaming about it until Iris woke her up.

She'd also dreamed of outlaws stealing their money.

"Iris, let's hide our funds in our bodices and not keep it in our purses, lest we're robbed." She wouldn't scare Iris with the details.

"My bodice?" Iris glanced down. "But then I'll lose it for sure." She thrust her reticule at Emily. "Here, you keep mine too."

"Oh, all right." Emily removed her traveling jacket and unbuttoned her shirtwaist. Iris handed her the folded bills, and Emily placed hers on her left side, closest to her heart. That's how she'd remember which bundle belonged to whom. Stuffing the bills downward, she managed to tuck them securely into her tight-fitting corset. "Our funds won't go anywhere that I don't know about now." She hoped they wouldn't chafe any more than her corset did at times.

"Perfect."

Emily redressed while Iris read from a menu she'd procured when they boarded last night. Oatmeal, poached eggs on toast, fresh fruit, hot rolls, cocoa. Who would have thought a dining car could provide such a wide variety?

They made their way out of the ladies' parlor, crowded with women wanting to freshen up. As they entered the dining car, Emily spotted Jake sitting at a table set for two. He looked rough, like he hadn't slept much last night either. His gaze snagged hers, and she saw his tired, red-rimmed eyes. The male server, in white sleeves and cap, poured him another cup of coffee.

"Good morning, Jake." Iris waved cheerfully.

He finger combed his brassy-blond hair back off his forehead and dipped his head slightly.

"He must not be a morning person," Iris whispered.

Emily couldn't contain a smile. But Iris always had that effect on her. In fact, Iris could make even the grumpiest of their housemates grin at the breakfast table.

The server, with the coffee pot still in hand, approached them. "Please seat yourselves, ladies."

"Thank you." Emily and Iris spoke in unison, and Emily spotted a vacant table. She pointed it out.

"A pity we can't join Jake, but his table will only seat two." Iris whispered the comment.

"Something tells me he'd prefer if we didn't join him." Emily led the way down the aisle. On one side tables covered with white linen cloths were set for four patrons, and on the other side smaller covered tables were set for two, such as the one Emily had selected and like the one at which Jake sat.

The car was filled nearly to capacity, and sounds of people's chattering and dirty dishes being cleared from place settings caused Emily to have to speak above the din. However, she soon realized she'd lost Iris. Turning, she saw her friend had paused to speak with Jake.

Emily sat down, wondering if she'd eat alone. Would Iris abandon her to sit with Jake? The idea caused her appetite to wane.

Then, before she could even unfold her linen napkin, Iris made her way down the aisle. She pointed to a table for four, being reset by a server, and a moment later, Jake followed in her steps. So Iris's cheery disposition won even him over this morning.

Emily moved to the other table, claiming the chair beside Iris. Jake sat across from them, facing the entrance. He tossed his hat on the empty chair.

"Mornin'." Just a grumble.

"Good morning, Jake." Emily gave him a smile. Maybe he'd cheer up.

"I asked Jake to join us."

"How nice."

"Look, Em, the saucers say, *Good Morning.*" Iris's twittered out a laugh. "What a lovely way to start the day. Isn't it, Jake?"

"Lovely."

Who could miss the facetiousness in his tone? Emily glanced at the single-page menu beside her green and white porcelain plate.

"Emily said you're headed to the Pacific Ocean, eh?"

"That's right. Unless we get a better offer, of course."

"Iris!" Emily's cheeks began to flame.

"Another offer?" Jake sounded none too amused. "What's that supposed to mean?"

"Well..." Iris glanced at Emily.

"Wait, I get it." Jake raised a hand to forestall further comment. He narrowed his gaze, first at Iris, then Emily. "Do either of you know where in Idaho you're even going?"

"Idaho?" Emily pictured the map of the United States in her mind and felt sure the Pacific Coast didn't reach that state.

"We're not going to Idaho." Iris had just uttered her last syllable when a server came to take their orders. She and Emily ordered cups of tea, and Jake asked for more coffee. All the while Emily wondered why Jake thought they were headed to Idaho.

Andy! She dropped her gaze and ran a finger along the hem of the tablecloth, wondering how to tell him otherwise without betraying Iris in the process.

"Ladies, what do you call a woman who chases a man clear across the country?" Jake's voice was razor-sharp.

"Depends why she's chasing him." Iris didn't look a bit daunted.

"How about a woman who throws herself at a man? What would you call her?" Jake's dark gaze drifted to Emily.

Me? Emily tried not to react, but his comment met its mark like a knife in her chest.

He turned the blade. "I certainly wouldn't call her a *proper schoolteacher.*"

"Jake!" How could he purposely wound her like that?

Without another word Emily stood and strode from the dining car. She blinked back the now scalding tears and returned to the ladies' parlor, where, thankfully, a dressing room stood vacant. Inside, she put her head in her hands and sobbed.

"Even Ruth in the Bible came to Boaz and lay at his feet. Notice he didn't come to Ruth?"

Jake had heard just about enough of Iris's prattle. She'd been going on and on for several minutes now, defending the right of single women to pursue eligible men. "I think you'd best go check on Emily." He'd regretted his thoughtless remarks as soon as he'd spoken them. "She looked upset."

"And why wouldn't she? You insulted her integrity." Iris tipped her head and peered at him through her spectacles like he was one of her grade-school kids.

The waiter brought Iris her tea, and she thanked him with a smile before staring back at Jake.

He glared at her. "What are you doing on this train, Iris?"

"I told you last Saturday. I'm husband hunting, and for your information, this trip was my idea."

He sighed audibly. His body ached from lack of sleep and his heart ached too. "How ironic that Andy Anderson rode the same line to Idaho."

"Is that what you think? Emily is chasing Andy?" Iris leaned forward, wearing her sternest expression yet. "You couldn't be more wrong. She simply agreed to accompany me."

Iris needed accompanying, that's for sure. Jake shook his head in wonder.

"And if you weren't my destiny, I believe I'd hate you for hurting Emily so deeply. Except I couldn't in all good conscience. Hatred is a sin, and as you know in your line of work, many crimes are committed because of it. Look at Cain and Abel. Cain was so jealous of his brother because he'd found favor with God that he murdered him."

Spoken like a little Sunday school teacher.

Wait. Jake brought his coffee cup to his lips and halted. Did she just say he was her *destiny*? "Back up, Iris." He set down his cup. "What do you mean by I'm your destiny?"

"Must I really explain it to you?"

He laughed. So Iris's husband hunting had led her to follow *him*. "I'm not your destiny, Iris."

"I hoped you'd invite Emily and me to your ranch in Montana."

Jake froze, tipped his head. "What did you just say?"

"Surely you heard me."

"I'm doubting my own ears."

"Emily and I have never been on a ranch before, and if we visited yours, we'd have something to tell our students this fall."

"No."

She pouted ever so slightly.

Jake softened his tone and glanced around the humming dining car. No one seemed to have overheard his terse reply. "It's not my ranch, Iris. It belongs to my brother-in-law. Lots of hard work goes on there. It ain't no pleasure resort."

"We're your friends. We stuck by you when you needed us most. It would only be mannerly of you to invite us."

She'd resorted to guilt now. *Unbelievable.* "Iris, now look. I'm flattered you'd like to visit, but my answer is no." He sure didn't want to spend any more time around Emily than absolutely necessary. At Iris's disappointed expression, he stiffened his resolve. "The best thing for you and Emily to do is ride the train as far as Glendive and turn yourselves right around."

"But—"

"And I'm not your destiny." He aimed his forefinger at her and gave her a hard look. "I made my feelings known last Saturday. I don't know why you can't get that through that blonde curly head of yours."

"You just leave my blonde curls out of this." She appeared genuinely insulted.

Jake knew he'd lost control of this conversation. A man could start feeling crazy, talking to Iris Hopper. He stood. "'Scuse me." He needed to get some sleep before dealing with these ladies any further. *Lord, I'd rather deal with outlaws!*

CHAPTER 16

*E*MILY SPENT THE morning in the ladies' parlor, crying, praying, thinking. She'd presumed all along that Jake wouldn't be pleased when he encountered Iris and her on the train, but to say such hateful things was unforgiveable! She fingered the silver necklace he'd given her. Her anger ebbed. It was her Christian duty to forgive him…but she didn't have to speak to him ever again!

At lunchtime Iris entered the car and suggested they share a noon meal to save on money. Seating was limited in the dining car, so they shared a table with a friendly couple, Reverend and Mrs. Carlson. They were Minnesota natives who'd heard God's call to spread the gospel in a remote town north of Billings. After eating, they proceeded to the observation car where they could sit comfortably and enjoy the scenery. Two long padded seats ran the length of the car beneath the windows so more than just four passengers could converse.

"My dream is to someday open a school for all the children in the area," Mrs. Carlson said.

"Are you a teacher? Why, Emily and I are teachers too."

"Yes."

The two of them seemed even better company.

"We're excited about ministering to the people of central Montana." Enthusiasm shone in the reverend's face.

"I hope you know how to use a gun."

Emily started when she heard Jake's deep voice. Why hadn't she seen him enter the car? He sat down beside her, forcing her to scoot over, which caused Iris to slide down the padded bench.

"And I hope you're not afraid to use it."

Questions pooled in the reverend's eyes. "Do we know each other?"

Since Iris was busy bending Mrs. Carlson's ear, Emily introduced Jake.

"Deputy Edgerton is a friend of my family's." Certainly not hers—not anymore. "He hails from Montana."

The reverend's features relaxed, and he extended his right hand across the aisle. "We'll practically be neighbors." His blond brows drew inward. "So we are embarking on a rugged piece of country, eh?"

"That's right."

Jake removed his black jacket, eased back, and made himself comfortable. Emily wondered if he wasn't angry with her anymore. She fingered the delicate cross at her throat. Forgiveness. Jake caught sight of her actions and the taut lines around his eyes disappeared as if he understood. He sent her a short smile.

Then while Iris and Mrs. Carlson talked about teaching children, Jake and the reverend discussed outlaws, buffalo, and cattle drives. Emily sat in between the four of them, listening to snippets of each conversation but participating in neither.

"I'd love to be able to teach every child in town to read." Vonda Carlson's green eyes sparkled with enthusiasm, and Emily admired her goal.

"Typically cattle drives are in the spring and roundups are in the fall." The low timbre of Jake's voice resounded next to her. "I don't have anything to do with the operations though."

"You're a sheriff's deputy?"

Emily forgot to specify.

"US deputy marshal, but I assist the sheriff if need be."

"Gunfights?" The reverend leaned forward and all but whispered the word.

"Sometimes."

Emily glanced around the car. Every lady seemed blissfully unaware of the nature of the men's conversation. Lucky her. She got to hear it all. Worse, Emily's interest had genuinely been piqued.

After dinner with the Carlsons that night, Emily, Iris, and Jake returned to their seats in the passenger car.

"What an enjoyable afternoon." Iris sat by the window.

"Very nice." Emily lowered herself into the seat across from Jake.

He met her gaze for several seconds. "We're fortunate that it's been an uneventful ride so far." Removing his hat, he raked his fingers through his golden blond hair and dropped the Stetson and a newspaper into the vacant seat beside him.

"I thought our day was quite eventful." Iris extracted a book from her cloth bag. She stuffed her reticule inside it.

"Jake means as far as outlaws robbing and killing passengers."

"Emily, oh my! What a remark." Iris appeared aghast.

Emily realized she'd listened far too long to Jake's conversation with the reverend. "My apologies, Iris." She glanced at Jake and spied the grin tweaking the corners of his mouth.

"Let's only think of the blessings of this day, shall we?" Iris said.

"You're right, of course." With that, Emily removed her knitting from her bag and set to work. *Besta* always said idle hands were the devil's tools.

Jake watched the wooden needles in Emily's hands fly in and out of what appeared to be a man's sweater. Now and again she would glance up and smile, but she made no attempt at conversation.

In the adjacent seat Iris had nodded off and snored softly.

Realizing it, Emily deftly removed the book from Iris's lap and tucked it away. Then she resumed knitting.

"Making that for Andy?" Jake couldn't keep the edge out of his tone.

"Not anymore." She sent him a glare. "And for your information, I'm not chasing Andy. I couldn't care less about that man. But in the future I'll thank you to mind your own business."

Jake rubbed his jaw. So now it was his turn to feel the icy sting of the Sundberg woman's cold shoulder. Well, he probably deserved it.

He sat back and watched Emily resume her knitting. Glory, but this woman could stitch! "I'll bet your father is worried sick about you, just like Granddad was all torn up inside when Aunt Bettina ran away from home."

"You dare to compare me to your selfish aunt?" A glance at Iris's sleeping form. "How could you, Jake? And the cruel things you said this morning wounded me deeply. I thought you were my friend." She touched the silver cross, resting at her throat, and his heart bent. But when he saw tears glimmer in her eyes, he crumbled.

"Don't cry, Emily. I'm sorry." He leaned forward and touched her hand. "I am your friend, that's why I'm angry. Can you understand?"

She shook her head.

"I didn't liken you to my aunt, but rather your father's worry about you to my granddad's worrying over Bettina. See the difference?"

Again a wag of her head. Her chin quivered.

He tried another approach. "What if something bad happened to you, Em? How would your father feel—or the rest of your family, for that matter?"

"Something bad could happen to me just crossing the street. You know that firsthand."

"Reckon I do." He offered his handkerchief, but she refused it and fished a dainty hanky from her reticule. Then she dabbed the corners of her eyes.

"Emily, I'm sorry. I had no right to speak to you the way I did." He took her free hand in both of his, glad that she didn't pull it away. "Will you forgive me?" He couldn't be more earnest. "I wanted to drive home my point is all. You have such a fine family where mine is…well, I really don't have a family to speak of anymore. I just would hate for you to worry your folks or lose their trust."

"I left a detailed letter, Jake. Once Poppa gets over his initial outrage, he'll understand that I have to make this trip. He left home at age fifteen out of sheer rebellion, but I left simply to prove my independence."

"All right." He'd leave it at that, although he wouldn't be surprised if the captain boarded the very next train west. "But you didn't answer my question."

"I forgive you."

"Thank you." Releasing her hand, Jake sat back. Being Emily's friend accounted for something.

With nimble fingers, she unpinned her hat and placed it in her lap. Iris's head dropped onto Emily's shoulder.

"Look at her, Jake. She's so trusting and naïve."

Jake wanted to chuckle. *Look who's talking?*

"I couldn't allow Iris to go on her adventure alone. She bought tickets for both of us before she even told me her plans. She was so determined to ride this train west, and I know how she is." Emily didn't even try to whisper. "There's no talking any sense into her."

"I believe it. And what's this about my being Iris's destiny or some such nonsense?"

A pretty blush tinted Emily's cheeks. "How do you know?"

"Iris flat-out told me."

"Oh, my…" Emily closed her eyes in a moment of what seemed like brief embarrassment. "Jake, I'm afraid Iris has her heart set on you."

"So she says."

"You don't believe her?"

"Nope."

A frown puckered Emily's brow. "Why?"

"Because her admission lacked feeling and conviction. I suspect if she really felt that I was her destiny, she wouldn't have found it so easy to blurt it out. My opinion is Iris Hopper is a professional manipulator."

"No, she's not!"

"And you're a loyal friend to the end, Emily Sundberg."

She seemed to swallow an awaiting retort. "That much is true. And that's why I couldn't bear the thought of poor Iris on this train alone."

"Hmm...I imagine Iris would have fared all right by herself."

"I don't know, Jake." Emily pushed Iris into a better position, one in which her shoulder wasn't Iris's pillow. "As you can see, she sleeps through practically anything. She's a sitting target."

"Isn't her grandmother going to be worried sick?"

"Perhaps...at first. But Iris left a letter and promised to return home with a..." She paused.

"Yes?" Jake sat forward again. "With a...what?"

"Husband. Or at least a *forloveden*, that's Norwegian for fiancé."

He groaned.

"Mrs. Hopper has been pressing Iris to get married. She's afraid she'll pass on and Iris will be alone in the world, but Iris will always have my family and me. She knows that." Emily gazed fondly at Iris. "Still, Mrs. Hopper considers it something of a social stigma to have an unmarried granddaughter of age twenty-four."

"What about your parents, Em? They think it's a social stigma that you're not married?"

She smiled and Jake felt captivated. "You know Poppa. I'll die an old maid if it's up to him."

Once again Jake found the comment amusing. "Emily, I can almost guarantee that you won't die an old maid."

"How can you be so sure?"

"A hunch." He pulled the newspaper into his lap and decided he'd best change the subject. Still, a hope that maybe he'd win Emily's heart sparked deep inside of him. "Iris said she'd like an invitation to the Ready Web, my brother-in-law's ranch." He glanced up to see Emily gape. Obviously she hadn't been in on the plan. "At first I told Iris no."

"Quite understandable. She shouldn't have asked." Emily flicked an annoyed glance at Iris's sleeping form. "Such rudeness."

"Well, I've been thinking about it all afternoon, and I've changed my mind."

"Thank you, but that's not necessary, Jake. Truly. We planned to ride the train to the Pacific coast."

"I know." *Crazy idea!* "But maybe you'd like to stop off in Fallon and visit. I realized my sister would enjoy some female companionship, and I can show you both around. I've decided to take time off from my work in order to pray over some important things."

Jake saw a flicker of curiosity enter Emily's eyes, but she quickly lowered her gaze and didn't ask personal questions. "That's a kind offer, Jake." She looked up. "Let's discuss it when Iris wakes up in the morning."

"All right." He didn't see that there was much to discuss. It had been Iris's idea, after all. But it was nice of Emily to consider her friend's feelings. Again.

"And Jake?"

He raised his brows, expectantly.

Emily leaned toward him. "Perhaps you can show Iris the nitty-gritty of ranching and forever discourage her romantic delusions that you're her...well, you know."

He grinned. "I know." He wasn't able to contain a chuckle as he leaned forward. Their faces were mere inches apart, and what he saw in Emily's pretty blue eyes made him think of forever. "Good plan, Em."

"Think it'll work?" She searched his face. "Iris isn't easily persuaded."

"We'll make it work." *Lord, she's so lovely.* Jake fought the yearning to take her into his arms and kiss her.

But then a movement up ahead, behind Emily, caught Jake's attention. He straightened. Seeing the conductor heading their way, Jake touched his forefinger to his lips and mouthed the word, "Later." At this time of night conductors were quick with reprimands as others in the passenger car wanted to read quietly or sleep.

Emily seemed to understand and went back to her knitting. For now, watching her would have to suffice. But, God help him, Jake wasn't sure how long he could look and not touch.

CHAPTER 17

*E*MILY WATCHED THE sun inch higher in the sky. After numerous stops, the conductor finally announced they'd pull into Fallon mid-morning. Jake suggested they eat a hearty breakfast as their next meal would likely be supper this evening. So after washing up in the ladies' parlor, Emily and Iris met Jake in the dining car.

Emily tipped her head and watched him from a side-glance. She enjoyed his company and felt safe in Jake's presence, particularly now that he wasn't angry with her. She understood that he'd only been worried about her—them.

Jake looked her way, and Emily quickly returned her gaze to the passing scenery. A few hills were visible off in the distance, but mostly prairie stretched out before her. Occasionally the train rumbled over a trestle spanning a swollen, sparkling river.

"Would you ladies like me to give you some history about the Ready Web Ranch?"

Smiling, Emily turned away from the window. "Indeed."

Iris bounced in her chair and rubbed her palms together. "This is so exciting." She turned to Emily. "Isn't it exciting? A real ranch?"

Emily laughed at her friend's childlike exuberance.

Iris got immediately serious as though she remembered her age as well as her manners. "You're a true gentleman, Jake Edgerton."

"I try." Jake wiped the linen napkin across his mouth. "Now then, the owner is Boyd Webster. Everybody calls him Web except my sister, who, for whatever reason, insists on calling him by his given name. Web purchased the ranch after Pa died and named it Ready Web on account of the fact that Web considers himself ready for anything. Coincidentally he married my sister, Deidre, in the process. They live in what we call the main house, and that's where you two will stay. As I said, I'm sure Deidre will enjoy your company."

"And what about you? I hope you won't be sleeping in the barn on our account."

"Nice of you to think about that now, Iris." Jake chuckled lightly.

Emily smiled and picked at her blueberry muffin.

"But, fear not, I kept a parcel and built a small cabin in back of Web and Deidre's house." Jake continued to grin until he took a drink of coffee. "Okay, where was I?"

"You told us about your brother-in-law and sister," Emily reminded him.

"Right. Then there's Charlie, who's the ranch foreman. He was Pa's friend, and he's what's known as a wolfer. He kills the wolves and coyotes that terrorize farms and ranches. The State of Montana and occasionally even townsfolk pay him for each hide he turns in. After Pa died, Charlie stayed around to help us. Then Ma died." Jake paused. Pain shadowed his face. "Charlie was a big help to Deidre and me. After Web took over with intentions of ranching instead of farming, he and Charlie built a bunkhouse, and Charlie moved in there, whereas before he stayed in the barn or camped close by."

"He sounds like an interesting man." Emily tried to picture what he might look like. An image of Buffalo Bill Cody came to mind. Emily had read a book to her class about the bison hunter and soldier turned international showman.

"You'll like Charlie. He looks mean, but he's got a good heart. And then there's Greg Flores. Folks call him Rez. He hired on as a ranch hand a few years ago." Another swallow of coffee. "Rez came up on a drive from Texas a long while back and decided to stay in

Fallon, seeing as the town was founded by his same kind—Texas cowhands."

"Really? Fallon was started by Texas cowhands?" Emily found the information astounding really.

Jake nodded and grinned. "You'll believe me when you see it. Pa settled here because land, far and wide, was up for the taking. Pa set out to have a bigger and better farm and more land than his older brother in Manitowoc."

"Are there Edgertons in Manitowoc?" Emily thought she knew most of the residents either through church, school, or one of the family businesses.

"Nope. My uncle and his wife are dead now and they never had children. Pa could have returned and taken over the farm on which he'd grown up, but he loved the beauty and ruggedness of Montana."

"Just how exactly does a ranch like the Ready Web make its money?" Iris adjusted her eyeglasses on the bridge of her nose. "Or is it a self-supporting enterprise?"

"It's both, I'd say. Self-supporting, although Web's in the cattle business. Web and his men recently got back from driving eight hundred head up from Wyoming. They'll get the cattle fattened up over the summer, and then in the fall they'll round up the ones Web wants to sell and drive 'em into Fallon. The town is the central hub for cattle drives."

"So will you be gone during the roundup and drive?" Emily felt disappointed at the thought, although she and Iris would be back in Manitowoc by then anyway.

"Nope. I don't help with the outfit. But Web, Charlie, and Rez will be gone a few days. Maybe a week. They don't have far to drive the cattle." Jake glared at Iris. "And, no, you cannot go. Understand?"

Iris blinked. "Well! I wouldn't dream of it."

Emily lifted her napkin and laughed. Knowing Iris's lack of ability as a horsewoman, the idea was quite hilarious.

"Oh, quiet." Iris gave her an annoyed glance. "It's not that amusing."

She laughed all the more as she imagined Iris on a cattle drive. Last Sunday she'd all but gotten lost on her parents' small acreage. And try as she did, Emily couldn't teach Iris to stay up straight in the saddle as the gentlest of horses trotted. "Iris on a cattle drive?" Oh, the idea was just too funny!

Jake chuckled from Emily laughing so hard.

"Stop it at once, Emily Sundberg." Iris glared at her like any good grade-school teacher.

"I apologize." Emily dabbed the tears from the corners of her eyes and concentrated on taking a few deep breaths. But when she looked at Jake, her giggles returned.

He chuckled and shook his head.

"Stop it, Emily. You're hurting my feelings."

She wouldn't hurt Iris for the world. Emily stymied her chortles.

"Aw, Emily's just laughing *with* you, Iris." Jake sent a wink Emily's way.

"That's right." *Breathe. In and out.* "And you know how once I start laughing I can't seem to stop." She was only too glad that the din of the voices and sounds of plates and flatware being removed from tabletops covered her hysterics.

"It happens in church all the time."

"It does not." That did it! Emily sobered and looked over at Jake. "I was a child when I last giggled in church."

With a satisfied smirk Iris readjusted her glasses, which had, again, slipped a ways down her nose. "So why don't you participate in the cattle drives, Jake?"

"Not my calling." The amusement hadn't quite dissipated from his expression as his gaze danced between Emily and Iris. "The only time I'd get involved is if there's horse thieving going on or some heads of cattle are stolen and the local authorities ask me to step in."

"But you're a deputy US marshal," Iris said. "Why wouldn't you step in even if you weren't asked?"

"I'm mindful of not crossing jurisdictional lines. Unless a federal offense has been committed, I have to leave matters in the hands of the town marshal or the county sheriff. Now, on occasion, he asks me to lend a hand and I do."

"How often do these crimes occur?" Iris queried.

"All the time." With his elbows on the table, Jake held his coffee cup between his hands. "Plenty of cowboys are out of work these days, so they make trouble in towns and turn to drunkenness, gambling, robbing banks, and...*trains*."

"You can't scare us, Jake Edgerton."

Emily lowered her head to hide her smile at Iris's bravado. Far be it from her friend to accuse her of laughing at her again.

"Fine. But you might keep my words in mind, Iris, as you're *husband hunting*."

"Iris and a...*a cowboy*?" That did it. Emily began laughing all over again.

The train pulled in to Fallon, Montana, around ten o'clock that morning. Emily and Iris disembarked onto the wooden platform.

"Wait here, ladies." Jake's hand held Emily's elbow. "Will you do that for me?"

"Of course." She watched Jake set off on whatever business he needed to tend to. "But don't forget us here."

Jake sent her a glance from over his left shoulder.

"Dear God, don't let him forget us here." Horror and wonder caused her to stare at the landscape again. Prairie spread out as far as the eye could see, although the town of Fallon consisted of no more than the train depot and platform, a grain elevator, a general mercantile, a grocer's, and a saloon. "Maybe this wasn't such a good idea after all." She glanced at Iris.

"A step back in time, isn't it?" She sounded just as awed but hardly deterred.

Railroad men in blue caps emptied the freight cars. Emily spotted her two alligator-leather Gladstone bags. Her parents had given them to her after she'd earned her teaching certificate. She'd used them only to visit Grandpa Ramsey in New York before acquiring her job, and then to move her clothes into her room at the boardinghouse so she could feel more independent and live closer to school.

Iris recovered her two tapestry-covered valises, and together they waved good-bye to the Carlsons who sat near the windows of the passenger car. Standing at the end of the platform, Jake finally waved them over to where a wagon sat parked on the dusty road. Two men leaned up against nearby hitching rails, wide-brimmed hats covering their features.

"Ladies, please meet my brother-in-law, Boyd Webster, and his ranch hand Greg Flores."

The two men wiped their hats off their heads.

"Please to meet you both." Mr. Webster nodded to each of them. Strands of his sun-brightened hair stood on edge.

The ranch hand stepped up to the platform. "Welcome to Fallon." Emily detected a hint of a Mexican accent in the younger man's voice. Lanky and dark-headed, he gave them each a wide smile.

"This'll be a surprise for my wife, Deidre—a nice surprise." Web gave a nod at Jake. "Like I said, you're welcome to stay as long as you'd like."

"How very kind of you to say so." Emily thought a week should suffice.

"We'll stay as long as you're willing to have us as your guests," Iris blurted. "Maybe even all summer."

Emily felt a measure of alarm and glanced at Jake, who

acknowledged her with a curious light in his dark eyes, but he remained unmoving and calm.

"We're hardworking," Iris prattled on, "so your wife won't feel put out. Right, Emily?" Iris nudged her.

Emily forced herself to nod.

Jake finally spoke up. "Emily and Iris are schoolteachers on summer break. They want to experience a ranch firsthand so they can tell their pupils about it this fall."

Mr. Webster scratched his jaw, looking impressed. "Well, okay then! We'll show you a ranch." He grinned.

"Yes, it will be a pleasure." The ranch hand smiled. "You'll be like sunflowers among weeds."

"How poetic." Iris folded her gloved hands and tucked them beneath her chin.

Emily frowned at her best friend's sudden bedazzled expression.

"Just so I make myself clear, I ain't a weed, cowboy." Mr. Webster sent his man a dark glance. "Remember that."

"Right, boss." Mr. Flores tucked the brim of his hat, albeit his grin never wavered.

"How 'bout let's get that second surprise for Deidre loaded into the wagon." Jake faced his brother-in-law. "Then we'll load up the ladies' things."

"Jake?" Emily caught his duster's sleeve. "Is there somewhere I can send a telegram?"

"Uh-huh." He gave a nod and pointed across the street. "See that little house behind the grocery store, there across the road?"

"The log house with the postal sign?"

"That's it. You can send a telegraph there."

"Thanks, Jake."

"And come right back. Don't let Iris get herself into trouble."

Emily saw the teasing flicker in his gaze. "A tall order to be sure." She whirled around and strode over to Iris. "Let's send telegrams home. Jake pointed out the way."

They crossed the road to the rustic home in which the postmistress and her husband lived. The slim woman was eager to help them and wrote down their messages. She promised to wire them right away.

With that accomplished, Emily and Iris strolled back to the wagon. Scores of people had disembarked the train and stood in clusters on the platform or on the unpaved street. To the north, a ferry, operated by pulleys, took a small crowd across the Yellowstone. Emily wondered on which side of the river the Ready Web was located.

Watching the action, Emily saw it took three additional men to help load the crated stove and oven that Jake purchased for his sister. Mr. Webster complained about the wagon springs, but Mr. Flores was convinced they'd manage the weight.

With a smile sent their way, Mr. Flores tossed their bags to Jake, who threw them at Mr. Webster, who placed them strategically into the wagon's already overloaded bed.

Mr. Flores approached them. "Shall we go?" He offered his arm to Iris.

"Yes, thank you." Two steps later Emily overheard her say, "I'll bet your wife is so grateful to have such a strong husband."

"Oh, I'm not married."

"What a coincidence." Iris laughed her fluttery laugh. "Neither am I!"

Emily blinked. Her jaw dropped. What in the world? She set her hands on her hips and planned to sit Iris down tonight and have a good, hard talk with her, for whatever good it might do. This husband-hunting business had gone too far. Besides, hadn't Iris said that Jake was her destiny? Why was she flirting so brazenly with Mr. Flores? Here Emily had been feeling so guilty for having feelings for Jake...

She gazed over at him. Removing his hat, Jake watched Mr. Flores assist Iris into the wagon. He scratched his blond head then walked slowly toward Emily. "Looks like I might be off the hook."

He chuckled and swung his gaze at her before donning his Stetson. Then he held out his arm. "May I assist you, Miss Sundberg?"

"Why, yes, but—"

"Don't even wonder, Em. You'll never figure it out."

"Oh, Jake! I don't know what to say!" Deidre's eyes danced with happiness as she stared at the brand-new stove. "Thank you!"

Jake chuckled when she threw herself into his arms and kissed his cheek.

"You're the best brother ever."

"Helps that I'm your only brother, I imagine."

His quip was lost on Deidre, who went back to admiring the gleaming ACME Steel Regal Range. It had doors and drawers and an oven that baked food evenly, whatever that meant.

"When can we get it into the kitchen, Boyd?" Deidre was the only one who called Web by his given name, and it always gave Jake a start to hear it. "I can't wait to begin cooking on it. Just wait and see what tasty meals I'm going to make for you now."

"There's incentive, Web." Jake grinned.

He muttered something under his breath and then sent a look at Rez. "Can you rustle me up some muscle for tomorrow morning?"

"Sure, boss."

"All together we ought to be able to get that ol' relic out of the kitchen and this newfangled thing into the house and hooked up."

Squealing with excitement, Deidre hugged Web around the neck. He laughed and swung her a few inches before setting her down. If two people ever loved each other and weren't afraid to show it, Deidre and Web were them. Deidre, particularly. She was always good for a hug, and if Jake didn't watch it, she'd kiss his jaw a couple of times. Kinda embarrassing when it was for no other reason than he'd made it home alive and in time for supper.

"This is one of the best days of my life. A new, modern appliance for my kitchen and two new friends who have promised to help me learn how to use it." Deidre turned to Jake. "I'm so thrilled that you've brought them for a visit. You can't imagine. I've been needing to talk—things only ladies really care to discuss, although I've chewed off Boyd's ear."

"And that's all right, honey." Web winked at her.

"You're so patient with me." She looped her arm around his. "Even so, it's nice to have ladies to talk things over with. I can already tell the three of us will get along just fine. God knew I needed female fellowship, more than I get at church on Sundays."

Her admission caught Jake off guard. "Well, it certainly had to be of the Lord then because I had no intentions of inviting them…at first." He glanced toward the main house. "Where are Em and Iris now?"

"Getting settled in the guest room."

Rez removed his hat and wiped his forehead with his sleeve. "They sure are pretty ladies. Bluest eyes I ever saw."

Jake decided he'd best lay down the law right now. "Watch yourself, Rez. These two are husband hunting by their own admission—well, just Iris admitted it."

"Husband hunting?" The man grinned. "You don't say…" He chuckled. "I just might let myself be their prey."

"That's up to you. Just stay away from Emily Sundberg."

Three pairs of eyes fixed on him.

"I have it on good word that she's spoken for." That's the best he could do to recover, and it seemed to work.

"How did the funeral go, Jake?" Deidre peered up at him. "Did you manage all right?" Sadness crept into her gaze.

"All went smoothly, thanks to the Sundbergs, Iris, and the Schulzes. The service was a fine memorial and tribute to Granddad. Afterward the Sundbergs hosted a luncheon in Granddad's home with help from all the ladies at church. The house was full of friends. Even a state senator showed up to pay his respects."

"Is that right?" Web seemed impressed.

"To hear it does my heart good." Deidre smiled.

"I didn't have to do hardly anything." Jake would forever be grateful. "All I had to do was convince Aunt Bettina and Uncle Dwight to return to Chicago, which I managed with Mr. Schulz's help." Jake relayed the crux of the story.

"Ma would be livid!" Deidre stepped away from Web and dropped her hands onto her round hips. "After what Aunt Bettina put Granddad through all these years, you'd think she'd show some respect."

"She showed none." Jake stifled a yawn. "But can we discuss this in greater detail later? I'm tuckered out."

"Of course. Go take a nap. I swept up your cabin, washed the linens, and remade your bed." His sister transformed into a regular mother hen.

"You didn't have to do that in my cabin, but I'm grateful."

"You're welcome. Now there's plenty of time before dinner." She smiled and sighed at her new stove. "It'll be the last dinner I serve from my old stove, and I don't feel a mite sad to see it go. Not when this beauty is waiting for me." She rubbed her palms together. Anticipation glimmered in her gaze.

Web churned out a short groan. "And you'd best pray I can fit it into your kitchen tomorrow."

"I know you'll figure it out." Jake grinned and lifted his two leather suit bags, which had once belonged to Granddad. Rez picked up the trunk that Jake had filled with odds and ends from the house. He'd also placed the brass lockbox, containing his grandparents' jewelry, inside the locked trunk. He'd made sure to insure it with the railroad, although the contents were priceless and irreplaceable. Deidre would be happy to have Grandma's pretty things.

He strode the distance across the yard to his cabin. Inside his place, Rez set down the trunk.

"Thanks, man." Jake set down his suit bags.

"No problem." His gaze traveled the circumference of the living area and parked at the tiny hallway leading to the one bedroom in this place. "You want me to carry it farther?"

"Nah, I can manage."

"Okay, and it's nice to have you back, Deputy."

The title put Jake on alert. "Anything going on I should know about?"

"Tornado came through here last Sunday evening."

"Yeah? Web didn't say anything."

"Probably didn't want to frighten the ladies."

"Maybe. But, for your future reference, they get tornados in Wisconsin, and Em and Iris don't scare that easily."

"Good to know."

Rez rub his dark, stubbly jaw, reminding Jake that he could use a shave too. A bath and a shave and a set of clean clothes. He'd sure gotten soft those few days in Wisconsin, although he had to say he'd enjoyed all the refinements life offered there. He'd been content—first time in a long while. In fact he nearly forgot the pain he sometimes felt whenever he set foot on this ranch.

Rez touched the rim of his hat. "See you at supper." He grinned. "I'm happy there will be two more pretty faces at the table tonight. I can gaze on them while I eat instead of lookin' at ugly cowboys."

Jake wasn't amused. "Watch yourself, Rez. I ain't warning you a second time."

"Don't worry. I'll be on my best behavior."

Jake saw him out.

"But you don't mind if I would, perhaps, take a little stroll after supper with Miss Hopper?"

"It's up to her. But if she agrees, I'd keep in plain sight if I was you."

"I'll do that." Rez sauntered off the porch and headed toward the yard.

Jake closed the cabin door. *Lord, am I going to spend the next weeks fending off ranch hands and cowboys?*

CHAPTER 18

*I*RIS YAWNED. "I believe Mrs. Webster said she'd have a couple of men carry in a bathtub for us. Won't a bath feel wonderful after sitting on the train since Wednesday morning? It's Friday afternoon and I, for one, cannot wait until tomorrow night for a bath!"

"Iris, please listen to me."

"I *am* listening." She opened one of her bags and began unpacking her things, hanging her skirts on one side of the oak wardrobe.

"Jake is not your destiny."

"I beg to differ. I'm here in Montana, aren't I?"

Exasperation mounted inside of her. "Last night while you slept, Jake asked me to tell you again—he's not your destiny."

"He is my destiny, but I'm not in love with him. Did I forget to mention that?"

"Yes, I believe you did!" Emily's temper began to simmer.

Iris twittered out a laugh. "Of course I'm not in love with Jake. He's actually got his heart set on someone else."

"He does?" Emily felt her heart twist, as if it were being wrung out to dry. "What are you talking about?" Surely Jake would have mentioned that he was interested in someone else. There had been plenty of times he might have slipped in that bit of information.

"I imagine it'll come out soon enough. He'll likely be heading back to Manitowoc sometime soon."

Emily stared at Iris, wondering if she should believe her. "Is this a joke?"

"I'm not joking. In fact, I was initially very attracted to Jake's ruggedness, as you well know, but Friday night I could tell he was attracted to this other young lady." A look of remorse wafted across Iris's face. "A pity. But I soon got over my disappointment."

"I don't believe you."

"Do you think I would lie to you, Emily?" Iris met her gaze and held it. Her expression held not a single trace of amusement. "I would never lie to you, and I swear Jake has his heart set on someone from Manitowoc. I saw it with my own two eyes."

"At the dance on Friday night?"

Emily tried to remember who Jake danced with on Friday night, other than herself. There had been quite a few young women eager to be his dance partner. "Jeanette McCoy?"

"No." Iris rolled her eyes. "Jeanette prattles far too much. Besides, she's hardly a match for Jake."

Emily thought she was a match for Jake. But she couldn't be the person Iris was talking about or her best friend would have come right out and told her so. What's more, Emily already knew Jake was a practiced flirt.

Emily's breath caught. She'd been such a little fool, enjoying Jake's attention last weekend and their stolen moments on the train when Iris slept. To think that someone else had actually caught his eye! But that figured. Emily already proved she couldn't catch a man's eye, much less hold it.

"Tell me who she is." Emily sat down on the edge of the double bed they'd share tonight. "Ruth Ellen Porter? Geraldine Grant? Helda Tverberg?"

"I can't say, Em. It's not my news to tell. Jake will have to tell you." She gave Emily a pitying look.

"But—"

"I know we're best friends and we tell each other everything, but my keeping quiet is for your own good."

"I don't understand." She felt deflated.

"Well…" Iris paused, a petticoat in hand. "If I tell you, you won't believe me."

"I will. I promise."

Iris shook her head and then peered out their bedroom's window. "Why, here comes that Greg Flores. He's so handsome and strong. He's carrying that bathtub by himself!"

"You're not going to tell me, are you?" Emily felt doubly wounded.

Iris spun from the window. "Do you realize, Em, that if I marry Mr. Flores, my name would be Iris Flores." She laughed. "*Flores* means flowers in Spanish." Another fluttery laugh. "Get it? Iris Flowers?"

"Some best friend you turned out to be." Emily stared down at her skirt. She felt hot, tired, and quite crabby at the moment.

"You'll thank me later."

At the knock on the door, Iris rushed to answer it. Emily stayed where she sat on the bed, her back to the action. She heard Mr. Flores bring in the tub and Iris gush over his physical strength.

"Aw, it was nothing, Miss Hopper."

"Please call me Iris. My friends do."

"All right. I would like to be your friend. And please call me Rez."

Emily rolled her eyes then peeked over her shoulder at the pair when a moment of silence ensued. They both looked star-struck.

"Mrs. Webster is heating the bathwater. She'll be in shortly."

"Thank you, Rez. I'll see you later."

"Until then, Miss Iris."

"Oh, no miss, please. I'm trying to get rid of that title." She laughed.

Emily resisted the urge to gag at the overused pun. And if Iris thought for one second that Emily would play chaperone, then her friend had another think coming.

The ranch hand finally left, and moments later Mrs. Webster arrived with buckets of heated water. She made two trips, pouring all four into the tub.

"You'll find soap and clean towels over there by the washstand. Take the afternoon to bathe, get settled, and rest. Supper will be about six o'clock."

Emily sat quietly by, listening.

"Thank you so much, Mrs. Webster."

"Deidre. Please. And you're welcome. It's nice to have you here—both of you."

Emily sent a smile over her shoulder. She didn't want to appear rude to their hostess.

"I hope you'll be comfortable here." Deidre ran a hand over her straight brown hair, coiled and pinned at her nape, except for those shorter, rebellious strands that hung loosely around her face. "Originally this was my parents' room. Jake and I had rooms in the loft, but when Boyd purchased the ranch, he built an addition with a larger bedroom for us and a kitchen for me. Also, plenty of space for guests."

"We'll be quite comfortable." Emily stood and eyed the lacy curtains gracing the window. "It's a perfectly cozy room, and you're very kind."

"Not really. Just desperate for female companionship." She smiled. "We'll chat more later."

"Indeed." Iris's gaze widened with what Emily recognized as enthusiasm.

Leaving, Deidre closed the door behind her.

Emily liked her. As for her brother…was he really attracted to someone back in Manitowoc? He'd shared so much with her that Emily thought surely he would have said something about a romantic interest.

"Stop frowning, Emily. You'll get wrinkles before your time."

Sitting back down on the doublewide mattress, Emily didn't care if she developed a face like an old apple core. Who would care? She'd die an old maid for sure now. If she couldn't marry Jake, she didn't want anyone else. In truth, she'd fallen in love with Jake the summer he spent in Manitowoc with Mr. Ollie.

"And you're pouting. I sense it from here. Quit it. Proper school-teachers do not pout."

"Oh, please…" Emily hurled a glance at the ceiling. "I hardly deserve a scolding on propriety from *you*."

"I'm unconventional, not improper."

"I beg to differ."

"Tell you what." Iris walked around the bed. She tipped her head and the blonde curls around her face swung lightly. "You can take the first bath. Afterward have a nap. I'm sure when you wake up you'll have a new perspective."

"Thank you." Emily stood and gave her best friend a sharp look. "That's the brightest idea you've had in a very long while!"

❧❦❧

Iris had been right. After a bath and a nap Emily felt like a different person. No more moping and pouting. As long as she was here, Emily decided she might as well enjoy herself.

Dressing in a simple ivory shirtwaist and a navy skirt, Emily opened the bedroom door and walked into the main part of the cabin. Furniture, which appeared to have been made from sanded and refinished logs, had been placed cozily around a stone hearth that occupied an entire wall. No fire burned in it today, however; Emily guessed the temperatures outside had reached nearly eighty degrees. Nearby, a long wooden table had been neatly set for supper. A savory smell wafted from the adjacent kitchen, and Emily's rumbling stomach reminded her that her last meal had been breakfast.

Iris strolled in from the kitchen carrying a bowl filled with mashed potatoes. "You're awake." She smiled.

Emily returned the gesture, and Iris's features seemed to relax. "Are you feeling better?"

"Much better. Thank you."

Their hostess followed with a plate of biscuits. She placed it on the table then brushed straying locks of light brown hair from her handsome face, which, Emily saw now, appeared wind- and weather-worn.

"May I help you with anything, Deidre?"

"Nothing, thanks." She indicated to one of the four benches. "Make yourself comfortable while I ring the supper bell." She headed for the back entrance of the cabin. "The men should be already washed up."

Emily walked to the table and peered into the tureen. It appeared to be meat and vegetables in rich brown gravy. "Smells delicious." Her stomach gnawed at her.

"Doesn't it, though? I've never eaten hare stew before. Have you?"

"Hare—as in rabbit?"

"Exactly."

"No." Although Poppa, Eden, and Zeb talked of making a meal of roast rabbit on hunting excursions.

A bell clanged loudly for several seconds. Emily fought the compulsion to cover her ears.

Deidre returned and the men came traipsing in through both doorways. Emily kept her gaze carefully averted from Jake.

Jake greeted them. "You look real pretty this evening, Em. You too, Iris."

"How nice of you to say so," Iris replied.

The compliments made Emily bristle. What would his true love say about his flattering other ladies? She recalled how he told her more than once that she was the most beautiful young woman he'd ever seen. Of course, she took it as his way of trying to make her feel better. She'd been disappointed over Andy's behavior.

Iris gave her a nudge. "Jake complimented you."

"Oh, thanks." She sent a furtive glance his way. He looked fine himself, clean-shaven, his hair combed, and a loose-fitting beige shirt beneath a tan, leather vest.

He caught her eye and grinned. So much for averting her gaze!

"I don't believe you ladies have met Charlie Dietz yet."

Mr. Webster's voice drew Emily's attention. She noticed the older man beside Jake. His face resembled crumpled brown paper, and his short white hair provided a startling contrast.

"Welcome to the Ready Web." Mr. Dietz's voice sounded as coarse as gravel, albeit his tone was polite.

"Thank you, Mr. Dietz," Iris said.

"It's Charlie." He grinned and Emily saw that he had a front tooth missing.

"And I don't know if I ever said it—" Mr. Webster took a seat at one end of the long table. "—but you ladies can call me Web. Everyone does."

Emily sent a polite smile to both men, trying to imagine Mr. Ollie, the polite gentleman and sophisticated attorney, in this setting.

Rez walked in moments later and hung his hat on a peg near the doorway. "My apologies for being late." He moved in beside Iris.

Emily scooted over on the bench to make room for him.

"May I say all you ladies look lovely this evening."

More inane flattery. Looking down the way, Emily saw Rez flash a charming smile at Iris.

Deidre took her place at the other end of the table.

"Let's pray before this food gets cold."

At Web's request, Emily bowed her head, praying along silently as he asked the blessing on their food.

"And thank You, Lord, for Deidre's capable hands that prepared this food. In Christ's name…amen."

Placing the napkin across her lap, Emily's respect for Web grew because of his acknowledgment of Deidre's efforts in making this meal. Poppa always thanked God for Momma and the things she did around the house.

Emily felt sudden and unexpected pangs of homesickness.

The eating commenced around her, and Emily saw Charlie dig into his meal. She smiled at his exuberance. Momma liked to say there was nothing like watching a man enjoying a home-cooked meal. Emily served herself and passed the dish on. She wasn't the least bit skittish about tasting hare stew. Between Poppa's and Grandpa Ramsey's extravagant palettes, Emily and her brothers had tasted a variety of strange fares and delicacies.

"Jake told us that you're both schoolteachers." Accepting the tureen, Deidre smiled, ladled a portion onto her plate then handed it to Jake. "I'm sure it's a rewarding profession."

"Most certainly." Emily spoke up as Iris had just taken a bite of food.

"What grades do you teach?"

"I teach third grade. Iris teaches fourth, although we work at different schools."

"All the interesting people we get to know and situations that arise give us something to discuss at suppertime." Iris gave Emily another nudge. "Never a dull conversation around the table, right, Em?"

"Right." Emily couldn't help a smile, thinking of what their fellow boarders were saying tonight. *They up and left for the Pacific Coast…*

"How refreshing." Deidre glanced at her husband. "Web and Charlie aren't much for table talk, although when Jake joins us they perk up. The topics are usual centered on the ranch or Jake's work."

Having grown up with two brothers, Emily could relate to that outnumbered-by-men feeling. "While we're here, Iris and I are pleased to discuss more genteel topics with you."

"Oh, yes! And I have the June copy of *Vogue* magazine," Iris added. "I purchased it for ten cents during our layover in Milwaukee. We can admire all the latest fashions."

"Ten cents!" Web wore an incredulous-looking frown.

"That's nothing, Web." Jake grinned. "I understand that *some ladies* pay a dollar and a half for a hat."

"What?" Web pulled his head back. "For a hat?"

"A perfectly beautiful hat!" Emily knew he teased her. "One that Jake ruined."

His smile widened. "I reimbursed you."

"True." Emily accepted the plate of biscuits and passed it to Deidre. She hoped she sounded nonchalant, but inside she felt so hurt that Jake loved someone else.

"How did you ruin her hat, Jake?" Deidre's brown eyes lighted with curiosity.

"I landed on it." He shook his head. "Long story. I won't bore you with details."

"Oh, but I'm happy to tell you all about it." Iris wiggled with excitement.

Emily pressed her elbow into Iris's arm, but that didn't deter her. She relayed the entire incident, and then told of how she'd written an article about Jake's apprehending the wanted man and how he was related to Mr. Ollie, another of Manitowoc's heroes.

"Did you know that Mr. Ollie often defended clients who couldn't pay him?"

Both Jake and Deidre nodded.

"He was a man whose desire was to truly see justice served, even for the less fortunate among us."

"What a marvelous thing you did, writing that article, Iris." Deidre blinked back tears.

"Oh, honey, now don't cry."

"These are good tears, Web." She smiled right through them. "Don't be alarmed."

Emily had to swallow her own bit of emotion. Beneath the table she found Iris's hand and gave it an affectionate squeeze. She never felt more proud of her best friend than right now.

CHAPTER 19

SOMETIME AFTER SUPPER Jake walked home to collect the brass lockbox that Mr. Schulz had given him. He'd already selected the items he wanted and now left the rest to Deidre. He knew she'd adore the earbobs, sapphire pendant, and other trinkets that their mother's mother once wore. There was even a set of matching cufflinks for Web. He most likely wouldn't have much use for them out here, but one never knew when an opportunity might arise and then he'd have them.

In his cabin he walked to where he'd left his jacket over a small pile of his belongings, including the lockbox. Thoughts of Emily filled his mind. She looked awfully fetching at the supper table tonight. But she looked sad too. Or tired. A good night's sleep would fix that.

He picked up the lockbox and held it in his hands, felt the ornate carvings on the cover beneath his thumbs. He could practically hear Granddad's voice saying, *One day you're going to have to put your heart on the line, Jake. You'll find it's more difficult than risking your life.*

Put his heart on the line. But could he make a woman happy? Emily? What would it take? What if he couldn't please her no matter what he did? What if she got so forlorn that she took her life, like Ma? Jake didn't think he could survive the anguish.

Put his heart on the line. What if Em was being coy, suffering from the wedding bell blues, as Jake had heard it said. Almost at once he banished the idea. He knew Emily well enough to know she didn't fit coy. He hadn't always been a saint. And yet he'd also sensed her romantic interest in him—at times. But was it as fleeting as her interest in Andy? Maybe she changed her mind as often as the wind changed directions. No. Emily didn't seem that sort either. Emily was genuine.

A breeze fluttered the faded curtains Deidre had hung on his back window. They were about all he'd had in here to make this place a home.

Funny how he'd felt more at home in Granddad's house.

As he walked slowly back to the house, he thought about his visit to Manitowoc, how he'd remembered his manners, avoided saying the word *ain't*, which had always vexed Granddad whenever he and Jake were together. He would miss that old man. But Granddad would have approved of the way Jake had done his best to reveal the kind of man he really was, a man of faith, character, and moral principles. He wasn't a hardened deputy, like some men became. Granddad had taught him to do it all to God's glory, and Jake tried. He used his gun when his life or innocent people depended on it, and he saw every man, even the worst, as a soul.

Nearing the house, Jake spotted Deidre and Emily on the back porch. It was getting to be about the time of year when Deidre would want the eating table moved there so they could enjoy their meals out of doors. Ma used to teasingly put on airs and call it her "verandah."

He removed his hat as he stepped onto the covered portico. "Ladies."

Emily gave him a smile. "Hi, Jake. I wondered where you'd run off to."

"Just had to retrieve something from my cabin." He walked to the end of the porch to where they sat.

"Emily's showing me a new stitch." Deidre's expression looked more relaxed than Jake had seen in a long while. "I'm accustomed to sewing needles over knitting needles."

He sat on the rail. "I guess Em would be the one to show you, seeing as the women in her family are experts in the stitching field."

"I just learned about her grandmother's boutique." Regret strained Deidre's features. "I wish I would have visited Granddad in Wisconsin."

"Travel has come a long way even since I first ventured east with him a decade ago." Jake's gaze settled on Emily.

"It was my first trip west by rail," Emily commented.

"What did you think of it?" Jake was eager to find out.

"I'm glad you were there to protect Iris and me."

That made him feel good.

"It's nothing like riding the train out East," Emily continued. "I didn't realize what a collection of people rode the train, some not so decent."

She'd learned that lesson well. Jake felt a measure of satisfaction there. "What are you attempting to create, Deidre?"

"Well…" A blush crept into Deidre's face. "A baby's blanket."

"Who's expecting? He thought of the women in their congregation that met here on the ranch. Web owned the best accommodations, and Fallon didn't have a formal church building yet. "Must be Mrs. Vincent."

"Wrong. It's me!"

Jake stood. Had he heard correctly? "You?" His sister was twenty-nine, and that seemed rather old to begin having babies. "Are you sure?"

"Yes." Deidre's smile never faded. "Dr. Morrison in Glendive confirmed it a few days before Granddad died. I never got a chance to tell you since you hadn't been home much before you turned around and left for Wisconsin."

"Well, what do you know?" He lowered himself back onto the porch rail.

Deidre laughed and leaned toward Emily. "He's in shock."

"Seems so." Emily rolled her pretty blue eyes.

"When's the baby due?" Jake regarded his sister. She didn't have that full, ripe look about her, like he'd seen in some women.

"Around Thanksgiving, we figure."

"Are you sure, Deidre?" Seemed so incredible. She'd been married all these long years and no baby until now? Miraculous. But that was God.

"Of course I'm sure. Do you think I'd rush off to a doctor for nothing?"

"Well, no."

"And Dr. Morrison's the one who told me the baby's why I've experienced all these stomach ailments. Those and some other symptoms. All makes sense now. They weren't ailments at all."

"I'm sure you must be so happy." Emily placed her hand on Deidre's wrist.

"Oh, I am."

The news sunk in. "I'm going to be an uncle!" Jake let out a hoot.

Deidre kept smiling

"Listen to you. I should think you'd scare babies, Jake Edgerton." Emily jerked her chin in a teasing little way.

"Oh, children adore Jake."

"I'm not as scary as I seem."

"I suppose that's true enough." Emily sent him a grin before looking at Deidre. "He knows how to dance too. I guess that's *something* in his favor."

"I suppose." Deidre went along with the ribbing, but her eyes went from Jake to Emily as if she were figuring out another secret. His, this time.

"You're very gracious to praise my dancing, Miss Sundberg." Jake shook his head at her. He couldn't rid himself of the magnitude of his sister's news, though. "A baby. Imagine it."

Deidre quieted for several moments. "I must admit that I'm a little scared of this baby."

Jake stared at his sister. "Scared? Of the baby?"

"I mean...I wonder if I'll turn out like Ma." Deidre plunged her gaze into her lap along with her knitting. "Emily, I don't mean to make you uncomfortable, but I'm presuming you know the situation since your family was close to Granddad."

She nodded. "You're not making me feel the least bit uncomfortable."

"Everyone says Ma was touched, and I'm scared..." She looked up. "Well, Jake, what if Ma passed it on to me?"

Jake's mouth went dry. He'd never thought of such a thing.

"God does not give us a spirit of fear." The confidence in Emily's voice brought his reasoning back to life. "But He gives us the spirit of love, power, and a sound mind—or so the Bible verse goes. I don't recall it verbatim."

"She's right, Deidre." Jake recognized the passage. He sent Emily a grateful nod.

"Yes...love, power, and a sound mind." His sister gave Emily a large smile. "I'll search for that passage tonight and read it before I go to sleep."

"You might even repeat it to yourself all day long."

"Yes..." Deidre inclined her head. "I will. Thank you."

"My pleasure."

Deidre's gaze returned to Jake then to the lockbox he still held. "What have you got there?"

Jake lifted the lockbox. "This belonged to Granddad. Just after he fell ill, he instructed Mr. Schulz to collect his valuables so Aunt Bettina wouldn't get her hands on them." He ran his palm over the polished brass cover one last time. "I took Granddad's watch and...a couple of other things."

A pretty blush colored Emily's cheeks.

"Now I'd like you and Web to have the rest."

"Thank you, Jake…" Deidre set aside her knitting and accepted the proffered lockbox. She traced the carvings with one finger.

"Captain Sundberg said Granddad gave his daughters one just like it, but I never saw Ma's around here."

"I did. She kept important papers and money in it. But Ma hid it after Pa was killed. She feared it would fall into criminal hands, should our home be invaded again."

"So where is it now?"

"The Lord only knows, Jake. I've looked everywhere because the original deed to this property was in there. Boyd even crawled under the house checking for it." Deidre shrugged. "It's gone."

Jake thought it over. He hadn't been home a lot after Pa was gunned down. After school he worked on a neighboring ranch. On Saturdays he cleaned the sheriff's office in Terry. As the man of the house he had to bring in some sort of income, meager as it was. But his cleaning job at the sheriff's whetted his appetite for first revenge and then justice. The years went by. He watched and learned from various lawmen, practiced his gunmanship, learned Montana and federal laws. His mind as well as his body had been elsewhere until the day when Ma…

He turned to Emily and saw her thinking almost as hard as he'd been. Her blue eyes met his gaze, and a sort of little light burst into them as if an idea struck.

"Maybe that's what your mother was after on the day she died." She looked at Deidre then back at Jake. "Mr. Ollie and I always believed your mother's fall was an accident."

Jake hated to shoot down her optimism. "It's a good thought, Em, but unlikely. There's nothing up there on Suicide Bluff but a long and deadly way down."

Deidre agreed.

"Suicide Bluff?"

"Legend has it," Deidre explained, "that Indians, whenever they felt ashamed or they were terminally ill, would walk up the bluff, pray to their gods, and then fling themselves over the edge."

"How dreadful." Emily paled.

Jake couldn't abide this conversation any longer and changed the subject. "Open up that lockbox, Sissy, and see what's inside."

Carefully Deidre lifted the lid. Glimpsing the contents, she gasped with such delight that Jake smiled.

"Just look at these earbobs!" She held a glittering ruby dangle to her left lobe and an emerald one to her right. "How do I look?"

"Like you're all set for Christmas," Emily laughed.

Jake grinned and watched the two ladies pick through the treasures, although he mostly watched Emily. When she smiled, the whole world seemed a brighter place.

"Wouldn't Web, Charlie, and Rez have a shock if I started wearing fancy jewelry while I did my chores?" Deidre giggled.

"I'd say it becomes you, Deidre." The joy in his sister's gaze was priceless.

"Thank you." She smiled into his eyes. "You didn't have to share, but I'm so glad you're a generous man."

"You're welcome."

She stood and kissed his cheek. "I'll go put these away for now." She turned to Emily. "Excuse me."

"Of course."

Deidre walked into the house, leaving Jake alone with Emily on the wide porch. For whatever reason, it seemed unusually quiet. He glanced up the road and glimpsed Rez and Iris. All seemed well there. He turned back toward Emily, and she picked up her knitting.

"Haven't finished that sweater yet?"

"I keep getting interrupted." She widened her gaze to emphasize her point.

He grinned and moseyed across the porch. He sat beside Emily and caught a faint floral scent that didn't come from his sister's garden. He wanted to put his nose in her hair and inhale deeply.

"Don't tell me you're interested in learning to knit," she teased.

"All right, I won't." He stretched his arm across the back of the bench. "I'll just watch you, if that's okay."

"I don't mind." Her knitting needles clicked as she wrapped the yarn around the one and then wove it in and out, wrap around, in and out. Jake felt cross-eyed watching her work so fast.

Then he thought about what she'd said and smirked. "Me and knitting needles. That's about as funny as Iris on a roundup."

Emily sounded like she choked, but then her giggles came bubbling out just like this morning in the dining car. Jake basked in the sound of her laughter and his smile turned into a chuckle.

"What's so funny out here?"

Emily coughed in obvious discomfort as Deidre walked onto the porch.

"I'm just helping Em. She's got something in her throat." Jake hid his smile and gently rapped Emily between her shoulder blades.

"I thought I heard laughing." She knelt by Emily. "Are you all right?"

"Oh...yes...I'm fine." Emily's gaze shifted to Jake. "Thanks a lot." Sarcasm and a smile hung in her tone.

"Pleasure was all mine." Jake meant every word.

CHAPTER 20

*T*HE NEXT MORNING Emily awoke before dawn's first light. She'd stayed on the back porch with Jake and Deidre until Iris and Rez came back from their stroll. Once darkness fell, she and Iris retired to their room and readied for bed. Beneath the soft bedcovers Iris had talked and talked about Gregory Flores's marvelous qualities. Emily found out more about the man than she cared to, and she wished Iris wouldn't set her heart on marrying the first man who paid her some attention. She was certain to get her heart broken.

Yawning, Emily slipped out from underneath the thick quilt. She'd had a good night's rest. As she brushed out her hair, thoughts of Jake permeated her memory. Emily enjoyed sitting so close to him on the porch bench, teasing him about wanting to learn to knit. And he could have moved over several times, but he didn't. So what did that mean? What about the girl he had his heart set on back in Manitowoc?

Emily dressed in the dark, slipping into the same skirt and simple shirtwaist she'd worn last night. She opened the door slowly and then tiptoed across the plank floor. The boards squeaked beneath her weight as she made her way through the kitchen. Sliding back the heavy latch, she opened the back door and stepped out onto the porch. A cool breeze greeted her, but she decided against retracing her steps and retrieving her shawl at the risk of waking someone who wanted to sleep longer. She stifled a gasp when the two hounds bounded toward her, although their tails wagged and their tongues dangled eagerly from their mouths. She patted their heads, wondering why she hadn't seen them before.

"Sorry, fellas, I don't have any treats for you just now." They seemed friendly enough.

Smiling, Emily moved to the step and sat down. The dogs lay down, one on each side of her. They smelled vaguely of skunk. Nonetheless, she felt oddly protected by their presence.

To the east, strokes of magenta and gray swept across the sky. Birds sang and flitted from the treetops to the clothesline. They dove into the garden and flew to the barn roof.

The hounds suddenly stood, whined, and each leapt from the back porch. Emily heard a man's low, soft voice, and soon Jake came into view. He made his way up the path, and when he saw her he smiled. "Good morning, Em."

"Morning, Jake. I would have started coffee, but I'm not sure how Deidre does things around here yet."

"No problem." He mounted the three stairs, passed her, and entered the cabin.

In the silence that followed, she prayed for her family, remembering each one to the Lord. *Bless them, keep them, make Your face to shine upon them, Lord, and grant us peace…*

"Looks like it's shaping up to be a nice day." Jake walked to the steps and Emily spied his scuffed boots.

"It's a pretty sunrise, that's true. But Poppa always said red sky at morning sailors take warning."

"Hmm…never heard that one before." Jake sat down next to her. "But there aren't a lot of sailors around here."

She heard the smile in his voice.

"Coffee should be done soon. Do you drink coffee? I think I've only seen you with tea."

"Sometimes I drink coffee." She enjoyed the strong flavor but always thought tea was a more genteel choice. Besides, Momma hailed from London and had taught her the perfect way to prepare tea—a lump of sugar and a splash of milk.

"Would you care for a cup? Honestly, I don't know that Deidre has any tea and I don't keep any groceries at my place, since I do all my eating over here."

"Coffee is fine. Thank you."

"Cream? Sugar?"

"Just black." That's the way Poppa liked it too.

"All right then. I'll be back."

"No hurry."

Jake stood and walked back into the house, leaving Emily to wonder over his solicitousness. But whether or not he had his heart set on someone else, Emily enjoyed his company. Could he ever love her best, above that other young woman, whoever she was, or were she and Jake merely good friends?

He returned with two cups of coffee and, once more, sat on the step beside her, so closely, in fact, their arms collided.

"Thanks, Jake."

"Sure thing."

Emily blew into her cup of boiling-hot brew then inhaled its rich aroma.

"Pretty soon my sister's garden will be in full bloom." Jake pointed to their left. "She's got three acres of fruit trees and just about every kind of vegetable. Deidre cans as much as she can store and then goes into Fallon and sells the rest from the back of the wagon. She tries to catch the cowboys during drive time because they're usually desperate for fresh fruit and jarred preserves."

"Think she'll go this year? She'll be pretty far along."

"I don't know. I'm still in shock about Deidre expecting. Didn't think it would happen."

"Do you like children?" She could easily imagine herself as Jake's wife. She could almost see their children, running through the yard…except in her mind's eye it looked like her parents' yard on the farm, not this yard.

"I like children just fine." He turned to her. "Do you like children?"

Emily laughed. "I'm a teacher, silly. Of course I adore children."

"Hmm…just checking." He smiled and arched a brow. "Besides, I love to hear you laugh, Em. It's a happy sound."

"Laughter usually is, don't you think?"

"Not always. I've heard plenty of sinister laughs or cynical chuckles."

Was he thinking of his father as he stared into the yard? Emily yawned, slumping a bit.

"Don't tell me you're still tired."

"All right. I won't." She smiled. "Seriously, I'm not tired at all." She straightened and sipped her coffee.

"I own several horses that Web looks after whenever I'm gone. One of them is a spirited but well-behaved mare that I think you'd enjoy riding. Another is a mild-mannered sorrel who would suit Iris. Would you ladies care to take a ride after breakfast? I'll show you around the ranch."

"I'd love to, although Iris isn't much of a—"

"Cowboy?"

"Um…well, yes, that too." Smiling, she sipped from the thick porcelain coffee mug. Strong and a little bitter.

"A neighbor almost convinced me to raise polo ponies. He said there was good money involved, and it seemed like something I could do in between assignments. But I found I wasn't dedicated to the profession. Even so, I'd grown particularly fond of a number of horses and kept them."

Jake reclined on the steps. She'd never seen him dressed so casually before, tan, collarless shirt, dark-brown trousers whose suspenders hung lose around his hips. No vest, no badge, no gun, no hat. Slivers of sunlight fell over his sandy-blond hair. He looked less daunting, not that he'd ever intimidated Emily.

He caught her staring. When had she stopped admiring the sunrise? A grin tweaked the corners of his mouth.

"Never in my wildest dreams could I have imagined Emily Sundberg here, in Fallon, Montana."

"Why ever not?"

Jake assessed her. "Well, to be honest, I never thought of you as the pioneer type."

The comment gave her pause. "I never had call to be."

"True enough."

Emily began to wonder if the young lady, whom Jake had his heart set on, knew she'd end up a pioneer wife. That sort of woman, like Deidre, needed gumption, that's for sure. Emily wondered if she, herself, would be able to endure the numerous hardships that settling in the Fallon area would bring.

Jake glanced toward the house. "Deidre ought to be up in the next half hour."

Emily reached back and grabbed hold of her braided hair. It hung freely down her back. "Then I ought to go and finish readying myself for the day ahead." And it was about time she roused Iris, that lazybones. She wondered too if Iris had any idea of the perils life in eastern Montana afforded. Perhaps if she understood, she wouldn't be so quick to flirt with Rez.

She stood. "Thanks again for the coffee."

"You're most welcome, Emily."

"It's a great morning for a ride." Deidre smiled from her place at the table and glanced from Iris to Emily. "Good thinking, Jake."

In her haste to pin up her hair and meet Deidre in the kitchen, Emily had forgotten to mention the idea to Iris.

"While you're gone, Web, Rez, Charlie, and a few other men will get my stove in and operating." Her smile broadened. "Emily and Iris can help me fix supper and do some cooking for tomorrow."

"We'd be delighted." Emily smiled at Iris, who nodded.

"Be sure to take them for a ride along the Yellowstone, Jake. The cottonwood trees are blooming, and they're so lovely."

"I'll do that, Sissy."

"I'm an experienced horsewoman," Iris told Rez, who'd seated himself beside her on the bench like last night.

Emily squelched the urge to roll her eyes, but Jake saw her struggle and sent a wink across the table. Funny how they seemed to read each other so well.

"Just in case, Iris, I've got a backup plan."

Good thinking—at least on Jake's part. However, Emily remembered she hadn't packed her riding habit or boots. Had Iris?

"We may have a problem."

All eyes fixed on her. Emily dabbed the corners of her mouth with the white linen napkin and looked at her hostess. "Deidre, I wonder if you might own spare riding clothes that I can borrow so I don't have to ride sidesaddle. You see, I thought I was going to stay on the train all the way to the Pacific." Emily turned to Iris. "That was the original idea."

Iris's eyes blinked from behind her thick lenses. "Didn't I mention that I hoped we'd stop and visit the ranch on which Jake lived?"

Emily tried to recall their conversation. "If you did, I don't remember. I'm sorry." Her face heated with embarrassment as she flicked a glance at Jake. "I didn't pack appropriately for visiting a ranch."

"That's all right, Emily." Deidre smiled. "I have a divided skirt you may borrow."

From the other end of the table, Web chuckled. "Just see that you don't get arrested wearing it."

"A divided skirt?" Emily had seen a riding habit of that fashion once. "Why would I get arrested?"

"It's the funniest story, but once quite a scandal."

Emily surveyed the men's grins around the table.

"Our neighbor, Mrs. Cameron, who is quite unconventional, ordered a divided skirt from California over five years ago. When she first wore it into Terry, everyone was aghast, and in fact, the sheriff said he'd arrest her if she ever wore that split skirt to town again. The news of this most convenient skirt traveled from Terry to Fallon and up to Glendive. Mrs. Cameron allowed me to make a pattern from hers, and I shared it with my friends. We all love our divided skirts. They look every bit like proper full skirts when walking, but they divide conveniently so women can ride astride instead of sidesaddle."

"Sounds like my kind of skirt." Emily smiled.

Jake stood and stretched. "Reckon I'll let you ladies figure out the particulars while I saddle up the horses." He kissed the top of Deidre's head. "Thanks for breakfast."

"You're welcome."

Web, Charlie, and Rez excused themselves and sauntered off.

Emily and Iris helped Deidre clear the table, and then Deidre brought out the divided skirt, a pair of black boots, and a floppy suede hat. The boots were a size bigger than Emily usually wore, but better that than too small.

"Thank you so much, Deidre."

She smiled a reply as she prepared to wash the dishes. "You know, I haven't seen Jake this happy in a very long while. Wonder why that is." She sent a look at Emily over her shoulder.

Emily raised her shoulders.

"Must be spring fever, eh?"

"Must be." Emily took a step backward. Far be it from her to tell Deidre that whatever made Jake happy didn't have anything to do with her.

Or did it?

CHAPTER 21

*A*s THEY SET out, Emily had to admit that Jake selected two perfect horses for Iris and her. She patted her horse's neck. Rusty had a gentle manner and yet definite ideas about which way he'd like to walk. Emily continually coaxed him to follow Jake and his horse, Nickel, named for his silvery-gray coat. Her horsewoman skills were put to the test, particularly as Iris's horse, Cloud, was tethered to Rusty's bridle to ensure that Iris didn't trot off in the wrong direction.

"Experienced horsewoman, indeed." She flicked an annoyed glance at Iris.

She lifted her shoulders in a helpless gesture. "I didn't say I was a *good* horsewoman."

Jake turned in his saddle. "Keeping up, ladies?"

"Oh, yes. We're having fun." Iris's voice wobbled as she bounced up and down.

"Keep your feet in the stirrups and use your legs when the horse trots, Iris. Remember? Up and down. Up and down." Emily caught Jake's grin before he faced forward again.

As Deidre suggested, Jake led them along a trail that paralleled the Yellowstone River. Certainly the seeds on the cottonwood trees resembled cotton and the panoramic view was magnificent. Lush prairie spread out for as far as the eye could see. Jake pointed out the downed trees and broken fences, remnants of the tornado that ripped through the countryside last week.

They reached Fallon and crossed the river on the ferry. Jake called their attention to the swift and powerful current, which Emily hadn't noticed yesterday morning when they first crossed over. She watched how the ferry operator strained with the pulley system, but at last they safely disembarked on the other side. Emily and Iris learned the Ready Web was located west of Fallon, bordering what was known as the badlands.

After walking their horses and stretching their own legs, they mounted and rode for about another hour. Soon they arrived in the town of Terry.

"It's shearing season." Jake pointed out the crude, wooden shanties or shearing sheds in which the sheep men, as they were called, could work out of the hot June sunshine. Emily had seen sheep shorn before, but never to this magnitude. Sheep men and their animals filled the streets. The bleating of the sheep was nearly deafening. Nevertheless, Jake led them through the crowd.

"Once the wool is bagged," he called over the din of the people and animals, "it's loaded onto railroad cars." He inclined his head toward the depot and the long, seemingly endless train. Emily counted only one passenger car.

On Terry's main street, Emily spied a hotel, bank, land office, general store, dress shop, and a newer-looking building that had the word *RESTAURANT* painted across the top. Jake steered them to the side of the road, where they dismounted and tethered their horses.

"This is the Central Café. I thought we'd stop here for some lunch." Jake smiled. "My treat."

"My, but this ride has been so educational." Iris peered around, wide-eyed. Her gaze halted at the depot. "I wonder if there's room for one more passenger on that eastbound train." She looked at Jake. "Do you think?"

He hiked his hat up off his forehead and his dark eyes set on Emily. "Plan B."

"Ah…" She looked at Iris.

"Does that mean I won't have to ride this beast back to the Ready Web?" Iris pushed up her glasses.

"That's the thought, assuming there's room in the passenger car for you and, going east, there probably is. It'd be under a half-hour ride to Fallon."

"Thank God!" Relief spread over Iris's sharp features. "I can't bear to ride in this saddle a moment longer. I'm aching all over from all the jostling."

Jake turned to Emily. "Would you prefer the train as well?"

She took note of the challenge glimmering in his gaze and drew taller in the saddle. "Of course not. I'm having a wonderful time."

"Always have to keep up with the big boys, don't you, Em?" His teasing smirk only made her grin.

"Let's just say I can hold my own."

"I'd agree with that."

"High praise indeed." She smiled.

After dismounting and tossing Nickel's reins over the hitching rail, Jake helped Iris down off Cloud's back. She could hardly stand on her own.

Emily swung off her saddle and jumped to the ground. This divided skirt was truly a blessing. She hitched up Rusty.

"I'll lead Cloud home, Em."

"Thanks, Jake. I'd appreciate it." She sent him a look of gratitude. Rusty had been horse enough to manage.

Iris patted her arm. "Take heart, Emily. Every time I ride I get a little better at it. You're a fine teacher."

"And you just had your last lesson." She gave Iris a glare.

"Maybe Rez can teach you in time for the roundup." Jake had a good chuckle over that.

Emily giggled until Iris sent her a wounded frown.

After seeing the horses tethered, Jake faced them. "I'll go see about buying you a ticket, Iris. Why don't you ladies go on into the café and sit down? Tell Zelda I sent you and that I'll be along shortly."

Emily took hold of Iris's wrist and led her to the establishment's front door. Lace curtains hung in the two front windows; however, the nicety vanished when smells of raw wool and unwashed humanity assaulted her after she stepped inside. Her eyes watered.

She pulled Iris close. "I can't eat in this place."

"We'll get used to it, Em. Be brave."

"You're a fine one to speak of bravery, getting on the train instead of Cloud."

"We all have our ways of proving ourselves capable of living in Montana, don't we?" Iris stared her down.

"And riding the train back to Fallon alone is your way?"

"Perhaps. But perhaps there's someone on the train that God intends for me to speak with—a disheartened woman who can no longer manage the rugged life out here and is heading back east again."

Emily shook her head. Iris had quite the imagination. "Let me know how it goes."

A harried-looking woman approached them. "Ladies..." She smiled. "May I help you both?"

Emily spoke up. "Are you Zelda?"

"That'd be me." She smiled and the fanning of wrinkles at the corners of her eyes scrunched together.

"Jake Edgerton sent us for a table and said he'll join us shortly."

"Jake's back in town?" The woman looked old enough to be his mother, and she appeared just as pleased to hear the news. "I'll find you my best table right away. Wait here."

Making her way up the center of crowded tables, the woman stopped at a table of four unkempt men, playing cards. "You've eaten your meals, fellas, now out with you!" She moved her head toward the doorway, and Emily stepped to the side, pulling Iris along with her. "Go on. Out!"

The men grumbled but sauntered out of the café without incident. Then, with a wide scoop of her long, slender arms, Zelda cleared the tabletop and took the dishes to the back of the eatery. When she returned, she wiped the table clean and placed a bright yellow cloth over its top. At last she motioned for Emily and Iris to come and sit down.

The café quieted as they made their way to the table.

"Now, there's what I call dessert, Zelda."

Emily caught the leering grin of a dirty sheep man.

"You'd do well to watch your manners, Mr. Tate." Zelda set her hands on her small waist and sent him a withering stare. "These ladies are Deputy Edgerton's guests, and he'll be arriving soon. Besides—" Zelda turned her back on the man and placed her hands on the backs of Emily and Iris's scarred, wooden chairs. "—I'll tell your wife."

The other men in the café had a good chuckle over the glib remark, and their individual conversations ensued.

"I'll bet you both would enjoy a tall, cool glass of my spiced Ceylon tea. It's imported."

"Sounds refreshing." Emily's mouth did feel awfully dry.

"I brew in the early morning and let it cool. On a day like today, it tastes real good."

"Thank you, Miss Zelda." Iris smiled.

After the woman left to fetch their tea, Iris leaned toward Emily. "We're the only females in here."

"Yes, I see that." She smelled it too. But Emily felt safe enough, and all because Jake, evidently, was held in such high regard.

"I'm glad to be taking the train back to Fallon."

Emily didn't reply.

"Oh, now, Em, don't be miffed with me." A conspiratorial little smile curved her thin lips. "Maybe Jake will tell you the name of his young lady."

"If there is one." Emily wondered if Iris fabricated the whole thing.

"Oh, there is. I saw her with my own two eyes."

"Did you have your glasses on?"

"Hush." Iris gazed around the place. "What interesting men."

Emily held the checkered napkin to her nose, hoping to curb the stench.

"As my parents were missionaries in our remote village, I learned to adapt to almost any situation and people."

"A blessing for you." Emily's stomach turned.

Thankfully Zelda returned with their tea, and then Jake entered the café. He checked his saddlebags and rifle at the door and proceeded to nod greetings to some men, shaking hands with others as he made his way to their table. Reaching it, he placed a perfunctory kiss on Zelda's cheek.

"Jake Edgerton…my favorite customer." The woman's sunny expression bespoke of her delight.

"I thought I was your favorite customer," a man called from somewhere near the entrance.

Zelda just waved a hand at him, smiling fondly at Jake. "My special today is antelope stew."

The announcement combined with the earthy smells made Emily want to gag.

"We'll all three take a bowl, Zelda. Thanks."

"Coffee for you?"

Jake nodded. "And a glass of water too."

Zelda rushed off with their orders.

Emily sat forward. "Jake, I'm not feeling well."

"What's wrong?" He appeared genuinely concerned and placed one hand on the back of her chair.

"It's this place. I mean no insult and normally I can put up with almost anything."

"I admit it's raw in here today."

Emily held the spiced tea to her lips and inhaled. It relieved the oncoming nausea.

"Poor Emily." Iris leaned forward. "She's so sensitive."

She narrowed a simmering gaze at her friend.

Iris regarded Jake with the sweetest of expressions. "Were you able to get me a train ticket?"

"Yes, ma'am." He pulled it from his inside vest pocket, showed it to her, and then tucked it safely back away. Then he glanced at Emily. "Need some air?"

She nodded.

"Iris, behave yourself while I'm gone. If you need anything, call for Zelda."

"I'll do that."

Jake helped Emily up and led her out of the café. Once on the boardwalk Emily gulped fresh air, still wooly from sheep, but far better than inside the eatery.

"You okay, Em?"

She leaned against the side of the building. "This trip to Terry reveals Montana life, Jake, but I think our plan backfired." She held her stomach. "I'm the one who seems unsuited to the place." So much for her bravado over the horseback ride.

"Come on and sit down in the shade." He led her to a bench a short ways away and sat down next to her.

Down the road, Emily spied a dress shop. It would smell nice in there if it was anything like Aunt Agnes's boutique. She pointed to it. "How about I wait in there?"

"Your choice."

"Please make my excuses to Miss Zelda. She went out of her way to make things nice for Iris and me...and you too."

"Zelda will understand." Jake helped Emily to her feet.

"I apologize. I'm usually not so sensitive." Would he think she couldn't handle the rough life of ranchers and sheep men?

"Don't be. Even I could barely stand it inside. I might even opt to eat my stew out here on this bench."

Emily smiled. Perhaps he thought no less of her. It was only the smells that bothered her, after all.

Taking her hand, Jake molded it around his elbow and escorted her to the dress shop. "Iris and I will stop back for you in about a half hour."

Emily nodded, feeling ever so grateful.

With a tug on the brim of his hat, Jake turned and walked back to the Central Café.

Hearty laughter wafted to Jake from inside the café, alerting him to the fact he'd left Iris unattended so he could walk Emily safely to the dress shop. He entered Zelda's place with quick strides, but stopped short, seeing Iris standing in front of the entire group of men, telling one of her stories. Some of the roughest sheep men he knew gaped like children as they listened.

"And then he burst out the front plate window, knocking the criminal unconscious and apprehending that nefarious man once and for all." Iris sent him a fond smile. "I wrote a newspaper article all about it."

"Why, Jake…" Carl Buford stared at him, looking impressed. "You're famous in another state, even!"

Chagrin welled inside of him. "It was nothing." He made his way toward Iris. "Go back to whatever you were doing, men."

Iris sat down and smiled. Jake had to hand it to her, she was neither afraid nor repulsed by the foul smell in here, and it was a far sight worse than he even imagined it'd be during shearing season.

"I shouldn't have brought you and Em in here. Should have gone over to the Terry Hotel for lunch."

"No, this place has…character." Iris's gaze sparked. "I can't wait to tell my students all about this day. I never saw sheep shearing *en masse* before."

Jake set aside his Stetson, shrugged out of his jacket, and then tucked his napkin inside his shirt collar.

"I already asked a silent blessing on my food," Iris informed him, indicating to the steaming bowls on the table.

After an acknowledging nod, he did the same. Next he lifted his spoon and ate his stew without participating in much conversation, although he listened to snippets around him. Iris, on the other hand, chattered with Zelda awhile. A customer hailed her and Zelda returned to work. Moments later a rugged-looking fellow in a full beard, seated at the next table, relayed his life's story—in case Iris wanted to write about him too. Turned out, J. T. Johnson worked almost every job on almost every ranch in the area. Jake made a mental note. A guy like him would see a lot of things and know a lot of other men and their whereabouts.

"Well, that's very interesting, Mr. Johnson." Iris behaved as though she were at a tea party.

"Today I'm helping out the Lazy Day Ranch with the shearing."

"You're a busy man."

Johnson replied with a toothless smile.

"I reckon we'd best go fetch Emily." Jake stood. He waved to Zelda and when she came over he handed her a dollar for their meals. "Good and filling as always." He kissed the older woman's cheek. "See you again sometime."

"Thanks for stopping in." She turned to Iris. "I'm sorry your friend wasn't up to eating."

"She missed a fine lunch and good company." Iris clasped hands with Zelda. "God bless you. Take care."

Jake led the way out and, once on the boardwalk, glanced at his watch. "Got an hour and a half before the train leaves."

"I'll find something to occupy my time, I'm sure."

"Stay out of trouble."

ANDREA BOESHAAR

"Of course. Why would you even say such a thing?"

"Oh, I don't know." Jake grinned and started toward the dress shop, but came to a dead halt. There, standing just outside, was Emily, and she was conversing with Andy Anderson.

"Look, Jake!" Iris pointed to them. "Why, Andy looks just as handsome as ever!"

Something cold and deadly coursed through his veins.

Iris quickened her pace and Jake kept up, but she reached Emily and Andy first.

"Andy Anderson. Imagine running into you here in Montana." Iris batted her lashes and smiled while her cheeks turned apple-red.

"Hello, Iris." Andy removed his hat momentarily and then his blue eyes jumped to Jake. A sense of unease spread over Jake. "Hey, Jake, how're you?"

He shook Andy's hand in silent greeting before glancing at Emily. A heavy frown marred her brow. Something was wrong. "What are you doing in Terry? Thought you were headed to Idaho."

"I was until I heard that silver mining is the way to get rich. So I got off the train."

Jake gave a wag of his head. "Gotta go to the western part of the state for that. Should've stayed on the train a ways farther."

"So I've discovered." Andy's gaze darted around in a way that made Jake wonder if he'd gotten himself into a fix.

"So climb back on board. What's stopping you?"

He chuckled and plunged his hands into his jacket's pockets. "I just told Emily this same thing. I spent my last dollar at the hotel." He raised his hands in a helpless gesture. "I had to sleep somewhere."

"I'm sorry I couldn't help you out today, Andy." Emily spoke with a pained expression on her face. "I didn't think to carry along my reticule."

Asked her for money, did he? Jake's respect for the man plummeted to a new low. Plenty of work around here that a man could do to earn his keep. "Andy, as you can see from the state of things

206

here in town, there's a lot of shearing going on, and there's bound to be a rancher who would hire you."

"Oh, yeah. I suppose so."

So why didn't he? Andy had grown up on a farm. He knew how to handle animals, so he'd learn quickly. Well, Jake wasn't borrowing trouble.

"Ready to go, Emily? We've got a long ride back."

With a single nod, she stepped to his side.

"Iris?"

"I'm all set." She faced Andy again. "So nice to see you. I hope you'll write and let me know how you're faring out here."

"Write to you?"

Her blush deepened. "So I can tell Granny and our friends in Manitowoc."

"Oh, sure. I'll write."

Jake doubted he really would.

"Say, um…" Andy backed up and motioned for Jake to follow. "Can I have a word?"

Jake inclined his head, and when he moved around Emily, he gave her elbow a gentle squeeze. "Be right back."

A goodly distance down the boardwalk Andy stopped. Jake positioned himself so he could keep an eye on the ladies.

"What's up, Andy?"

"You don't look pleased to see an old friend."

He wasn't.

"I, um, get the feeling that you're sweet on Emily Sundberg, eh?" Andy grinned. "Good luck getting past the captain."

"He's the least of my worries."

Andy appeared impressed. Then he chuckled. "I remember a time when I came calling for you at your grandfather's house, back when we were kids. The old man showed me into that big ol' music room, and I looked out the window, only to see you and Emily kissing.

Whoo-whee." Andy wagged his head, slapped his knee, and hooted. "It looked like some kiss too."

Jake quickly put all the pieces together and clenched his fist. Not only did Andy relay the story to the boys at Sunday school, but also he stood by and watched Emily wrangle with the guilt and shame for months on end. "Thought that was funny, did you? I'll bet all your friends did too."

"Yeah, they did." Andy kept chuckling while glancing over his shoulder from time to time.

Jake wanted to break the man's jaw for hurting Em. "What do you want, Andy?"

"Can you lend me fifty dollars? Just a loan."

"Fifty? That's a lot of money."

"I've got debt at the hotel, and I'll need a train ticket."

"I'm going by the depot so I'll buy a ticket and leave it there in your name. Get on the train when you're ready. But I am not paying your debt. Work it off."

"But Jake…" Andy rubbed the sole of his boot against the edge of the boardwalk. "See, the truth is, I got into a card game last night, and if I don't come up with the money I lost by this evening, the fella's gonna kill me."

Jake didn't feel a shred of sympathy for him. He gave Andy a parting rap on the shoulder. "Good luck." With that he walked to Emily and Iris, who were peering into the dress shop window, discussing the gown on display. He clasped their elbows. "Shall we go, ladies? Iris has a train to board."

CHAPTER 22

*E*MILY STOOD NEAR the platform with the horses while Jake saw Iris safely to the station to await her train. She'd overheard his stern warning that once Iris reached Fallon, she was to walk to the post office and stay with "Aunt Susie," as the postmistress was known to all in the area. Iris promised she would.

Jake strode toward Emily. "Are you sure you wouldn't rather ride the train back to Fallon?"

"I'm sure." She grinned. "Do you think I'd ever be able to look my brothers in the eye if I didn't?"

Jake grinned at her retort, but it wasn't his usual. Emily could tell that their meeting with Andy had aggravated him, and it didn't appear that Jake loaned him the money for his badly needed operation.

"Jake?"

"Hmm?" He came around Rusty's left side.

"Is Andy going to die now?"

"Die?"

"Without his operation?"

The etchings around his eyes smoothed as his gaze softened. "Is that what he told you?"

"Yes, and I feel guilty for not doing my Christian duty and helping him."

"He lied to you, Em. He owes someone money that he lost in a card game or he owes some debt here in town. He tried both of those stories with me. Never said anything about needing a doctor's care."

Emily felt stunned. "What a rotten thing to do, that scoundrel!"

"I'd say so. Want a leg up?"

"No, thanks. I can manage." She mounted Rusty.

Jake climbed astride his horse and collected Cloud's reins. "Ready?"

Emily nodded and followed him out of town. But instead of riding parallel with the river, they crossed it before leaving the town of Terry behind them. Emily thought of Andy and wondered why she ever imagined he'd make a suitable husband.

Jake slowed his horse and motioned Emily beside him. "I thought I'd take you through a part of the badlands."

"Another lesson, Deputy?" She couldn't hold back the teasing.

"In a way, yeah. A lesson."

She saw him smile.

"Ever see buttes before?"

Emily shook her head, nearly unsettling the floppy-edged hat that Deidre lent her.

"You'll see them today and you can tell your class all about them this fall."

"I'm up for it."

"I hoped you'd say that."

For a number of miles they rode side by side with Cloud placidly trailing. Soon the terrain became rocky and uneven. The trail vanished. At one point they dismounted and walked their horses up an incline. Jake reached back for her hand, and Emily accepted the assistance over a particularly difficult area. When the land evened out, Emily realized they stood on a ridge. Strange reddish-brown rock formations loomed around them.

"These are buttes. And those—" He directed her attention to a number of dead tree trunks. "—are petrified trees."

"Petrified?"

"That's right. They're hundreds of years old and solid as rocks."

They tethered the horses, and Jake pulled his rifle from his saddle. Then they climbed a worn path through one of the buttes. Holding his gun over his right shoulder, he reached for Emily with his left gloved hand.

"Why do you need your gun?"

"Precaution is all."

Reaching a plateau, carved between two steep formations, she gasped as a panoramic view greeted her.

"I can see forever."

Jake pointed out the river to their southeast and the adjacent railroad tracks. Emily took a step forward in order to peek over the edge, and the stony ground below her feet crumbled. Jake clasped her upper arm.

"Not so close, Em." He pulled her beside him and cinched his arm around her waist.

"You rescued me again." She peered up at him and then leaned against him. She felt safe and protected. But did Jake think of her as only a friend—a friend he rescued quite routinely?

"Sorry for taking you to the café." His voice sounded close to her ear and a delightful shiver ran down her spine.

"No need to be sorry. I enjoyed visiting the dress shop anyway, and I told Mrs. Drew about my *Tante* Agnes's shop in Wisconsin. I explained where the state of Wisconsin is on the map." Glancing up at him again, she glimpsed his grin. His gaze captured hers for a long moment before Emily stared out over the wide landscape once more.

An ominous thunderlike growl and grumble shook the ground. Jake's hold around her waist tightened.

"What is it?"

"Watch."

Moments later Emily saw it. The train. Its shrill whistle split the peaceful afternoon.

"There goes Iris."

Hearing the smile in his voice, Emily grinned as the train rumbled past on the tracks below.

"Granddad was always fascinated by this place. He said it's where he could watch the world go by."

"A nice memory, Jake."

A weighty pause. "I can't hardly believe I'll never see him again." Sadness crept into his voice. "But that's the truth in this life. We're all appointed once to die…"

"…but after this the judgment," she completed the verse from Hebrews. "To think someday we will come face-to-face with the Lord Jesus Christ." She looked up at Jake once again. "I know it will be a judgment for some, but for those who know Him I like to think it'll be a sweet reunion. Isn't that what grace means, that with all our sins covered by Jesus, we should have no fear of death?"

A rueful smile inched across his face. "That's because you haven't faced death yet, Em."

"Think so?"

"I know so. But me? I've seen too much death in my lifetime." His gaze roamed the craggy landscape. "Frankly, I'm weary of it. I need a fresh start."

"Hmm…thinking about settling down, Deputy?" Maybe Iris was right and Jake would reveal the identity of the woman back home for whom he'd set his cap, except…Emily wished it was her.

"As a matter of fact…" Jake's gaze jumped to something over her head. "Look there, Em."

She turned and saw an enormous beast with a full rack stemming from his head. It looked like a strange cross between a moose and a deer. Two more came into view, obviously females as they bore no horns. Another of the same creature appeared. Four total.

"What are they?"

"Elk."

The bull brought his large head up and stared at them for several seconds before continuing on his way.

"If we didn't have to meet Iris in Fallon, we could hunt. Your father and brothers would be sorely envious of you."

"Too bad." She hated to pass on such an extraordinary opportunity, even if she disliked hunting. "This is a majestic view. I wish I owned a camera so I could capture it." *Or I wish I could live here. With you.*

But did she? Really? Emily couldn't be sure she'd survive the vastness of the badlands and prairies. Fallon was no town to speak of, only a handful of women resided in the area, and Montana winters were at least as long, snowy, and cold as Wisconsin's.

But Jake…

Emily disliked the thought of living the rest of her life without him.

"If you want a few keepsakes, our neighbor, Mrs. Cameron, photographs eastern Montana and sells her pictures at Aunt Susie's." The warmth of Jake's voice touched her ear and neck, and she smiled. "I'm sure you can find some pictures to your liking."

"Oh, yes, I remember seeing them displayed when Iris and I sent our telegrams." She turned and faced him and something bold and familiar awakened in Emily. Was it wrong to wish that he'd kiss her? Did he want to? She held his gaze. *Kiss me, Jake.*

His dark eyes narrowed. "I think we'd best get going." His words lacked conviction.

Forget about that woman in Manitowoc. Let's stay so you can kiss me.

"Iris might find more adventures."

Emily forced herself to lower her gaze and nod. Disappointment washed over her, but she tried not to let it show.

Jake helped her down through the butte. The gravelly path beneath her boots caused her to slide unless she stayed pressed against his muscled arm. By the time they reached the horses, Emily couldn't shake an idea made manifest by her conversation with Deidre last night.

"May I ask you something personal?" She folded her gloved hand around Rusty's reins.

"You may certainly ask." He tucked away his gun and grinned.

"Last night Deidre mentioned your mother. Did we just stand where...I mean, is up there where..."

"No. Suicide Bluff is nearer to the Ready Web, and I'd never take you there, Em."

"Why not? I'd like to see it."

A shadow of wariness drifted over his face.

"It's more than some morbid interest, Jake. Mr. Ollie and I talked about your mother's death at great length."

"It's a dangerous place. Too dangerous for a sweet lady like you." He smiled.

"I'm not easily persuaded by flattery."

"I'll remember that."

"Seriously, Jake, why won't you take me there? I owe it at least to Mr. Ollie's memory."

He pushed back his hat back and regarded her with a wounded expression in his eyes. "I haven't been back there since..." He swallowed and glanced off in the distance. "Look, Emily, I was the one who had to scale down to the rocky valley below Suicide Bluff and collect Ma's broken body. Couldn't just leave her lying in the crevasse."

Emily fought to hide her grimace, but she didn't pull it off.

"I'm sure you can understand why it's a place I never want to revisit. My granddad understood, so I expect you can too."

"Of course." His words shook Emily to her core. Collecting his mother's broken body? "That had to have been very traumatic for you."

"It was." He set his jaw as if fighting back the pain he still felt.

Obviously it hadn't healed with time. He rammed his dark gaze into hers. "Any more questions?"

She wetted her lips and shook her head.

"Then we'd best be on our way."

Emily climbed into the saddle and patted Rusty's neck. "I appreciate your candidness."

He mounted and sidled his horse up beside her. "I don't share particulars of my life with just anyone, Emily."

"You can trust me not to repeat them."

"That's not exactly what I meant, but—" His lips moved as he wrangled with his next words. But in the end he merely gave a tug on the brim of his hat. "Let's go."

As they rode back to Fallon, sometimes side by side, sometimes with Emily following, she got lost in her thoughts. Jake certainly was a complex mix. She pondered everything she knew about him, but more so what she didn't know. Then all at once she simply *had* to know the mystery woman's identity.

She nudged Rusty until she rode right beside him. "Jake?"

He slowed.

"One more personal question?"

"All right." He kept riding but leaned his palms against the saddle horn.

"Iris said that you're romantically interested in a young lady back in Manitowoc that both she and I know. Is that true?"

A puzzled grin turned to a broad smile. Then he chuckled, and its rich sound made Emily feel foolish. "Iris said that, huh?"

"Yes." She leaned forward and glimpsed his smile. Folly or not, she wasn't about to stop asking now. "So? Who is she?"

"Iris wouldn't tell you?" He still sounded amused.

"No. And that's so unlike her. We share everything—well, almost."

"Been thinking about it, have you?"

"Yes." Impatience nipped at her. "Who is she?"

"Well...you keep thinking on it, Em. It'll come to you."

"You're not going to tell me?"

"Nope."

Disappointment crashed over her.

He chuckled again, only this time he gulped back a portion. "I can't believe Iris told you such a thing. But I reckon I shouldn't be surprised. Beneath that harebrained head of hers is an abiding, special sense. A God-given quality that lets her know certain things before others do."

"We're still talking about my best friend Iris Hopper?"

"The very one."

"Are you in love with...*her*?"

Jake twisted in his saddle. "Have you lost your very mind?"

"Just making sure."

"Keep guessing." Jake's amused expression rankled Emily's nerves. "How about we discuss the love of *your* life now."

"It's not Andy Anderson, that's for sure, and I wasn't chasing him across the country either."

"So you've said." Jake's smile eased her defensiveness.

"But I did throw myself at him, and I'm ashamed of it. I'm embarrassed you witnessed it."

"Forget it, Em. Forget him."

"I did, up until this afternoon."

"No special feelings for him?"

Emily thought about it. "Irritation." She saw Jake grin once again.

"So...is there anyone you do have special feelings for?"

She decided to be honest, at least in part. "Yes, actually."

"Oh? What's his name?"

"I'll tell you if you tell me."

"No deal, Emily Sundberg."

She tossed a gaze heavenward. "You're still impossible, Jake."

"Yeah? Are you still ticklish?"

Wide-eyed, Emily gaped. "None of your business!" The memory of Jake pinning her down in the tall grass and tickling her until she couldn't breathe flashed across her mind. Eden had sat by and cheered him on.

"I'll take that for a yes."

"Don't you dare!" She heard him chuckling. "You're quite fresh, Jake Edgerton. When I find out who that young woman is—and I will find out—I'm going to tell her."

He turned her way and smiled, wide and full. "You do that, Emily. But for now we'd best quit talking and ride if we want to make it back to the ranch before supper."

Emily picked up his increasing pace, holding steady with little problem. Soon the rustic log buildings known as the town of Fallon appeared on the horizon.

CHAPTER 23

*H*OW WAS THE ride?"

"Good."

"Good?" Deidre turned from the kettle that simmered on her shiny new stove.

"Yeah, good." Jake smiled, seeing the interest in her eyes. "What are you cooking? Smells delicious."

"I love my new stove and oven. See the bread I baked?"

"I see." It had been one of the first things he'd smelled as he walked in.

"And to answer your question, I'm making venison and gravy over biscuits for supper, and later I'll bake a couple of chickens and a cake for tomorrow's Sunday meeting." She tipped her head. "You'll be in attendance, right?"

"Wouldn't miss it."

"Because Emily Sundberg will be in attendance?" she whispered. "Or because there will be a lot of food since everyone brings a dish?" Again that glimmer of interest in her gaze.

"Because I want to praise God with friends and family and get fed from God's Word." Jake knew his sister, and she'd likely pester him all night if he didn't tell her the details of this afternoon's ride with Em and Iris—at least some of the details. He glanced toward the closed bedroom door of the room Emily and Iris shared. The ladies had decided to change their clothes and take a rest before supper, and he didn't want to disturb them.

"I took them to Terry and into the Central Café to meet Zelda."

"You did what?" Deidre shook her head. "It's shearing season."

"I know. Em and I thought it'd be…" He didn't want to mention their plan to discourage Iris. "…educational."

"And? Was it?"

"Quite." Thoughts of Emily beside him on the butte, her upturned face and the interest sparking her sky-blue eyes filled his mind. It had taken every ounce of will he possessed not to kiss her. If he wasn't mistaken, she'd wanted kissing, and—Lord help him—he wanted to oblige her!

And then her trying to guess who he was in love with. Funny! As for their meeting with Andy Anderson—well, he wasn't about to tell Em that Andy was the culprit of the gossip that wounded her so badly. Best to let it die. But what Jake saw in Emily's actions and in her eyes made him believe that she genuinely hadn't ever been in love with the man. His initial inklings were right.

"Jake? You've got a funny grin on your face."

"Sorry 'bout that. Yes, our ride was quite educational." He smiled and dipped his forefinger into the cake batter.

"Now, stop it. That's for tomorrow."

"Mmm, tastes good."

"Thank you." She moved the bowl out of his reach. "But any more tastes and I won't have a cake to bake."

Jake straightened from where he leaned against a counter. "Then I guess I'll leave you to your cooking on that new stove."

"Oh, I'm so pleased with it. Thank you again."

"You're welcome." The happiness on his sister's face was worth ten times the amount he'd paid for the modern appliance. He thought of Ma and how much she would have enjoyed a new stove. Even Deidre's former one had been steps up from the old black iron thing Ma cooked on. "I'll go wash up before supper."

"Won't be too long now."

Jake headed for his cabin, heavy thoughts and memories pressing down on him. Em asked him to see the bluff, but how could he take her there when he couldn't muster the courage to ride out there himself? He went so far as to ride out of his way to avoid passing it.

He stood still on the path and made a slow circle, eyeing everything, seeing nothing but sadness on this ranch. Like a prevailing dark cloud, it didn't seem to matter what improvements Web made; Jake still saw the place where Pa was murdered, where Ma ended her life. Suicide Bluff taunted him, mocked him. Little wonder he stayed away.

Comfortably seated on the porch after supper with Jake, Iris, Rez, Charlie, and the Websters, Emily knitted a sweater, enjoying the feel of the soft, chocolate-brown yarn in her hands. She looked up to see the same color eyes watching her.

"That's not really my style." With a smirk, Jake glanced at the sweater then back at her.

"You have a style?"

"Hard to believe, isn't it?"

Emily smiled. "You'll be relieved to know I'm not making this for you. But I do love this color, so rich, like the promise of fertile soil in springtime."

Iris spoke up. "Emily always has been a little different when it comes to colors."

"Thanks, *best friend*." She gave Iris a pointed stare.

Iris smiled and waved a hand at her. "It's not your fault. It's from growing up with a twin brother."

"A twin?" Deidre looked up from the far end of the porch where she worked on her mending. "That's right. I'd forgotten that you have a twin."

"Shared the womb with my brother Eden."

"Even though he's younger than I am," Jake remarked, "Eden and I were great friends the summer I spent with Granddad. Mischief makers, the two of us."

"I remember." Emily had never forgotten.

The other three men didn't seem to be paying much attention, however. Web and Rez hummed along to the tune Charlie played on his harmonica, although Rez watched Iris as if he couldn't get his fill. The sight was worrisome to Emily. Things between Iris and Rez were happening much too quickly. What about their futures? Did Iris want to live in Montana, married to a ranch hand? Or were they both merely engaging in shameful flirtations?

"So you're partial to that color, huh?" Jake seemed interested in her yarn and the sweater she knit as he stood across the way. He leaned against a thick square support, which ran from the porch to the roof.

"Yes. Very much."

"How about a short stroll, Iris?" Rez stood and held out his hand, helping her to stand.

"What a fine idea." She set her slender hand into his calloused palm.

Emily watched them cross the porch and step down to the path that wound through Deidre's garden. Emily shifted on the bench.

"Are you making that sweater to sell in your aunt's shop?"

Jake's voice pulled her focus from Iris and Rez. "No, not the shop, but I do have plans for it."

"Oh? Like what?" He folded his arms across his chest.

She glanced at Deidre and Web, sitting next to each other, talking between themselves. "Jake, may I ask for yet another favor?"

"You can always ask." Smiling, he sent a nod toward the back door. "Want to step inside the house and talk?"

Emily thought that would be best and set her knitting aside to follow him.

When they faced each other in the great room, Jake asked, "What's on your mind?"

"I decided to finish the sweater with Deidre in mind and give it to her as a thank-you gift for hosting Iris and me. With a few minor alterations, it'll fit her fine. And it'll keep her warm this winter."

"That's real thoughtful of you, Em."

"You don't mind?"

One of his brows dipped. "Why would I mind?"

A rush of embarrassment flooded her face.

Jake leaned toward her. "Because you started it for...*someone else*?"

She stared at Jake's ivory cotton shirt with its brown and tan crisscrosses. "I was such a little fool..."

"Hardly." Jake wagged his head. "Just a mistake. The important thing is you learned from it."

"Indeed I did. Thanks to you, pointing things out that I'd known all along about Andy but didn't want to acknowledge."

"No need to bring it up again." Jake set his hands on his hips as she looked up into his face. She read earnestness in his expression. "As for the sweater, I think my sister will be very pleased."

"I'm glad you think Deidre will like it."

"So what's the favor?"

From her skirt's side pocket, Emily pulled a folded list of what she needed along with money. "Deidre mentioned you're going to Glendive on Monday. When the train made its stop there, I saw it's a larger town."

"That's right."

"Will you pick up these things for me?" She handed him the list. "That is, if it's not too much trouble."

"Five silver buttons, two yards of lace..." He glanced up at her. "That sweater will look real pretty on Deidre."

"Matches her eyes." *And yours.* Emily's heart skipped half a beat.

Jake held her gaze. "I'd be happy to."

"Thank you."

He inclined his sandy-blond head.

Several awkward minutes passed as they regarded at each other. How easy it would be to get lost in his stare. Curious thoughts ran through Emily's mind. If she were the one Jake loved, she'd be angry that he looked at another young lady the way he looked at her right now.

She placed her hands on her waist. "I should tell that girl in Manitowoc about your flirting with me."

"I don't flirt and play games, Emily." His gaze narrowed, and she glimpsed that hardened, serious side of him. "I like to think my actions are deliberate."

"What does that mean?" Her heart skipped a beat. *He isn't a flirt?*

"It means I enjoy staring at you. I don't mean to be rude. I think you're the most beautiful woman I've ever seen."

"Jake!" She laughed, hoping to cover the sudden rush of discomfort—and pleasure—she felt at his compliment. She touched the hair at her temple.

"I've told you that before. At least three times now."

His honesty embarrassed her, and Emily felt her face heating up as fast as Deidre's new oven.

"I'll pick up these things you've asked for." He pocketed her list.

"Thank you." Still flustered, she turned and walked back out onto the porch. She gazed out at nothing in particular as she tried to figure out what Jake's compliment and statement meant. But maybe they simply meant he found her pleasing to the eye. Emily had heard that before. Perhaps she read too much into it. Besides, they were friends.

"Are you all right, Emily?"

She blinked and looked at Deidre. "Oh, I'm just fine." She smiled for her hostess's sake.

"Don't worry about Iris. Rez is a good man."

"Oh?" Emily followed the direction of Deidre's nod and saw the couple walking toward the side of the ranch, toward the river. A moment later she felt a presence behind her then saw Jake as he moved to stand one step down. He faced her and held out one hand.

"It's a nice evening for it. Would you care to take a walk?"

Friends taking a walk.

Emily relaxed. "I'd enjoy that another time, Jake, but I'm rather tired from our ride today."

"Understandable." Amusement danced in his gaze. "After all, you didn't abandon the outing and hop on the train like someone we know." With a dip of his head, he indicated to where Iris walked, her arm linked with Rez's.

The evening breeze caused a rustling in the budding treetops. Emily smiled. "And I'm glad I didn't take the train. I had a nice time."

"Me too."

The rounds of his cocoa-brown eyes softened in that same way as on the afternoon of Mr. Ollie's funeral. They had stood by the window in the music room, facing each other, and he'd asked her if she wanted him to return to Manitowoc someday.

Before she could begin intellectualizing things all over again, Jake placed his hand beneath her elbow and guided her back to where Deidre and Web sat. Charlie was still perched on the porch rail and played his harmonica. Emily sat and lifted her knitting into her lap and Jake seated himself beside her. His left arm came to rest across the top of the bench behind Emily. She gave him a stare that said, *Do you mind?* Evidently he didn't because he didn't move.

Truth to tell, she didn't mind either.

"I'm amazed when I watch you knit, Em. I've never seen a woman's needles work so fast."

Charlie stopped playing and stared. "Why, sure 'nough."

Emily hadn't meant to show off. "I've been knitting since I was old enough to hold knitting needles."

Jake's gaze hopped to his sister and brother-in-law. "Emily's grandmother started a business—"

"A boutique."

"Beggin' your pardon. A boutique."

Emily smiled inwardly. Jake was fun to tease.

"Anyway, it's called Sundbergs' Creations, and now Em's aunt runs the place, and that's just one of the Sundberg family's businesses. Her father runs a shipping and freight company."

"Actually Grandpa Ramsey, Uncle Will, and his father are part owners as well."

"That's right. I remember now."

Emily smiled at him and kept knitting but sent a glance Deidre and Web's way. "Poor Jake met almost everyone all at once. My family can be overwhelming."

"I'm sure he handled it just fine." Web stretched.

"Em's brother-in-law's family owns two hotels in town." Jake continued bragging on her family. "I stayed at one, since Aunt Bettina and Uncle Dwight took over Granddad's place for a time."

"I still can't believe Aunt Bettina had the nerve to return after everything she and that leech of a husband put Granddad through." Deidre caught herself. "Oh, my apologies, Emily. I shouldn't be airing our family troubles."

"It's quite all right, Deidre." She meant each word. "I understand. Even Sundbergs have skeletons in their closets, so to speak."

"Sure, honey." Web pressed a kiss to Deidre's temple. "There's trouble in every family."

"What sort of trouble lurks in the Sundberg ancestry?" Jake asked.

It wasn't a secret, so Emily told him. "My mother's older sister in London had been ruined by the master's spoiled and selfish son. Feeling as though she had no other choice, she made one bad decision after another and then died a lonely drunkard."

"How sad." Deidre's features fell. Her dark gaze clouded.

"Then Momma had to run for her life, and she ended up on

Poppa's ship, heading for America. The rest…well, you can imagine, as here I sit today."

Charlie tipped his head. His bushy brows furrowed. "You making that up, little Missy?"

"No, it's the truth."

Seconds of silence ticked by.

"Well, like I said, there's trouble in all families," Web said.

"You're right." Deidre's eyes fixed on Emily then hopped to Jake. Emily turned to find him staring at her knitting. She hesitated and his gaze met hers. He smiled and Emily was reminded again how nice it felt to sit beside him.

"Say, Jake, will you help me move the table out here to the porch?"

"Sure."

"I think I only have one more heavy move in me for this week. That stove took everything I got."

Jake ground out an amused-sounding guffaw.

"But I'm so very grateful, Boyd." Deidre glanced Emily's way. "After the table is out of the way, perhaps you and Iris will help me with the final preparations for the Sabbath tomorrow."

"I'd be happy to." Emily looked toward where Rez and Iris still strolled on the edge of the garden. The evening breeze carried her friend's quivery laugh. Emily set aside the sweater she made. "I'll go get Iris right now."

CHAPTER 24

WAGONS FILLED WITH families and men on horse-back began arriving early on Sunday morning. Emily inserted the last pin into her thick hair and sent a quick glance across the bedroom at Iris.

"Ready?" Emily turned and inspected her appearance one last time in the beveled mirror above the bureau. She smoothed out the last of the wrinkles in her two-piece silk ensemble with its lace trim. Momma always said the dress's peach color complemented Emily's complexion and caused the color of her hair to stand out.

"I'm ready. How do I look?"

"Lovely as always." The blue-and-white-striped dress with its wide white belt looked summery, and Emily envied her friend's tiny waist.

"Thank you. You're lovely as always too." After a smile, Iris pushed up her glasses and moved the curtain to one side. "I don't see Rez, but there are plenty of other men in the yard, several children, and...only four other women."

"I'm sure Rez will be along soon." Emily opened the door.

"Oh, dear...I think we may have overdressed."

She closed it again and strode to the window, peering outside. The four women she glimpsed wore dark skirts and crisp light-colored blouses. Floppy bonnets covered their heads.

She stood back. "So now what? I washed out my everyday skirts last night. They're still drying."

Iris shrugged. "We'll just be examples of city fashion."

"I hope we're not perceived as snobs."

"We'll just have to be extra friendly."

"But not too friendly to the men, Iris. You heard Jake's warning last night. Some men take a smile to mean you're willing to get married."

"And isn't that just something!" Iris giggled softly. "I never heard such a thing."

"Women are scarce out here, and men need help on their farms and ranches." She wagged a finger at Iris. "So be careful. Jake said he wasn't rescuing any damsels in distress today." She smiled again at his pun.

"Oh, that Jake—he's got such a facetious wit, doesn't he?"

Before Emily could reply, Iris walked forward and then led the way into the great room. It looked even more spacious with the dining table removed.

Deidre spotted them and waved them outside where she introduced them to her friends, who each held a picnic basket or a kettle. But that wasn't the last of the foodstuff. As the wagons were unloaded, the kitchen filled with jars of pickles and preserves, smoked ham and beef, roast chicken, fresh breads, and sweet treats. However, Emily knew from experience that in the presence of hungry men it wouldn't last long.

The service was held in the yard. Chairs were brought from the porch and blankets spread on the grass. Emily steered Iris over to where Deidre and Web planted themselves in the shade of the unpainted barn. Jake, Rez, and Charlie sat nearby. A man in a white shirt and brown vest stood, Bible in hand.

"That's Reverend Taylor." Deidre leaned partially over Emily so Iris could hear her whisper. "His wife died in childbirth a couple of years ago, leaving him with four children to care for and a farm to manage."

"How tragic." Iris's hand fluttered to her throat, and Emily could practically hear the gears turning in her friend's head.

She nudged Iris and gave her a stern look. She wouldn't dare pit Rez against the reverend...would she?

Iris batted her eyelashes.

The reverend delivered an informal but eloquent message from Philippians chapter four on the peace of God that passes all understanding and keeps our hearts and minds through Christ Jesus. Emily figured the man ought to know, having experienced such loss in his life. She looked at Iris, who had also experienced tremendous loss and grief. At fifteen she'd lost her parents, missionaries. Emily supposed that out of the two men, Rez or the reverend, Reverend Taylor would make the most likely choice of husband for Iris.

But what did Emily know?

Her gaze drifted to Jake. Whom was he interested in, and just what would that woman say when she learned of his *friendship* with Emily? If in her position, Emily wouldn't allow her *forloveden* to have such a good female friend. And if Emily knew of this young lady, as Iris claimed, then the woman had to reside in Manitowoc. So would they write to each other, or did Jake plan to give up his job and move back to Wisconsin to court her?

Jake glanced her way and Emily started. She'd been staring so hard that it was little wonder Jake felt it. They exchanged smiles before Emily refocused on the reverend's message.

When the minister finished speaking, everyone stood and sang a hymn together. Another man said a closing prayer, adding a blessing on their noon meal. The children scattered, the boys chasing each other. Emily noticed that she and Iris garnered more than a few curious stares. Web saved himself the trouble of making individual introductions and shouted a general announcement.

229

"We have guests today. Miss Emily Sundberg and Miss Iris Hopper all the way from Wis-con-sun."

Emily grinned at his pronunciation of the state. However, when she saw interest light up several men's countenances, she decided to heed Jake's warning and stay close to the house, assisting Deidre and the other women with serving lunch and cleaning up afterward. Iris wisely did the same. Then they congregated on the back porch to sew, knit, and share bits of news. One of the men found a round, thick piece of wood that sufficed as a bat, and another used his new wife's biscuits as baseballs, much to her chagrin.

"I just can't get that recipe down no matter how hard I try."

"There, there…" Emily put her arm around the plump young woman who didn't look much older than herself. "I can't cook at all, so don't feel bad."

"What?" Deidre obviously overheard and stepped toward them. "You don't know how to cook, Emily?"

"Well, I'm sure I'll learn when I have my own kitchen. But Momma only knows the basics and isn't much of a cook. My grandmother always prepared our meals." Emily smiled. "Turns out that I'm better at climbing trees than baking biscuits." She gazed at the woman who now dried her eyes. "So you see? You're a far better domesticate than I am. Even if you bake baseballs." It was rather amusing.

A contest ensued to see which man could wallop the biscuit the farthest. Women and children watched from the back porch, cheering on their favorites.

"Excuse me. May I have your attention?"

Hearing Iris's voice, Emily watched in horror as her friend stood in front of the men. "What are you doing?"

Iris ignored her. "I will give a kiss on the jaw to the winner—provided he's not married, of course."

The men cheered and chuckled.

Emily gasped. Her mouth fell open. Unbelievable! She turned to Deidre. "We have to stop her."

"I'm afraid it's too late."

Emily's gaze followed Iris's sashay up to the porch. She longed to shake that girl until her senses returned. She stepped toward Iris, but Deidre halted her by clasping her wrist.

"You can't always protect her, Emily."

"I'm not, but—" She tried to pull out of Deidre's grasp and failed. The woman had a surprisingly firm yet gentle grip.

"Let her be, Em. She's a grown woman who's made a public offer. Now she'll have to pay any consequences that arise."

"Iris is naïve. She needs protecting."

"But not from you, Em." Deidre pulled her into the house and then into the room Emily shared with Iris. She closed the door.

Emily sensed a reprimand coming on. "I've done something wrong?"

"No." Deidre shook her light-brown head. "You have been a good friend to Iris. But she and I had a chance to talk, and Iris mentioned that she's felt as though she's been living in your shadow for years. You're the pretty one, the privileged one... the protected one. Here in Montana Iris hopes to find her place and her time to shine."

"By behaving like a hussy?" Her time to shine, indeed! Emily took umbrage at Iris's remark. She and her family had done everything in their power to be Iris's surrogate family.

"She's not behaving like a hussy." Deidre folded her arms and gave Emily a soft grin. "She's giving Rez a little incentive." The grin became a smile. "You know he'll win, right?"

Emily rolled a shoulder. "How would I know that?"

"Well, I guess there's only one way to find out." Deidre opened the door and motioned Emily to follow. But then she paused near where the dining table once stood. "Jake said you're spoken for already, so I—"

"Spoken for?"

Deidre momentarily pressed her lips together. "Oh, dear…is it a secret?"

"I guess so." And one kept from Emily. She tipped her head, curious. "Did Jake say who's done the speaking?"

Deidre shook her head. "But I'm pretty sure I know. I mean, it's obvious."

"Is it?" Emily feigned a laugh. "Of course it is." She had no idea.

"My brother never could hide his feelings, at least not from me."

Emily blinked.

"Like I said yesterday. I haven't seen Jake this happy in a long time." She tugged on Emily's wrist. "Come on. We're missing the fun."

Me! How had she been so blind, such a dunce? Or perhaps she'd been afraid to hope that Jake would feel for her what she felt in her heart for him.

Smiling to herself, Emily recalled their friendly banter as they rode toward Fallon. No wonder Jake had laughed so hard. And the way he'd held her so close to him while they stood on the butte. How he enjoyed watching her knit. *Absolutely amusing!*

A hearty cheer drew Emily's attention, and she walked onto the porch. With one arm around a support post, she looked for Jake and found him watching the sport a short distance away. He seemed to sense her presence. His gaze found her, and he grinned. She replied with a tiny wave. *Jake's love interest from Manitowoc.* Really? Could it really be? Yesterday he said he considered settling down. But what about his job? Did he plan to live out his future here on this ranch? But he said ranching wasn't his calling. Did he have other plans?

Emily's mind filled with questions, although she knew first things first. As soon as she got the opportunity, she'd corner Jake and tell him she'd guessed the riddle—the identity of his mystery woman. It was…*herself!*

✾✾

"You sure you want to do this, Jake?"

"I'm sure."

Fellow deputy Roy Gentry fell silent for several moments as they ambled down the road leading to and from the Ready Web. "I'm disappointed to say the least."

"I appreciate it, but the fact is I want to settle down."

"You can do that and still be a deputy marshal. I have."

"I realize that and don't think I didn't consider it."

"You've been deputized by four different marshals. Know why? Because folks around here know that you're honest, trustworthy, patient, and fair—even to the Indians."

"I've tried, Roy, so I'm glad that I'm leaving the profession with a good reputation."

His burly friend, a man who'd been part of the posse that tracked down Pa's killers, worked his thumbs under his suspenders. "It's more than that, Jake. We need you."

"No, you don't. There are plenty of other good men who can step into my place." When Roy started to debate, Jake held up a forestalling hand. "My mind's made up. Tomorrow when I report for duty in Glendive, I'm turning in my badge."

"Wish you'd at least give it another thought."

"Done thinking on it, Roy." Jake's tone was sharper than he'd intended.

"All right then." He snapped up a long piece of prairie grass and chewed on the end of it. "So who's the lucky girl?"

Jake grinned. He knew that question was coming. "Emily Sundberg."

"That red-headed filly?"

"Right." Although Jake would say her hair was more russet than red.

"Pretty little thing." Roy gave him a sideways glance. "Seems kinda quiet, though. You sure you want a quiet woman? A man never knows what them quiet ones is thinking."

Jake laughed. "Emily is not quiet. Trust me."

"Okay." Another hesitation. "It's good you found a woman to love, Jake. I'll admit that Verona and I sometimes worry about you. God said it ain't right for a man to be alone. And you're young enough yet, not so set in your ways that a woman can't share your life."

"I plan to move to Manitowoc, Wisconsin, and live in Granddad's house. He left it to me. It feels like…like home."

Roy stopped and stroked his grizzled face. "You're leaving Montana too? That's quite a blow you've hit me with. If you leave, that's one less God-fearing, law-abiding soul in the county."

"I know. And I apologize for the disappointment you feel. But I've got to follow my heart on this one, Roy. Besides…" Jake grinned. "I can always visit."

"And speaking of…" They resumed their slow amble. "Have you been over to Suicide Bluff yet?"

"Nope, and I don't plan on going near it any time soon."

"I think you might want to reconsider."

Jake gave Roy a glance, but didn't reply.

Again Roy halted. "You can't begin a new life until you've made friends with the past, Jake."

"The past ain't been any sort of friend to me."

"And that's my point. You can't carry all the hurt and anger that's inside you into your marriage. It'll haunt you there as much as it does right now."

Jake's temper simmered. His friend walked a precarious edge right now. "We'd best get back to the house."

"You never struck me as a coward, Jake. Not in any situation."

"You can't goad me, Roy." He turned and strode toward the house.

"I'm your friend, Jake, and it's my duty to tell you the truth."

Jake stopped so the man would quit his hollering. With his back to him, he waited for Roy to finish his rant, mentally protecting himself from the words sinking too deep. This wasn't the first time Jake heard this particular advice. But no one really understood what he thought and felt. The pain was unbearable. Miserable. And it wasn't so simple as *making friends*.

"It's a fact, Jake. A man has to go back in order to move forward. It's just like tracking a murderin' thief. You find out where he's been before you can figure out where he's at."

Several moments of silence, and then Jake walked back to the house alone.

CHAPTER 25

*T*HE GUESTS LEFT, and Emily assisted Deidre in cleaning up afterward. Just light duty, as Deidre believed in resting on the Sabbath. They retired to the porch where a cool breeze greeted them along with Charlie's harmonica playing. A ways off, near the fruit trees, Emily spotted Iris and Rez, strolling along. He'd got his kiss on the jaw, but Emily still felt a bit hurt that her best friend thought she cast an oppressively tall shadow over her. They'd been best friends for more than eight years. Whatever Emily had, she'd shared with Iris, including her dreams and disappointments. But, on second thought, she'd never told Iris about kissing Jake under the oak. She'd been too ashamed. If Iris ever heard gossip or rumors about it, she'd never said, so Emily never had to explain.

Thinking of Jake caused Emily to realize she hadn't seen him in a while. Where'd he run off to? An afternoon nap in his cabin?

"Come on over here and sit a while, Emily." Deidre called to her from the left end of the porch where the dining table stood.

She smiled and headed that way. But about that same time Jake came from the barn, leading Nickel and Rusty. Both animals were saddled.

His gaze found hers as he walked across the yard. Nearing the porch, Emily glimpsed his fallen features, darkened by the brim of his Stetson, and somehow knew things were amiss.

"Want to go for a ride?"

She nodded. "Wait here while I change. It'll only be a few minutes." She faced Deidre. "May I borrow your split skirt again? It's hanging in the room I share with Iris."

"Of course." A little frown puckered Deidre's brow. "Anything wrong, Jake?"

"Nope." He put one booted foot on the first porch step.

Emily hurried inside to change. Without so many petticoats to wear, changing into the split skirt was a simple task. Next she unpinned her hair, allowing it to fall down her back in one thick braid, like yesterday. Chances were she'd lose the pins during the ride anyway.

Back outside she smiled at Jake as she approached Rusty. She rubbed the horse's nose. "I'm ready."

Jake handed her the reins and politely assisted her into the saddle. Then he mounted Nickel.

As they rode slowly out of the yard and down the dirt road, Emily waited for Jake to say something. A good minute went by before he did.

"Will you ride to Suicide Bluff with me?"

Surprised, she looked his way, but his gaze remained straight ahead. "Of course I will." So many more questions filled her, but the time didn't seem fitting to ask.

They steered their horses the opposite way as they'd gone yesterday and then made another turn, away from the river and going farther into a stretch of badlands.

Finally the path became impassable on horseback. They dismounted and walked up a steep incline, using the boulders on either side of them for leverage. Then suddenly they stood on a narrow ridge. Another steep incline lay ahead, but a weathered wooden fence blocked their entrance. The word *DANGER* had been painted across one plank.

"That's it up there." Jake stepped up to the fence. "If you look over there—" He pointed to the right. "—you can get a sense of how deadly the fall might be."

Emily strode to a short, hip-high rocky formation, looked over its width, and glimpsed the stony crevasse below. She looked back at Jake's bowed head. He'd removed his hat and held it against his chest. His other hand gripped the top plank of the wood barricade. Emily felt his sorrow. Her heart ached for him.

She walked to his side and hugged his right arm. He moved and pulled her against him, holding her so tightly that Emily could barely pull in a breath.

"Can I hold you a minute?" He spoke the words into her shoulder. She felt each one.

"Yes, and squeeze me as hard as you want if it helps." She pressed her hands into his muscled back. "I won't break."

His shoulders moved in a way that made Emily think he was...crying? She'd never seen a grown man cry. Was it possible? A rugged, experienced deputy marshal? Tears filled her own eyes. He had to be in an enormous amount of pain.

She said nothing. No words came to mind that might soothe him.

His left hand cupped the back of her head, and she heard him exhale then sniff as if he had a cold. Long moments passed before he relaxed his hold around her. His breathing slowed.

"This has been a long time coming." Jake kissed the side of her head and gently pushed her away. One arm remained around her waist, the other on her shoulder. "I spent the last hour praying about something a friend said earlier. As much as I hate to admit he was right, he was."

"About what?"

"About...making friends with the past." He gazed off in the distance before looking into her face once more. "You see, I never let myself grieve for Ma. That is, I never let it out. I avoided it—and this place. Does that make sense?"

Emily nodded.

"But you're the only one I trusted to be with me right now."

"I'm glad." High compliment indeed! She removed the borrowed riding gloves, letting them drop, before reaching up and wiping a spot of moisture from his face. "Do you feel better?"

He appeared to think it over. "Maybe." His right shoulder moved up and down. "Guess I do."

Emily smiled. As fickle as a female, as Poppa liked to tease.

Jake's gaze narrowed as if he read her thoughts.

Emily stepped closer and hugged him around the waist. Her ear to his heart, she heard its strong, steady beating. *Lord, I love him.* Jake pressed a kiss on her forehead. *And he loves me.*

"I figured out who your true love is." Maybe now wasn't the time or place, but Emily couldn't rein in her own feelings a second longer.

"About time."

She straightened and longing filled her as she looked in his dark eyes. She cupped his face, stood on tiptoe, and kissed him on the mouth. The instant their lips made contact, Emily knew without a doubt that she'd loved Jake for almost half her life.

"Mmm…" Jake pulled back and wagged his head. A grin twitched the corners of his mouth. "Emily Sundberg, bold as brass."

"Not usually." Her hands slid around his neck, and she sagged against him.

"I'm glad to know that." He made no attempt to free her—or be freed.

"The truth is I gave my heart away to you when I was thirteen years old. I tried to forget you, but I never could. That's why I was so angry to see you again. Just when I thought that maybe Andy Anderson might fill the void you left in my heart, you burst back into my life."

Jake stared at her, vulnerability pooling in his eyes.

"I love you, Jake."

"You mean it?"

"From the depths of my being. Maybe knowing this will help heal your heart. Admitting it has helped heal mine."

He leaned slowly forward, his lips seeking hers, claiming them. The magic happened all over again. Emily closed her eyes and kissed him back until the air left her lungs.

Jake moved slightly back. They shared a breath. "I guess my fate is sealed." He sounded breathless himself. "At least according to your father."

Emily smiled and snuck another quick kiss.

Amusement danced in Jake's gaze, and then Emily glimpsed forever there too. "I love you, Emily, more than words can ever say."

"I know."

He gave her braid a little tug as payback for the sassy reply. Then he gazed up at the bluff; however, the sadness had been erased from his face. "I think my heart is healing, Em."

She clung to him. "What was she like?"

"Ma?"

"Uh-huh."

He rested his head on hers. "Soft-spoken, sweet, caring. Like Deidre, only not as talkative."

Emily tried to imagine what Jake's mother looked like.

"She was nothing like my aunt! Just the opposite. And she would have liked you, Em."

"I have a feeling that I would have liked her as well."

Jake talked on about his mother, and Emily didn't interrupt him. With arms still around his waist, she stared up at the bluff, listening to him and yet pondering the same question that plagued Jake, Deidre, and Mr. Ollie all these years. *Why?*

A glint of something in the rock caught a ray of evening sun, and Emily blinked. And then she saw it.

"Jake!" She gasped. "It's there. It's truly there!"

"What?" His body tensed.

"The lockbox. I see it, hiding in the rock at the top of the bluff. Look!"

"Emily—"

"Look!" She broke free and pointed, hoping she didn't lose sight of it as the sun sank deeper into the sky.

Jake shoved his hat onto his head, and then with forearms on the barricade and a booted foot on the lowest plank, he stared upward.

"Do you see it?" She saw his eyes searching the rock formation. "See it?"

He pursed his lips and squinted.

Emily tugged on his elbow, pulling him several steps to his right. "See it now?"

A second later, Jake's eyes widened. He saw it!

Relief mixed with excitement coursed through her. "Let's get it. If we're careful, we can climb—"

"No."

"No?" Emily wouldn't accept the answer. "But we owe it to your late grandfather, to Deidre and your unborn niece or nephew to get the box. It proves your mother fell. She didn't jump."

Jake's gaze jerked to hers, and she sensed he weighed his options.

"We need to get that lockbox tonight."

"Not 'we,' Emily. There's no way I'll let you risk your life." He reached for her hand. "You're too important to me. Let's go back to the house."

"You can't be serious?"

"I am. You mean everything on earth to me."

"Thank you, but don't you think we'll all sleep easier tonight if—"

"I'll get that lockbox before nightfall, but I need Web, Charlie, and Rez to help." They reached the horses. "I also need a passel of dynamite."

"Isn't that extreme?" Emily swung her leg over the saddle.

Jake grinned. "Not if I intend to blow Suicide Bluff to kingdom come!"

"But the lockbox! Won't it be blown to kingdom come too?"

"Don't you worry." Jake sent her a smile. "I'll safely retrieve it before I blow up the bluff."

Emily awoke the next morning and immediately smiled. Many miracles occurred last night. It seemed to take forever, but finally she, Iris, and Deidre felt the consecutive blasts that shook the very house in which they waited for the men to return. The china clattered in the cabinet, and glass panes rattled in windows, but Deidre was so relieved to learn her mother's death had been an accident and not suicide that she said she'd willingly suffer with any collateral damage, although there was none. And while the men were blowing up Suicide Bluff, Deidre carefully leafed through the lockbox. It was weathered, but it was identical to the one Mr. Ollie left to Jake.

A sigh passed through Emily's lips. But the best part of the night was that she'd found out he loved her—and she loved him.

And it had been with great delight that Emily told Iris that she'd guessed the identity of Jake's *mystery woman*. Afterward they'd giggled as if they were sixteen again!

A rooster crowed, and Emily remembered that Jake was leaving for Glendive this morning. She wanted to see him before he rode off.

Taking care, she slipped from beneath the bedcovers. Iris still dozed peacefully, no doubt dreaming of Rez the ranch hand. Emily had heard only good things about him thus far, and she wouldn't dare interfere. It still hurt, though, to think Iris had harbored feelings of inadequacy all these years when Emily loved her as much as if they were sisters.

She dressed in a red and ivory pinstripe walking dress with empire waist. Probably too fancy for a day on the ranch, but most of Emily's wardrobe had been tailored for teaching school and afternoon garden parties. After brushing out her hair, she twisted it into a knot and let it hang between her shoulder blades. She'd pin it up later. She simply couldn't miss seeing Jake off.

As she hoped, she found him drinking coffee on the back porch. He looked every bit the US deputy marshal in his white shirt, coal vest, and black trousers. She guessed he'd don a dress jacket to complete his ensemble.

"Good morning, Jake." She spoke softly so as not to wake anyone else.

He stood from the step and faced her. "Morning, Em." His gaze ran the length of her. "My, but you're a pretty sight."

"A bit overdone for my visit here at the ranch, but I was, um, misled when I packed."

Jake grinned. "You're beautiful."

"Thank you." She stepped forward and clasped his outstretched hand with both of hers. "How are you feeling this morning?"

"Like a new man."

He didn't appear to be teasing either. "Good."

"Want some coffee?"

Emily shook her head. "Is your assignment today dangerous?" She hoped not—prayed not.

"No. I'm giving testimony in front of a judge today regarding a man I apprehended."

"Did he kill someone?"

Jake shook his head. "Stole some livestock and drove them into North Dakota to get back at his second cousin who, supposedly, stole them first."

"Well, please be careful."

Jake set down his coffee cup and caressed her cheek. "Don't worry, all right?"

Emily nodded, wondering if deputies' wives ever grew accustomed to their husbands' often-perilous professions. Did Jake plan on continuing his role as a deputy marshal, even though it was, as he said, a widow-maker?

"I've been wondering if you should send a message to my father...about our...you know, courtship."

Jake drew in a breath. "I ain't interested in courtship, Em."

A stab of disappointment. "I see." Had she misunderstood something?

"I want to marry you." The huskiness in his tone sent an exquisite shiver down her spine. "I'm praying you want the same thing."

"I want it very much." She stepped closer and slipped her fingers between his. "I can't imagine my life without you."

He gave her hand a gentle squeeze.

"Will you kiss me again?" She tipped her chin upward.

"Yes, but not this minute." He grinned before his gaze skipped to the cabin door. "G'morning, Sissy."

A shot of embarrassment flamed her cheeks. Had Deidre overheard?

"Well, good morning, you two."

Emily turned to see Deidre step onto the porch.

"I hope you slept as well as I did."

Emily nodded and smiled, hoping her blush wouldn't give her completely away.

"I see you're ready to leave, Jake."

"All set." He tossed the remainder of his coffee. "I'll be back at suppertime."

"Wonderful. In the meantime, I'll do my best to entertain Emily and Iris. Cooking lessons, perhaps." She winked at Emily.

"Cooking...*lessons*? Am I to understand that you can't cook, Emily?"

She shrugged. "It can't be that difficult, and I'm an expert assistant. *Besta* tells me that all the time."

Jake didn't seem too worried about starving to death. "Listen, you two, just keep Iris out of trouble. And I've got your list, Em."

She smiled her thanks. Even with everything that happened yesterday, he hadn't forgotten about the buttons, ribbon, and lace that she needed for Deidre's sweater.

Jake handed his sister his empty cup. "See you ladies tonight."

CHAPTER 26

*J*AKE FIXED HIS thoughts on Emily for most of the way to Glendive, although he kept a watchful eye on his surroundings and his shotgun close at hand. Wasn't heard of for lone riders to get ambushed, robbed, beaten, or worse. Jake never feared death, but for the first time that he could remember, he had something to live for, something tangible and real: Emily Sundberg. He almost didn't feel worthy of such a blessing, and he soon imagined her setting up housekeeping in Granddad's house. Had he mentioned it? What if she didn't want to live next door to her family? Was she and Deidre teasing him about Emily not being able to cook? What woman didn't know how to cook?

Emily Sundberg. Jake chuckled to himself.

Reaching Glendive, his guard went up. Couldn't afford distraction. After giving his sworn account of the night he arrested Jimmy McJeevers, he walked over to the general store and purchased Emily's buttons, lace, and ribbon. Afterward he strode to the marshal's office. He was glad to see Marshal Lloyd was in his Dawson County office today. The man owned a dairy farm and ranch near Butte but made monthly appearances in Dawson County, as it was one of the state's largest with a vast amount of open territory. His visits usually corresponded with the judge's appointments, although Marshal Lloyd had only been in office four months now.

"Nice to see you again, Edgerton."

"Likewise, sir." Jake shook his hand but didn't mince words. He gave his resignation and turned in his badge.

The conversation that followed echoed the one he'd had with Roy yesterday afternoon. Was he sure? The marshal was sorely disappointed to lose such a valued deputy.

"But I'm glad to write you a reference, Jake." The clean-shaven man with white-blond hair opened the side drawer of the wide oak desk, reached in, and extracted a piece of official stationery. Pen in hand, he scribbled out a few sentences, and as the ink dried he found a matching envelope. "Kind of a shame, though. You were sworn in by three of my predecessors as well as myself, although I assure you, I've been much more selective than they were."

"Thank you, sir." He respected Marshal Charles Lloyd, a West Point man who'd fought in the Sioux Wars. He'd only been appointed to his current position earlier this year, but Jake had a hunch they would have seen eye to eye on most things. Not all, but most.

"I'm partial to Wisconsin. My family moved there from Sweden when I was an infant."

"Thought I heard you grew up in Iowa." Jake tucked the marshal's letter into his coat's inner pocket.

"We moved to Iowa when I was about twelve, and I have connections in the Midwest still, so my reference should prove valuable."

"I appreciate it, sir."

They shook hands again before Jake left the office. Standing on the boardwalk, the world looked like a different place, now that he no longer was a US deputy marshal. The job had consumed him. He'd given it his all, done his best, and his efforts hadn't gone unnoticed. Feelings of intense satisfaction spread throughout his being.

He strode up the walk and stepped into a local eatery, ordered some lunch. He figured he'd best send off a telegram to Captain Sundberg. No sense in waiting, and it'd cost him less to send it in Glendive than in Fallon. He doodled as he ate, playing with the wording of his telegram. Maybe something like, *Permission requested to propose marriage to Emily.* He should send an official missive in the next couple of days. *Formal letter to follow.* Might be good for Emily to write to her parents as well.

Thinking back on their conversations, Jake didn't think Captain Sundberg would be surprised.

"Help!" A man stormed into the establishment. Jake turned and viewed the well-dressed, long-faced banking clerk. "Someone help. The bank's been robbed!"

Two days later Emily stood on the shady porch and wiped the perspiration off her brow with the hem of her apron. Supper was nearly done, thank goodness! Cooking took a lot of effort, and today's heat made the kitchen an uncomfortable place. However, they'd eat in a half hour, and hopefully Jake would be home by then.

Worry picked at her. Was he all right? On Monday he'd sent a message stating he was detained and that he'd be back in a couple of days. Did testifying put him in some sort of danger? Web didn't think so, and Deidre said this sort of thing happened frequently. Emily couldn't help but wonder if she'd calmly abide Jake's unplanned absences when they married…or would she worry herself sick over him every time he went away?

The latter. Most definitely. *Lord, forgive me. I know fretting is a sin. Please give me Your peace that passes all understanding…*

She blew out a weary sigh and reflected on the past two days. They'd been filled with lessons learned from domestics to matters of the heart. While Emily had grown up on a small farm, Iris hadn't, and the daily chores exhausted her. Then starting yesterday Rez seemingly lost all interest in Iris, discouraging her further. Worse, she seemed to resent Emily. Deidre said that Iris was just hurt and envious that Emily wouldn't be husbandless for too much longer.

The statement evoked great happiness in Emily as well as huge sorrow. She loved Jake but didn't want to lose her best friend.

A lighter lesson learned today was that three women in one kitchen were more bother than helpful. Iris, God bless her, was a teacher at heart, and she wanted to show Deidre all sorts of new ways to create Web's and Jake's preferred dishes.

The only trouble was, Iris had book and magazine knowledge, but lacked experience, so Deidre's Very Berry Pie, one of Jake's favorites, didn't turn out exactly right. The filling was too runny and the crust got overdone.

But Iris took care of the problem by giving the entire pie to Charlie's hounds, Beet and Buster. Consequently there would be no dessert tonight. As for cooking lessons, Emily decided to learn from *Besta* before she and Jake married.

But how could she learn from her grandmother if she lived out here? On the outskirts of Fallon?

Emily eyed Jake's log-sided cabin in the distance. From the stories she'd heard, her great-grandfather, Karl Sundberg, lived in such a cabin in Brown County, Wisconsin. Seemed a step back in time. Would she be able to survive such a rudimentary existence?

Sounds of hoofbeats and a rattling wagon wafted through budding treetops from a short distance off. Emily strained to see if it might be Jake just as Charlie appeared, shotgun in hand. Around his neck hung field glasses, the kind Poppa and her brothers used when hunting.

He peered through them. "It's Jake coming!" He cupped his free hand around his mouth and hollered toward the house. "He's got someone in a wagon bed. Injured man, looks like."

Emily pulled off her apron and tossed it onto a nearby chair before making her way into the yard. Web and Rez jogged from the barn. Deidre and Iris rushed from the kitchen.

"Stay back, ladies." Web held up a hand.

Emily, Iris, and Deidre did as he bid them as Jake drove the buckboard up the long drive. Nickel trailed, tethered to the back of the wagon.

Jake pulled the team to a halt near his cabin. "Doc Fenske will be along shortly," he called to Charlie.

Charlie gave a nod.

Emily moved forward, but Deidre took her hand.

Straining to hear, Emily couldn't make out anything Jake said to Web and Rez, but the two men carried the injured stranger out of the wagon bed and into to Jake's cabin.

"That's Andy!" The horror in Iris's voice made Emily take close scrutiny. Still she couldn't quite tell.

While Charlie tended to Nickel and the other two horses, Jake strode over and confirmed it. "A couple of no-account gamblers robbed the bank in Glendive Monday and bungled the job. One of them confessed to beating a third man and throwing him off the train south of town." Jake glanced down at his dusty boots. "I had a hunch it was Andy. I went searching and…sure enough, I found him."

"Oh, my stars!" Iris's hands covered her heart. "Poor Andy."

Emily folded her arms. God forgive her, but she had a difficult time feeling sorry for the man.

"I took him to the doctor in Glendive," Jake continued, "and stayed at the hotel until Andy's conditional stabilized." He aimed a gaze at his cabin. "The doctor tending to him said Andy was all right for light traveling this morning, so I rented a rig and a team, made up a pallet in the wagon bed. Even so, during the trip home Andy started bleeding again." Jake glanced at Emily, then Iris, and finally Deidre. "I stopped in Fallon and told Aunt Susie to get a message to Doc Fenske, asking him to come."

"Why did you bring this man all the way here?" Deidre appeared perplexed.

"He's a friend of ours," Iris answered quickly. "A good friend."

Emily resisted the urge to roll her eyes at the *good friend* part and regarded Jake. "How on earth did Andy end up north of here near Glendive? Last we saw him, he was in Terry."

"From the little I was able to get out of him, Andy hopped on the northbound train early Monday morning, since I'd left a ticket for him. Andy owed a gambling debt to a fellow who hired the outlaws to kill him when he couldn't pay up. The men followed Andy onto the train, beat him, threw him off, and left him for dead. Then the outlaws disembarked in Glendive with plans to rob the bank."

"Poor Andy," Iris repeated.

"I'll heat some water and find bandages before the doctor arrives." Deidre ran back into the house.

"I'll go see about Andy." Iris stepped around Jake.

Jake's dark eyes fixed on Emily. "I feel like this is my fault. Maybe if I would have given Andy the money he'd asked me for, he wouldn't have gotten himself beat up. It's just that he'd lied so many times that I—"

"Jake, you're not responsible for what happened to Andy." Emily reached for his gloved hand. "If you would have given Andy the money, he would have, in all likelihood, spent it and still gotten the same sort of beating—maybe worse. I hate to say it, but perhaps this is the only way he'll finally learn to change his ways."

A little grin twitched the corners of his mouth. "How'd you get so smart?"

She smiled and hugged him around the waist. Hands on her shoulders, Jake moved to kiss her, but Iris's sobs banished any romance of the moment. Emily looked across the yard in time to see her run from Jake's cabin.

Disappointment wove through the concern she felt for her friend. "I'd rather stay here with you, Jake. I missed you, but I should look after Iris." Seeing a hint of something akin to confusion in his gaze, she added, "Rez has been avoiding her for two days, and this morning one of the dairy cows knocked Iris to the ground. And that's not all."

Jake chuckled. "In light of Iris's trauma, I reckon you'd best tend to her." He let loose an audible sigh. "Maybe you and Iris can sit on the porch. I'll let you know what Doc Fenske says."

"Good idea, and…thank you."

He sent her an affectionate wink before striding toward his cabin.

Emily met Iris inside and walked beside her to the chairs at the far side of the porch. Iris continued to cry, so Emily draped her arm across her friend's narrow shoulders.

"How could someone beat Andy so badly?"

A moment passed before Emily replied. "You heard Jake. Andy got himself in trouble with men of no integrity." She'd never told Iris that Andy lied about why he needed money. The subject never came up again after they departed Terry.

Iris trained her eyes on Emily, searching her face for an answer. "You know something more about this, don't you?"

"I only know that Andy asked both Jake and me for money when we saw him in Terry and that he'd lied about why he wanted it." Emily paused.

"Jake didn't lend Andy the money? Money that might have spared him?"

"Or money that might have killed him for sure." Emily refused to allow Iris to blame Jake. "God didn't allow Andy to die, did He? There's a reason why things happened the way they did. Jake found Andy and acted like the Good Samaritan. Maybe now Andy will stop his gambling and philandering."

"Emily!"

"It's true, Iris. Up until now Andy has displayed ugly penchants for strong drink, gambling, and…well, you saw him with those women the night of the Memorial Day Dance. To be honest, I no longer respect the man."

"But you must forgive him."

"I do." After Saturday she hadn't given Andy another thought.

"And I pray he'll make good use of this second chance that God's afforded him."

They sat in silence for several long seconds.

"Em, something worse than Andy nearly losing his life has transpired." Moist, pale-blue eyes filled with accusation stared at Emily. "Something has shattered our friendship."

"Oh, please! Don't start with that nonsense about living in my shadow. Deidre told me you spouted such silliness. I'm hurt and annoyed. All these years you never let on that you felt...stifled by my family and me."

"The knife cuts both ways, Em. We're supposed to be best friends who don't keep secrets from each other."

"But we did."

"Yes, we did." Iris folded her bony hands tightly in her lap and shrugged off Emily's sisterly arm. "It seems I've outgrown my childhood best friend. I'm sorry, Em."

The remark wounded her, and yet, try as she might, Emily couldn't argue.

That night Emily laid wide awake, thanking God that Andy would most likely recover from his injuries. He'd regained consciousness enough to drink some broth that Deidre made, and Jake allowed Iris to visit for a few minutes. When she had left the room in which Andy convalesced, Iris looked drawn and pale.

"His face is simply hideous!" Iris's hand had fluttered at the base of her throat.

"I've seen worse," Jake had countered.

But Iris refused to be consoled, and tonight she'd cried herself to sleep. Emily wondered what had come over her friend. She'd never shown such interest in Andy before. Or had she been hiding her interest, knowing that Emily was interested in Andy too? She sighed. Why did relationships have to be so complex?

She turned onto her side and stared into the darkened bedroom. She and Jake hadn't found much time alone tonight. Even so, he managed to tell her that he'd posted a letter to Poppa, asking for her hand in marriage. At first he planned to send a telegram with the formal letter to follow. But he found time to write the latter as he sat by Andy's bedside.

Marrying Jake. The idea sent a pleasurable warmth through her veins. But how would Poppa respond? Would he be shocked? She didn't think he'd refuse Jake's request. And just wait until Eden and Zeb heard the news. Emily wished she could be present to view her brothers' astonished expressions.

An animal yowled somewhere outside. Emily pulled the quilt up under her chin and thanked God that Andy hadn't been left out in the Montana wilderness with the coyotes, wolves, and rattlesnakes. He probably would have died then—and maybe not of his injuries. Either way, it was a miracle that Jake had found him. Web had said that once Andy healed up, he could work on the ranch. Web added that he'd need an extra man come the fall roundup. Meanwhile Andy could regain his strength and learn the many particulars of a ranch hand's job.

As the faintest light of dawn Emily heard sounds coming from the barn. She slipped from beneath the bedcovers and strode to the window. Peeking out, she saw Jake leaving for Glendive to return the team and wagon. *Keep him safe, Father God.*

It was late afternoon when Jake returned to the ranch. Emily stood from where she'd been sitting on the porch, knitting. She'd almost completely finished the sweater for Deidre.

Setting it aside, she walked out to greet Jake.

"You're back safely." She smiled. "I began to wonder if something happened."

"No…no need to worry." After tethering his horse, he removed his hat and leather riding gloves while crossing the yard.

Emily glimpsed the creases lining Jake's forehead and suspected something wasn't right. "More bad news? Is it about Andy?"

Jake shook his head and took her hand in his. "How is he today?"

"Iris took a couple meals to him and reported back that he ate."

"A good sign."

"I haven't gone to see him yet." Emily rolled one shoulder and gazed toward Jake's cabin. "I don't feel the need." She looked at him, feeling less confident than of late. "Am I wrong?"

"All things considered, I'd say you're spot on." Jake set his arm around her shoulders. "But I need to speak with you. Aunt Susie waved me down as I waited for the ferry this afternoon. A telegram arrived from your father."

"Poppa?"

Jake gave a single nod. "Let's you and me take a little stroll through Deidre's garden so I can share it with you in some privacy. I need to stretch my legs anyhow."

As they headed toward the spring garden, aggravation sparked inside of her. "So Poppa has already sent a reply, and he doesn't approve. Is that what you're going to tell me?"

"No."

"What then?"

Jake stopped and searched her face. "Em, your grandmother is ill."

"What do you mean she's ill? With what?"

Jake reached into his jacket's inside pocket and pulled out a folded note. He handed it to Emily. "We'll have to pack today and board the eight-fifteen train tomorrow morning. That's the soonest the eastbound train makes a stop in Fallon. I've purchased our tickets."

Her heart pounding, Emily opened the message and read the neat script. *Emily must come home at once. Bestamor's heart is failing. Discussion of wedding plans postponed.* It was signed, *Captain D. Sundberg.*

She blinked back the sudden tears and stared up at Jake. "I'll start packing right away."

"Emily…"

He folded her into an embrace, but she didn't want to be still and coddled. She wanted to run and pack—maybe sprint all the way back to Wisconsin.

Besta? Her heart was failing? But she'd been so strong and spirited only weeks ago.

"Take a moment and let it sink in."

"No, I can't."

Jake tightened his hold.

"Let me go!" She tried in vain to push him away. "Why isn't there a train leaving this afternoon or tonight?"

"Shh…I'll get you back home. I promise." His soft voice and patient tone had a calming effect on her. "We'll pray for your grandmother. I love you, Emily."

"I love you too." She swallowed hard. "But *Besta*…she can't die!" She stared up into Jake's face. "What if this is my fault?" She ignored the shake of his head. "Maybe I upset her by leaving Manitowoc."

"No. It's easy to think that way, but, trust me, torturing yourself does nothing to change things."

Emily clutched the front of his jacket and dropped her forehead onto his chest.

"Go on and cry, honey. You'll feel better once you do."

Part of her wanted to. But oddly his permission only made her gulp back her tears. "Crying won't do any good either." She peered up at him. "I have to be strong. For *Besta*'s sake."

"That's my girl." Jake smiled.

"What about Andy?"

"You worried about him?" He searched her face as if trying to look into her very heart.

"You're the one I love, Jake. But I'm concerned about Andy being left alone in your cabin—a cabin containing a trunk of treasures from your grandfather. I don't trust Andy."

Jake's features relaxed. He looked relieved. "Web'll keep an eye on him. Dr. Fenske promised to check back in a couple of days. Once Andy is on his feet again, he can move into the bunkhouse with Charlie, Rez, and the other cowboys hiring on for the roundup."

After a nodded reply, Emily rested her cheek against Jake's heart and listened to its strong, steady beat. "The one I can't help fretting over is *Besta*."

"I know, Em. I've been praying for her ever since I got the telegram."

"I realize my grandmother is elderly, but I'm not ready for God to take her home yet."

"I understand all too well how you feel."

Of course he did, given Mr. Ollie's recent passing, not to mention his parents' untimely deaths.

"Come on." Jake steered her toward the house. "Let's tell the others that we'll be leaving."

CHAPTER 27

*E*MILY BEGAN PACKING at once. When Deidre gonged the dinner bell, she headed outside to the table, set with a pretty embroidered cloth. A pottery vase containing a spring bouquet made for a lovely centerpiece.

After Web asked the blessing, Jake explained the situation involving *Besta*, and everyone promised to pray. Emily could barely choke down her meal. In addition to worrying about *Besta*, Emily sensed Iris's disappointment at the news of their hasty departure. Even so, Emily had to return home.

When supper ended, she reentered the guest bedroom and finished collecting the last of her things. Then she took up her knitting and headed for the back porch. She'd at least have a small gift for Deidre as gratitude for the past few days.

On the way out she met Iris. "I need to speak with you," Iris wore a stern expression.

Emily backtracked. Inside the room they shared, Iris closed the door.

"I'm not leaving with you and Jake tomorrow."

"But—"

"I'm staying on at the Ready Web."

"I don't understand."

"Deidre and Web extended an invitation, and I feel I have more of a chance of finding a husband out here in Montana than back in Manitowoc."

Emily didn't argue. She wouldn't overshadow her friend any longer.

"You must admit, I was right." Iris pushed up her eyeglasses and blinked. "Jake was my destiny. I love it out here."

"And what's your grandmother going to say when I arrive back home without you?"

Iris lifted her slender shoulders. "The truth is, Em, if I don't come back at least betrothed, Granny will be the one with heart failure."

Emily's gaze fell to the knitted sweater in her hands.

"But look at you, Em. Why, you're practically engaged already. It's only a matter of time before Jake speaks of marriage to you."

Emily withheld the news that he already had spoken of marriage. "It's bittersweet to find my true love only to lose my best friend."

"No, God has given you a new best friend, Em. He's given you Jake." Iris sat on the end of the bed. "I knew the Saturday morning after the Memorial Day Dance when I interviewed him that he was in love with you. He couldn't keep his eyes off you. Still can't. He watches your every move, ready to protect you if need be."

"I love him too, Iris." There. She'd admitted it.

"I know." Her eyes twinkled. "Why do you think that I concocted the crazy idea to follow Jake here? Truly my motives were twofold. But, Emily, I want a husband and family too. It's what I've always wanted. When my parents died, I wanted it all the more. Can't you please understand?"

She did. She nodded. "Yes, Iris, I understand."

The next morning Web drove Emily and Jake to Fallon's small depot where they boarded the eastbound train, heading for St. Paul, Minnesota. But to Emily it seemed like forever before the train rattled and swayed into North Dakota and then another eternity as it crossed the plains. Emily felt like she could run faster than this train moved.

She glanced at Jake in the seat beside her. He read the newspaper and every so often paused to tell her about an article he thought might be of interest. Thus far he'd been a perfect new best friend.

"I've been meaning to speak with you about something important, something we should come to an agreement about before reaching Manitowoc. I expect your father will have plenty of questions for me."

"He certainly will." To Emily's great relief, Jake knew what he was in for.

Jake leaned closer. "I never did sell Granddad's house."

"You didn't?" All this time Emily assumed Poppa purchased it.

"I kept seeing a vision of you in the music room, playing that beautiful piano, like you did at Granddad's funeral luncheon." A rueful-looking smile snaked across his face. "I couldn't sign the papers when it came time."

You mean I won't have to live in Montana? Joy flooded her heart, but she disguised her response. "What was Poppa's reaction?"

"Oddly he seemed to understand, although I gave no specific reason. I wasn't sure how you felt about me and if my feelings were mere infatuation." He gave her fingers an affectionate squeeze. "They're not."

Of that Emily was certain. But she was curious about one thing. "If I hadn't followed you to Montana, would you have come back to Manitowoc? Or would you have written me?"

"Come back, of course. I'd have invented some crazy excuse to see you again." They shared a smile. Then Jake continued, "I'm wondering if you'd object to living there, in Granddad's house."

"Of course not." She'd prefer it to ranching.

"Next door to your family?"

Emily grimaced in jest.

Jake chuckled. "I also plan to work for Mr. Schulz's law firm and learn Wisconsin law."

Emily sobered, thinking of all Jake would be giving up. "Won't you miss Montana? The excitement of being a US deputy marshal?"

"I've thought about this good and hard, and I think eventually I'll run for public office."

"Sheriff?"

"I'm thinking more along the legislative lines. I know what federal laws work and don't work, at least in eastern Montana. You see, I enjoy a mental challenge as well as a physical one."

"Are you thinking of becoming state representative? A governor? Maybe president of the United States?"

He chuckled at her enthusiasm.

"Seriously, Jake, I'll support your decision, whatever it is, and help in any way I can."

"I hoped you'd say that because there's bound to be some schooling involved."

"A fortunate thing you're in love with a teacher."

"Fortunate is right. God sure is smiling down on me."

His statement warmed Emily's heart. How grateful she felt to see Jake at peace after he'd suffered so.

"Does Deidre know of your plans?"

"Yes, and she promised that she and Web and my baby niece or nephew would visit. Web even said it might do everyone some good if he got away from the ranch and left Charlie and Rez in charge for a spell." Jake glanced around the passenger car then brought his gaze back to Emily. "We'll talk more in detail about this in private." His voice was low and hushed. "But Granddad left me enough money to get a good start. We should be fine financially during the transitional stages."

"May I continue to teach school?"

"If you wish."

She did. She'd worked hard for both her certificate and her position.

"Anything else that I didn't address?"

"I don't think so." She did wonder over an official proposal of marriage and a wedding date, but of course they needed her parents' blessing.

"What's the first question that you think your father will ask me?"

"Easy."

"And?" Jake arched a brow.

Emily tried to imitate her father's deep voice. "Did you kiss my daughter?"

A snort of laughter. "Well," he drawled, "at least I know the answer to that one. 'No, sir. She kissed me first!'"

A dark, cloudy sky greeted them in Manitowoc on the night they arrived. The summer wind off Lake Michigan had a bite to it. Emily hoped it wasn't a predictor of things to come. After collecting their baggage, Jake hired a driver to take them home. Emily would have stopped in at Sundbergs' Creations for an update on *Besta*'s condition, but in the shop and back apartment in which her aunt, uncle, and cousins lived, not a single lamp shone through the windows.

Dread dropped like a rock inside of Emily. "What if *Besta* is gone?"

Jake collected her in his right arm and held her beside him while they passed the familiar scenery. When they rolled by the street on which Andy Anderson's family lived, Emily thought of how she saw him, supposedly penniless, and how he'd lied about why he needed money. She wouldn't speak of it to anyone, although Iris might let the news slip in the form of a letter to friends. Leaning her head against Jake's shoulder, Emily thanked the good Lord she hadn't caught Andy's eye. Good thing Poppa scared him off when he did.

She smiled. She never dreamed such a thought could run through her head.

At long last the buggy pulled up into her parents' drive. Lamplight shone through the gauzy drapes. Emily staved off the desire to leap from the conveyance and rush into the house. Instead, she allowed the driver to open the door for her and assist her descent. She thanked him properly and then...whirled around and ran for the house!

"Poppa? Momma?" She ran to the parlor. Empty. By the time she turned toward the sitting room, the less formal of the two, Momma met her with outstretched arms.

"My darling, are you all right?" She held her at arms' length. "Let me look at you."

"How is *Besta*? I've been so worried."

"She's resting now, but she gave us all a fright when she swooned at the dinner table."

"Oh, my!" Emily headed for the front stairs when she glimpsed Poppa as he rounded the corner of his study. She smiled. Was he terribly angry?

"Emily..." He came forward and hugged her tightly. He smelled like fresh linens and spice. He held her by the shoulders then and gave her a mild shake. "Don't you ever pull a stunt like that again, you hear?"

"I hear, and I promise. I learned many valuable life lessons. Believe me!"

"You'll have to tell us all about it."

Momma interrupted. "But you must be famished. I'll fix us a pot of tea and a snack for you."

Jake entered the opened front door and removed his hat. "Mrs. Sundberg." He politely inclined his head. "Captain."

Momma smiled at him before looking back at Emily. "I'll fix two snacks."

Poppa shook Jake's hand. "Thank you for seeing my daughter home safely."

"Entirely my pleasure."

"So I'm to understand."

Emily expelled a weary sigh. Leaving her parents and Jake behind, she climbed the stairs to check on *Besta*. Just as Momma said, the elderly woman slept peacefully. She appeared just the same as when Emily had seen her last. How could her heart be failing? How could she be dying?

As if sensing her presence, *Besta* turned her head and opened her age-lined blue eyes. "Emily!" She smiled. *"Alt er vel nå som du er hjemme."* All is well now that you are home.

"Ja, Besta. Sov godt—sleep tight." Emily bent and placed a kiss on her grandmother's cheek then tiptoed from the room. In the hallway relief overwhelmed her to the point of tears. But downstairs, she could hear Poppa's booming voice—not the words he spoke, but she figured she ought to rescue Jake just the same.

Emily descended the stairwell. In the parlor Poppa was lighting a third lamp when Emily entered. She glanced at Jake. He appeared none the worse for wear. Crossing the room, she sat beside him on the settee and arranged her skirt.

Poppa clasped his hands behind his back. "How was your trip?"

"Fine." There was so much more to say, but, in truth, she longed for news about her grandmother. "What did the doctor say?"

"He said her heart is failing. She's growing weaker by the day."

"Just like that?" Emily found it difficult to believe.

"Evidently she's had symptoms but never mentioned them."

Momma walked into the parlor, carrying a tray on which her polished tea service sat. She set it down on a nearby table. "Daniel, pour out, will you? I'll bring along the snacks."

Emily didn't feel much like eating, but she gratefully accepted the cup of tea her father handed her. Jake declined the offer.

"Eden and your cousin Jacob are on their way as we speak." Poppa sat down in an armchair. "I expect them some time tomorrow morning. Grandpa Ramsey decided to accompany the fellows. Over the years he and your grandmother have become friends."

"Grandpa Ramsey's making the trip?" More proof that *Besta*'s condition was serious.

Momma returned with plates of sliced peaches, bread and butter, and cubes of cheese. "I'm so relieved you're home safe, Emily. And Jake? Thank you for protecting her and Iris."

"Again, it was my pleasure."

"I presume Iris is settling in at home with Mrs. Hopper?"

At Poppa's inquiry, Emily shook her head. "I'm afraid she refused to come back home."

Momma gasped and Poppa sat forward, a frown pushing his thick brows inward.

Emily explained the situation.

"My sister and brother-in-law," Jake said, "will do their best to keep an eye on her."

"No small task, believe me." Poppa smirked. "How does Iris expect to get home?" He took a swallow from the teacup he held and looked first at Emily and then at Jake.

"I guess that'll be something Iris has to figure out on her own," Jake said. "Hopefully, she'll make the right choice when it comes down to it."

"Let's hope and pray she does." Momma smoothed away the worried lines from her forehead. "A pity her grandmother pressures her to marry. She's liable to snatch up anyone just to cease the nagging."

"And speaking of choices..." Poppa set aside the teacup. He wore that certain look that told Emily the interrogation would soon begin.

"So tell me, Jake...did you kiss my daughter?"

Emily sent a glance upward then caught Momma's grin.

"Yes, sir, I did."

"In spite of my warning?"

"That's right. And I'm fully prepared to bear the consequences of my actions…"

Emily heard the note of light sarcasm and grinned.

"…for the rest of my life."

CHAPTER 28

J AKE SLOWED HIS horse as he rode past the Sundbergs' property. Nine days had gone by, and he was slowly adjusting to
living in Granddad's house and riding to work each morning. He
timed it so he'd see Emily—as he did this morning. She walked in
the yard near a row of flowers with the elderly Mrs. Sundberg, who
clung to Emily's arm. The older woman's heart hadn't given out
yet. In fact, she seemed better. And Emily hadn't had any qualms
about leaving the boardinghouse and giving up her independent
lifestyle. Now she was back into the thick of things with her family
and enjoying it.

Just as she did each morning, Emily blew him a kiss. Jake reined
in the gelding at the end of the drive and gave a tug on the brim of
his hat. He glimpsed her smile; it would have to satisfy him for the
day. It was part of his agreement with the captain, allowing some
time to pass and having carefully supervised contact with Emily.
The captain called it a "cooling off" period in which they could all
pray. Make sure. Seemed a reasonable request from a concerned
father, although Jake felt confident about marrying Emily. And
what was a few weeks compared to the rest of their lives?

Fortunately he'd been invited to dine with the Sundbergs almost
every night. He enjoyed meeting George Ramsey, Emily's grandfather. It was great seeing Eden again and getting reacquainted
with both him and Zeb. The couple of times he didn't dine with

ANDREA BOESHAAR

the family, Jake had business dinners with Mr. Schulz and the law firm's clients. So far things worked out. Jake served as the aging attorney's eyes, ears, and legs, researching, interviewing, and investigating—everything Jake found rewarding. Of course he still had a few things to settle in Montana, but he was building the springboard from which he could launch a solid career.

He spurred his horse on down the road and into town.

The torrid month of June melted into July, bringing the Fourth of July holiday, which Emily and her family, along with Jake and *Besta*, celebrated on the deck of the *Sea Princess*. Even Momma had gone aboard, although they never left the dock. At the end of the month Emily received a letter from Iris, stating that she was sure to have a marriage proposal soon—and that it would be a big surprise. Deidre felt good and wore the knitted sweater that Emily gave her whenever the evenings were cool. What's more, due to Iris's help, Deidre was able to put her feet up and rest in the middle of the day. Happy for her friend, Emily wrote a reply and posted it.

As the month of August brought with it days of rain, Emily shared buggy rides into town with Jake. He let her off at school so she could prepare her classroom and herself for the upcoming school year. On the way home they laughed, talked, and planned their future together. But Poppa still withheld his blessing.

But then one Sunday afternoon, as she relaxed in the parlor with her family, Emily sensed something was up. Change was in the air, and the coming autumn season had nothing to do with it.

"I think you ought to go for a stroll, Em," Eden said.

Surprised by the comment, she glanced up at her twin. He stood beside the parlor window, his hands stuffed into his trouser pockets, looking every bit the important executive. Poppa was so proud.

"A stroll will cheer you up. Guaranteed."

"How do you know I need cheering?"

"Because you look glum." Eden glanced at Poppa and Momma. "Does she look glum?"

"Mmm…" Poppa inclined his head. "Probably because Jake couldn't join us this afternoon."

Discomfort blew right through her, and Emily shifted on the settee. She and Jake shared so much, and yet he refused to tell her after church this morning why he couldn't join her and her family for noon dinner. Perhaps Poppa's holding back finally discouraged him, although she'd seen Jake yesterday. They'd met beneath the oak tree… with *Besta* standing in the near distance.

"Well, maybe it's not meant to be, huh, Em?"

She heard the teasing note in Eden's voice before she glimpsed his smirk. "Isn't it time you went back to New York?"

"Grandpa, Jacob, and I want to be sure *Besta* makes a full recovery before we leave."

"It'll never be that, I'm afraid." Momma looked up from her embroidery. The scarlet skirt she wore blended well with the armchair in which she sat. "But her health has improved greatly."

"I'd like for my grandmother to be in attendance at my wedding." Emily sent Poppa a mild glare.

"Emily, I gave Jake my blessing weeks ago." Poppa's voice beheld a tender note. "If he hasn't formally proposed marriage, the reason has nothing to do with me."

The news made Emily feel as though she stood onboard a tossing ship. "Honestly?"

"Honestly."

Was Jake having second thoughts?

"On a different note, Mrs. Hopper stopped me at church this morning. Apparently Iris is engaged to be married—and you'll never guess to whom she's betrothed."

"On the contrary, I'm sure I know." *Rez.*

"We should go on a hunting expedition with Jake," Eden

interrupted before more could be said. "Perhaps before I return to New York. Grandpa would enjoy it."

"I understand Jake is extremely busy with his work these days."

Too busy to think of marrying me. Emily staved off a pout but stood and silently left the room. She heard Grandpa, her uncles, Zeb, and three of her cousins, Kjæl, David, and Jacob, talking out on the front lawn about fishing. *Tante* Adeline and *Tante* Agnes chatted nearby. She found her grandmother in the kitchen, slicing a cake. Her two youngest cousins held out their plates.

"*Besta*, you're supposed to be resting."

"Oh, Emily, there you are!" She turned from the table and set down the knife. "It's a lovely afternoon. How about a stroll? Will you accompany me?"

"Of course." The doctor permitted short walks as long as *Besta* moved slowly. "Eden's been trying to convince me that I need some air. He said I look glum."

"You do!" Kate grinned.

Emily bristled at the teasing. "Oh, go eat your cake, you imp."

"And you're crabby too."

Emily swallowed further retort. It would only encourage her young cousin.

Besta shooed the girls to the table. Once they sat down to enjoy their pieces of cake, *Besta* hooked elbows with Emily, and together they strolled to the overgrown path that led to Jake's home. Emily fought back the confusion she felt. Jake didn't seem as though he'd had any doubts. Quite the opposite. But Poppa gave his blessing weeks ago? How could that be? Poppa wouldn't lie.

"Look across the long grass, Emily."

She did. Lush and green, it rippled on a gentle gust of late summer wind.

"I remember when not a single structure stood for miles around. My Sam brought me here from Brown County. He built the house we live in. I had my babies in it, your father being the first, as you know."

Emily nodded. She'd heard the story many times before. *Besta* liked to retell it, and Emily found herself paying more attention as she knew her grandmother wouldn't be around much longer.

"I watched my grandchildren enter the world here and saw them grow." *Besta* smiled and the blue of her eyes deepened. "I have lived a full and wonderful life."

"With many more happy memories to come." Emily disliked it when her grandmother spoke as though she was about to depart for heaven on the next soul train.

"*Ja*, and many more happy times to come. Love is the thread that binds us together in the fabric of time."

"Beautifully said."

Besta's smile widened. "Go take a quiet stroll by the stream, Emily. Walk as far as you can, remembering that your grandfather and I did the same. Your parents did too."

"Not today, *Besta*." She wasn't feeling particularly nostalgic. "I'll take you back to the house, though."

"I'll escort *Besta*." Eden came up behind them. "Go take your stroll."

"I'm not up to it, but thanks anyway." She sent her twin an annoyed glance.

Besta's gnarly hand gripped Emily's. "Go. Walk. You'll find the answers to your questions."

Had she really been so transparent?

"Go and walk."

Emily shook her head.

"Listen, Em, I believe your answer is waiting beneath a certain oak tree." Eden glanced at his pocket watch. "And has been since precisely 3:30."

Her jaw slacked.

"You've been clueless all day despite the hints we've dropped."

"Don't tell her." *Besta* whispered as if Emily couldn't hear. "It's a surprise."

She understood at once. Turning, she saw Grandpa Ramsey, her parents, brother, aunts, uncles, cousins, all congregating at the side of the house. Obviously she'd become the main attraction.

"I told Jake a surprise proposal wouldn't work. You're not exactly cooperative when it comes to surprises."

Emily felt stunned. Speechless.

"Emily's gonna get married. Emily's gonna get married." Kate's singsong teasing drifted across the way.

Eden chuckled. "You know you and Jake love each other. Go on already."

She set off on the path. The only consolation was that the oak wasn't visible from her parents' home. Located in back of Jake's property that bordered her family's, it stood near the stream.

The tree came into view, and Emily spied Jake sitting beneath it, his back up against the base of the wide trunk. He smiled as she neared and got to his feet. "I hoped you'd come."

She hated to tell him that Eden had to spell it out for her. "It's a lovely day for a stroll."

"Hmm…" His gaze tapered, and Emily could tell he figured she knew. "You'll never guess what I heard after church service this morning."

"What?"

Jake held out one hand and Emily clasped it. "Iris is engaged to be married."

"Poppa told me. So Rez finally came around, eh?"

"Nope. Not Rez."

"Oh?"

"Andy Anderson."

Emily gasped. "No!"

Jake nodded. "Word is that the beating really shook him up, and he's determined to turn his life around. Deidre confirmed it, and

Iris is insisting on a long engagement in order for him to prove himself. So I…I sold him my property in Fallon."

"Was that wise?" She hoped Jake didn't live to regret trusting Andy. Iris, either.

"We'll see." He searched her face. "I believe in second chances, don't you?"

"Of course." She brought her fingers up and touched the delicate silver cross she always wore.

Jake pulled her close. "I never thought I could be as happy as I am."

Emily smiled and locked her arms around his waist. "I'm happy too, Jake, although I was fretting that Poppa scared you off."

"Not a chance. In fact, your father's given me his blessing, Em. I just wanted to feel somewhat settled in my new life before I made another big change." His gaze intensified. "Will you marry me?"

"You know I will. In a heartbeat."

"Oh, wait…"

"Wait?" Hadn't she waited long enough?

A grimace. "I think I was supposed to get down on one knee."

She smiled. "Don't bother."

He fished in his trousers' pocket and pulled out a small sapphire-blue velvet box. Emily opened it. A diamond engagement ring sparkled.

"It's beautiful."

Jake placed it on her finger. It fit.

Happiness filled every ounce of her being. She cupped his clean-shaven face and silently urged his lips to hers. His kiss was so filled with promise that Emily barely heard the whoops, whistles, and cheers from her family. All that mattered was that the man she loved held her in his arms and God Almighty held them both in the palm of His hand.

Also Available From Andrea Boeshaar

Threads of Hope

BOOK ONE

FABRIC *of* TIME

SERIES

CHAPTER 1

September 1848

*I*T LOOKS LIKE *Norway.*

The thought flittered across nineteen-year-old Kristin Eikaas's mind as Uncle Lars's wagon bumped along the dirt road. The docks of Green Bay, Wisconsin, were behind them, and now they rode through a wooded area that looked just as enchanting as the forests she'd left in Norway. Tall pine trees and giant firs caused the sunshine to dapple on the road. Kristin breathed in the sweet, fresh air. How refreshing it felt in her lungs after being at sea for nearly three months and breathing in only salty sea air or the stale air in her dark, crowded cabin.

A clearing suddenly came into view, and a minute or so later, Kristin eyed the farm fields stretched before her. The sight caused an ache of homesickness. Her poppa had farmed…

"Your trip to America was good, *ja?*" Uncle Lars asked in Norwegian, giving Kristin a sideways glance.

He resembled her father so much that her heart twisted painfully with renewed grief. Except she'd heard about *Onkel*—about his temper—how he had to leave Norway when he was barely of age, because, Poppa had said, trouble followed him.

But surely he'd grown past all of that. His letters held words of promise, and there was little doubt that her uncle had made a new life for himself here in America.

Just as she would.

Visions of a storefront scampered across her mind's eye—a shop in which she could sell her finely crocheted and knitted items. A shop in which she could work the spinning wheel, just as *Mor* had...

Uncle Lars arched a brow. "You are tired, *liten niese*?"

"*Ja*. It was a long journey." Kristin sent him a sideways glance. "I am grateful I did not come alone. The Olstads made good traveling companions."

Her uncle cleared his throat and lowered his voice. "But you have brought my inheritance, *ja*?" He arched a brow.

"*Ja*." Kristin thought of the priceless possession she'd brought from Norway.

"And you would not hold out on your *onkel*, would you?"

Prickles of unease caused Kristin to shift in her seat. She resisted the urge to touch the tiny gold and silver cross pendent suspended from a dainty chain that hung around her neck. Her dress concealed it. She couldn't give it up, even though it wasn't legal for a woman to inherit anything in Norway. But the necklace had been her last gift from *Mor*. A gift from one's mother wasn't an inheritance...was it? "No, *Onkel*."

She turned and peered down from her perch into the back of the wooden wagon bed. Peder Olstad smiled at her, and Kristin relaxed some. Just a year older, he was the brother of Kristin's very best friend who had remained in Norway with their mother. She and Peder had grown up together, and while he could be annoying and bad tempered at times, he was the closest thing to a brother that she had. And Sylvia—Sylvia was closer than a sister ever could be. It wouldn't be long, and she and Mrs. Olstad would come to America too. That would be a happy day!

"You were right," John Olstad called to Uncle Lars in their native